MW00979261

Denver Aquarius

Alan W. Lehmann

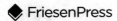 FriesenPress

Suite 300 - 990 Fort St
Victoria, BC, V8V 3K2
Canada

www.friesenpress.com

Copyright © 2019 by Alan W. Lehmann
First Edition — 2019

All rights reserved.

No part of this publication may be reproduced in any form, or by any
means, electronic or mechanical, including photocopying, recording,
or any information browsing, storage, or retrieval system, without
permission in writing from FriesenPress.

Editor and Cover Designer: Elaine Fleischmann

Author photograph: Aloys N. M. Fleischmann

ISBN
978-1-5255-3326-6 (Hardcover)
978-1-5255-3327-3 (Paperback)
978-1-5255-3328-0 (eBook)

1. FICTION, LITERARY

Distributed to the trade by The Ingram Book Company

BOOKS BY ALAN W. LEHMANN

Hamlet the Novel   2015

"A fresh retelling of William Shakespeare's *Hamlet* . . . a well-crafted adaptation that offers readers richly developed, relatable characters."

—Kirkus Reviews

Inca Sunset   2017

". . . lovingly detailed, world-building adventure."
—Eden Robinson, author of best-selling
Monkey Beach and *Son of a Trickster*

Denver Aquarius   2018

"Thank you for letting me be 'first on the block' to read *Denver Aquarius.* Readers will stop, roll their eyes back in reminiscence, and go 'yeesss' as their own versions of Danny's experiences drift up from their fading memories."

—K. Gosse, Beta Reads

"Entering the Age of Aquarius, both individuals and societies will experience needed transformation. It is a chaotic time, one of adventure and discovery, with both increased freedom and responsibility."

—the Optimistic Astrologer

"Diseases desperate grown, by desperate appliance are relieved, or not at all."

—King Claudius in *Hamlet*,
by William Shakespeare

"This, too, shall pass."

—Attar of Nishapur

TABLE OF CONTENTS

PREFACE

As the psychedelic 1960's bled away into the self-absorption and personal development preoccupations of the 1970's, many young people indulged a restless movement from idea to idea and from place to place. Their motives were as diverse as their backgrounds. As always, cultural change took place within the web of international events. Possible nuclear annihilation was an ongoing preoccupation for many, especially after the Cuban Missile Crisis. A long, drawn-out misery both at home and abroad, the Viet Nam War's daily horrors entered our living rooms through the evening news. Watergate's administrative criminality began the extended, slow contamination of citizen trust in government.

Bewildered parents watched and tried to adapt, as their offspring wandered in the wilderness of unpredictable cultural change, riding wave after wave of innovation (psychedelic drugs, novel cults and religions, scientific exploration and discovery). Progressive politics continued to stretch to accommodate expanding demands for rights and freedoms from previously marginalized and persecuted minorities, and from a rising feminism.

The rapid spread of televised entertainments reinforced traditional American mythology (through Westerns such as *Bonanza* and *Gunsmoke*, which ran for twenty seasons and celebrated gun violence as the preferred solution to social problems). It also introduced new norms of social possibility through satires like *All in the Family*, and through fantastic shows such as *The Twilight Zone* and *Star Trek*, whose initial series ended the year American astronauts first set foot on the moon.

It was a period underlain by a sound track of rock 'n roll and other forms of hit music. One of the songs celebrated the absurd optimism promoted by astrologers in their "explanation" of the arrival of the so-called Age of Aquarius, in which celestial alignments would bestow ecstasy on the world. Other music presented less sanguine commentary on the state of society, touching on the emptiness of consumer desire (the Rolling Stones' *Satisfaction*) or expressing the personal/political angst evident in the songs of Paul Simon (*America* and *The Sound of Silence*, for example).

Alternate forms of psychology emerged from the aridity of behaviorism's straight jacket, actually recognizing the phenomenon of consciousness(!), with all of its potential for joy and pain. And as dharma came west, numerous frauds and tricksters came with it, harvesting fortunes from Americans' gullibility and personal longing for even further freedom and fulfillment.

Amid all this social roil, many individuals were simply troubled, plagued by anxiety and other forms of mental "illness." As in most times and places, these individuals did their best to cope using whatever resources became available.

Danny, the protagonist of this novel, was one such person, perhaps luckier than most, in that he found sufficient support to pursue relief. This is his story.

As always, any resemblance of characters to real individuals, living or dead, is purely coincidental.

CHAPTER ONE

Dark Side of the Moon

I'm afraid, thought Danny each morning as he groped his way out of bed, wishing he could go back to sleep. *I'm afraid,* as he brushed his teeth or combed his hair, staring into the mirror at the mystery he knew to be himself. *I'm afraid*, as he walked to his high school biology class (currently focused on the nervous system), wondering how axons and membranes and organelles could combine within him to create the mess of his experience. *I'm afraid*, as he struggled to concentrate on the history of Confederation, or those bewildering German genders. At the end of each day he would sometimes tremble as he was fighting to get to sleep.

Most of his acquaintances were unaware of the level of his desperation, even if some were puzzled by his tense reserve. It was difficult to read him, to get a true sense of his feelings. On the surface, he appeared curiously unreactive to the social world around him, although he seemed easily fixated on music or books, an artistic sensibility that wasn't uncommon in young people in the 1970's, but that Danny experienced more as a life preserver than as a diversionary pleasure.

In a way, he was hiding in plain sight. Very few who knew him noted his tension, his controlled affect, or if they saw it, they didn't perceive it for what it was, a nearly debilitating horror. Instead, it seemed a humble kind of shyness. Years before university, Danny reached his own clear recognition of his personal anxiety when Bobby Fortnum, an occasional high school friend, had provided a unique exception to the general obliviousness in Danny's social circles.

"You're so nervous," Bobby had remarked to him one day after their high school classes had ended for the day.

They were sitting in the hotel coffee shop, drinking milk-shakes and discussing girls, that 'undiscovered country' that bridges childhood speculation and adult experience. For Danny, girls (and boys' confused and diverse reactions to them) were still a subject for contemplation and discussion rather than interpersonal immersion. By contrast, Bobby was proudly fond of describing his backseat explorations of girls' tits and thighs. "You should see the rack on..." was one of his favorite comments, delivered with a joyfully lecherous grin, but Danny hadn't begun dating yet.

At Bobby's comment, Danny suddenly imagined the shapely calf of Diane Martin wavering in and out of the corner of his vision in the math classroom aisle behind his desk, and he thought momentarily of his compulsive masturbation in the darkness of his bedroom and in the privacy of his toilet at home. He dismissed the image.

"I'm not nervous," Danny replied, but even while uttering the words he knew with sudden certainty that he was lying, and in his shock at Bobby's perceptive comment, he wondered momentarily whether or not he might any day now dissolve into a tremor-filled paralysis. *I'll see you on the dark side of the moon* sang Pink Floyd on the radio behind them. Bobby looked at him skeptically. *They lock the door, they throw away the key; there's someone in my head, but it's not me...*

At first the inklings of his fear had struck Danny only as a shortness of breath or momentary paralysis of action. He perceived these incidents as failures of the body to obey the injunctions of the mind. Toward the end of high school, however, he began to recognize that something more serious was going on, something almost out of his control.

Throughout his teens he had been bullied, the severity of which was tempered (he thought) only by his status as 'a teacher's kid;' there was no telling what school staffs or administrations were likely to do to a student seen to be bullying one of said staff's children. When he was younger, he thought just being a teacher's kid was the liability that caused older, tougher kids to pick on him. But that wasn't necessarily the case. Walking home from the movies one night, Danny heard the dreaded voice.

"Hey, dink!"

Danny felt his guts turn to water. *Shit,* he thought. *It's Cory!*

Cory was a rough and tumble, marginally school-worthy adolescent who took particular pleasure in tormenting Danny and a few other of Danny's hapless peers. Cory's mother, with whom he lived, was divorced (his father had bailed out on them with a waitress from the local bar; he was rumored to be working at a logging camp in BC). She kept Cory and his younger sister alive on her meager welfare cheque, living in a trailer behind the industrial yard of the utility company. They were the kind of family that most of the upright citizens of the community preferred not to notice, or perhaps might recognize with murmured "tsks" and the rueful shaking of heads, but without further specific comment.

That night Danny considered crossing the street to avoid any possible confrontation, but realizing that Cory would see it as an admission of fear (which it would have been), he decided against it. He could feel his heart racing as Cory sauntered up to him.

"What're you doin', Dink?" Cory stood in Danny's way on the dimly lit sidewalk, arms crossed, smirking.

"Just going home."

"How come you're not lookin' at me?"

Danny had been looking down to the side, as if the dandelions growing beside the uneven concrete walk needed attention. He looked up.

Uncrossing his arms, Cory stepped swiftly forward and punched Danny in the solar plexus. Danny doubled over and gasped to catch his breath.

"Don't ya know to look at people when you talk to'em?"

Danny felt almost all the tone in his musculature disappear, his guts churning. "Leave me alone," he managed to blurt out.

Cory slapped him, not a serious blow, but just a signal, the message that he could do virtually anything to Danny without any serious repercussions, and that both of them knew it. Cory gave a crooked sneer and spat to one side. "Just remember to look at people when they talk to you." He shoved Danny aside and walked past, on his way to God knew where.

Danny panted to catch his breath, holding his bruised abdomen gingerly, and then he continued on his way, looking only once over his shoulder to make sure that Cory was gone—for now, at least.

Bobby knew that Cory tormented Danny, and to a degree he sympathized. But he wasn't about to interfere. Instead he once asked Danny, "Why don't you just punch his lights out? The shit deserves it..."

Danny just looked away, kneading his knuckles together and murmuring softly, "No. No."

But Bobby was fundamentally correct, Danny knew, and he couldn't understand why he didn't fight back. His will to resist would simply disappear, melt into a kind of paralysis. Upon a confrontation he would feel the way you do in one of those dreams when you're being chased and you can't move your legs. He thought of reading in history class of how Jewish victims being taken away to the concentration camps in World War II had failed to resist, walking fearfully (but cooperatively) into their final "showers." Danny felt distinctly Jewish.

In the privacy of his fantasies he would dream in elaborate detail of smashing Cory's head with a baseball bat, to the general and sustained applause of Danny's fellow victims (he wasn't the only boy Cory bullied). In his imagined triumph, the blood would flow, and Danny would feel the celebratory joy of righteous revenge. Of course, in reality he knew he couldn't manufacture this response or anything like it. Nor did he truly wish to. It simply wasn't within his moral compass. But the daydreams had a wonderfully satisfying feeling to them.

Instead of standing up to the bullies in town, he submitted to repeated humiliations, like (in the coach's absence) being pissed on in the showers after hockey practice by the popular and high-scoring captain of the team, who sneered and laughed as Danny turned away. (Like any prairie boy, Danny loved to play hockey, but he wasn't the kind of kid who prowled the corners or picked fights at center ice. One or two of the tough farm boys on the team called him "Lady Byng," a jibe meant to comment on his clean style of play and his avoidance of any form of violence, in their simple view of the world a form of cowardice.) Danny gradually came to realize that although these events were ugly and painful, it was a fear *already present within him* that encouraged their occurrence, as if it were an odor that the bullies could sniff out, a disagreeable scent that would mobilize their antagonism.

The inklings of this psychological fact had gradually crystallized into a realization that could be verbalized. *I'm afraid!* And as the realization grew it expanded into the understanding that he had always, to a greater or lesser extent, felt this way, especially when he was around his father. All Dad needed to do was appear slightly cross, emitting a scowl or raising the volume of his voice, and Danny would feel the ugly ghost of terror rising through his spinal cord. As a result, he had become very adept at being where his father *wasn't*. Dad's in the living room? Go to your bedroom. Dad's in the kitchen? Go into the living room. Dad's in the yard? Stay in the house. Dad's at home? Go out with your friends.

His father's taciturnity, an inborn habit of exhibiting long, frowning silences punctuated only, for the most part, by expressions of displeasure, sometimes featured curses of varying levels of profanity along with corrections to the conduct of those around him. Danny's mother would wince at his outbursts, especially when he swore, a behavior that she thought unbecoming to a teacher, not to mention offensive to Christ (or so she believed). "Don't curse, Dear," she would meekly plead, and he would scowl guiltily.

But he was consistent in his ongoing campaign to perfect his children. "Don't waste the hot water! Clean your room! Stop leaving your books all over the house! Put your shoes away! Stand up straight—don't slouch! Do your homework! Eat your turnips! Watch your manners!"

Danny's childhood Biblical training had taught him the familiar psalm, "Yea, though I walk through the valley of the shadow of Death, I shall fear no evil,". But he *was* afraid, afraid of the control that he thought should be his simply slipping away, afraid of the unknown terrors that might follow. And he knew, absolutely knew, that despite the sardonic humor of the poster he had once seen exhibiting a sneering cartoon simulacrum of someone who might as well have been Cory, that he, Danny, wasn't 'the meanest son of a bitch in the valley.'

To Danny, this seemingly inborn fear inside himself was an incomprehensible mystery, the most bewildering part of which was that he was by most social measures surprisingly successful. He had always been near the top of his academic classes in school, and he was well read for his age. He loved music and played the piano. His friends and most of his classmates generally liked him, perceiving him as good-humored, intelligent, and reliable in a pinch. The point of the puzzle digging remorselessly into his failure to understand, a painful goad in the flank of his being, was best summarized by the question, "If I'm so smart and talented, why am I afraid?" He remembered all too well the plaintive queries of Willy Loman in Arthur Miller's play *Death of a Salesman*, "What's the answer?" and he constantly reminded himself how that play had turned out. And though he despised Willy Loman, angered by the hapless character's failures, he nonetheless felt a resonance for, indeed, he had almost been brought to tears by the pathetic man's struggles: *What's the answer?*

Danny's conundrum persisted beyond high school and into the early period of his university education (an academic process that he had always taken for granted would follow his public schooling into the future—his parents and the rest of his family assumed that as well; he was an exceptionally bright student). Day after day of classes slipped away as he read and pondered, slipping imaginatively into the minds of Lord Jim and Meursault, wondering sometimes whether his own 'tell-tale heart' could be heard thumping outside himself. And always echoing in the background was, *What's the answer?* and *I'm afraid.*

But aside from Bobby, Danny's friends and family were more or less unaware of his nervous condition. His brother and sister, both older, were preoccupied with their own marriages and children. His parents mostly left him alone to find his way, supportive in a measured way (both financially and socially), but largely uncomprehending of the emotional turmoil behind his uncommunicative face.

When Danny finally appealed to a favorite uncle for help, the man generously drove over 400 miles to talk to his nephew, demonstrating a loving concern that took even Danny by surprise. His uncle didn't understand the depth of the anxiety driving the boy, but he took the trouble to arrange a meeting with a psychiatrist of his acquaintance for Danny.

"Just talk to this doctor, ok, Danny? I've known him for many years. He's a fine man." Danny looked at his uncle's concerned frown.

"Thanks, Uncle Don," Danny said. "I will." He felt a rush of gratitude. He had always loved his uncle. But he knew the man really had no idea of the painful turmoil that plagued him.

Uncle Don took his coffee and sat down at the kitchen table with his sister, Danny's mother. She looked up at her brother questioningly, and the two of them began a murmured conversation. Rather than attempt to eavesdrop, Danny slipped outside and sat down heavily on a yard swing that was mounted crookedly on an uneven, brick patio. He brushed his hair out of his eyes and sat daydreaming uncomfortably as the swing rocked slightly back and forth.

Almost immediately upon meeting the consulting psychiatrist, a slightly balding, formal man named Dr. Brook, Danny didn't trust him. The doctor's demeanor was clinically devoid of anything resembling sympathy. After all, in the time-honored stance of *objective* science, there was no legitimate way for the man to demonstrate any feeling toward or about Danny within the phrasings of his gently probing questions, assuming that he felt anything at all. It was this antiseptic attitude that Brook maintained that offended Danny, and that merely served to amplify his sense of hopelessness.

Dr. Brook sat erectly at his desk, toying with a gold pen and gazing at Danny through gold-rimmed glasses.

"Why are you unhappy, do you think?"

Danny stared at the backs of his hands for a moment or two. "I don't know."

"Has something seriously gone wrong in your life?" Dr. Brook turned away from Danny, now keeping his eyes on the leather-bound notebook in which he was writing, slowly and carefully. He may well have been doodling.

"No." Then Danny added, "Well, yes, I guess. There must be something." He paused, then said, "I'm afraid." He hunched forward, head down. "All the time, it seems."

"What are you afraid of?"

"I don't know. Nothing. Everything." Danny lifted his hands and gave a wave that might have suggested dismissal if it meant anything at all.

"Everything. That doesn't seem very reasonable, does it?" Brook finally looked again at Danny, who avoided his observant stare by looking at a potted philodendron beside the desk. Four or five seconds passed.

"No, it doesn't," he finally said. "It's not. But it's the truth." He frowned, because he fully recognized that his fear *was* unreasonable. *Why are there unreasonable truths?* he wondered briefly. Despite having a sustained faith in the powers of logic and reason (wasn't that what education was all about?), he still had to admit that this unreasonable truth had him utterly flummoxed, the more so because his fears were debilitating, a terrible source of misery and tension.

He thought of the song in the musical *The King and I* that their high school drama class had staged only a few years earlier: *Whenever I feel afraid, I whistle a happy tune, so no one will suspect, I'm afraid.* The silly tune was in an unrealistic major key, at least as unrealistic as his fear. *Fear is foolish*, the song seemed to say, *so you have to fool it back by hiding it—or if you don't, you're a fool.*

"Are there girl problems?" Dr. Brook asked.

Oh, here we go, thought Danny. *Sex!* He lifted his head toward the doctor's blank face. "No," he said. "Not really," he added somewhat lamely.

Danny had begun dating a number of different girls during his first year at university. He would fall wildly in love at the slightest stimulus: a smile, a toss of hair, a glimpse of a pretty leg. Then he would mentally mock his own internal reactions, especially after finding out in the reality that followed his fantasies that the girl was utterly unsuited to his personality and temperament. Most recently he had become infatuated with a long-haired beauty named Cindy, a girl from his own home town who had gone through his high school only a few years behind him.

But he didn't say anything about her to Dr. Brook. She had dumped Danny only a month or two previously, a loss that made him ache with frustration, but the more so because this outcome was, in his honest reflection, more or less exactly what he had expected. He had felt utterly demoralized by her sincere yet clumsy efforts to let him down gently and yet firmly to push him away. He wondered if the ongoing tension in his solar plexus had been somehow readable in his face, or if she knew of his secret terror and would be repelled by him if she recognized his interior phantoms. *Is she afraid of me?* he wondered. *I'm afraid of her—of her leaving me.*

"It's time for you to go now," she had said, standing up from where they had been seated on the back steps of her wartime house, turning into the back doorway. Danny had watched her desirable backside move through the door into the shadowy interior. The door had closed with a convincing click.

So, I've lied to the doctor, he thought to himself. *Big deal. He wouldn't get it anyway.* Then he felt guilty for a few seconds, for not giving the man a chance. But he couldn't summon the least confidence that Dr. Brook would or could do anything to help him.

"Perhaps I should give you something to help you calm yourself, get your bearings, as it were." The doctor held out this tantalizing morsel of potential pharmacological relief like a life preserver on the end of a pole, something he could withdraw at any time, leaving Danny to struggle in the deep end of a long, strange, and dangerous pool.

One pill makes you happy, and one pill makes you small... He could hear Grace Slick wailing out *White Rabbit* in his imagination.

Danny looked at Dr. Brook for a long moment. "You're asking me?" he finally squeezed out.

"Not exactly," Dr. Brook said slowly, drawing out the syllables as if he were reconsidering the offer. "Just letting you think about it."

Danny thought about it.

"No," he finally said. The thought of bulling into his mind with chemicals gave him a twinge of even greater anxiety.

"So, you're ok, then?" The doctor looked at him expectantly, as if simply by mouthing a few questions, offering Danny a brief moment or two of opportunity to talk, he might have miraculously dispelled *any* problem. He was a doctor, a psychiatrist, after all. He gave Danny the faintest of smiles, perhaps the stifled expression of his own relief.

Danny felt the slightly greasy leather of the chair seat under his sweaty palms. He had unconsciously stuffed his hands under his thighs while pondering the doctor's questions. He pulled his hands out self-consciously, flexed his fingers, and got to his feet.

"Yeah, I guess so," he muttered. *Another lie*, he thought.

Dr. Brook jotted a couple of lines in his notebook, but hearing Danny stand up, he added, "Please call me again if there's anything I can do to help." He looked Danny in the eye. Danny looked at him blankly.

"Sure," Danny said.

"My secretary will give you a card."

Danny looked away at the window, and he felt a kind of longing surge through him at the sight of the blue sky beyond. Somewhere a car horn honked. "Thanks," he said, without much conviction.

Dr. Brook extended his hand to shake. Danny glanced at the extended appendage, pink and soft, with a signet ring of some kind on the fourth finger. He reached forward and allowed Dr. Brook to clasp his hand, the warmth of the skin an almost forgotten sensation. He thought of Cindy, the mild eroticism of her slim fingers in his own as they watched a movie together one evening. He looked up at the doctor's eyes behind the glasses, as if for a moment he thought it would be Cindy's face there.

The doctor withdrew his hand and looked back at his notebook, where he jotted a few words. Danny turned and made his way out of the room. The heavy door clunked shut behind him.

A woman in a grey suit, seated in an arm chair and with a sleepy poodle on the floor beside her, looked up from her magazine, a curious glance as if she wondered, *I wonder what he's in here for*? At the reception desk, the elderly secretary was turned away, talking on the telephone in low tones. At the sound of the door, she turned, clasping her hand over the telephone mouthpiece, and said to Danny, "Will there be another appointment?"

"I don't think so," he said.

He felt a pang of nervousness, even though the other patient had turned back to her magazine.

"Well, then," the secretary said. She looked at the office door as if to indicate he should use it.

It's time for you to go now, echoed in his imagination.

Seated in his used Volkswagen Beetle outside in the parking lot he sighed in the fetid summer air. He reached to the dash and turned on the Blaupunkt radio, tuned as usual to one of the popular music channels.

It is the dawning of the Age of Aquarius, Age of Aquariuuuuuus, Aquarius! Aquarius. The Fifth Dimension hit practically surged at him.

The song's energy lifted him out of his unhappiness for a moment. Trying to sing along, he started the car, released the clutch and pulled out of his parking space. *Crystal vision, revelation, and the mind's true liberation, Aquarius! Aquarius!* But even before the song had ended his imagination was already supplying, *Whenever I feel afraid,* ...

CHAPTER TWO

Looking for Relief

Several years went by during which Danny found little to no help. Even though he read and studied voraciously, he sometimes felt he was only going through the motions of his university studies. His fearful preoccupations dogged him daily with tremors and night terrors. Nonetheless, through sheer force of will, he managed to plug his way through an English degree with a minor in history and music.

Danny found these subjects thrilling. The explanatory power of language sometimes left him nearly breathless. Modernist writers were particularly powerful in his experience. Dostoyevsky's *The Brothers Karamazov* shocked and astonished him, and despite the detailed convolutions of his style, Joseph Conrad repeatedly prodded Danny's analytical thinking, forcing him away from his more childish demands for stories providing the opportunity for hero worship and happy endings.

History's collage of cultures and periods began to contextualize his own childhood conditioning—his religious background, and the wartime experiences of his parents and grandparents. It seemed to him that the past was little more than conflict after conflict, war piled upon war, with resolution always a goal somewhere in the future. His own adolescent experience of news from everywhere seemed to place him and his community at the center of a cyclone of global changes spinning around them: more wars (and threats of wars), draft dodgers (like his Grade 12 English teacher had been, a geeky yet academically proficient refugee from Texas), and the startling adventure of the American moon landing.

Music, especially classical music, seemed to wash through him in streams of sensory abstraction, tonal thought lines whose structures and timbres penetrated the center of his being. The Romantics were especially powerful, with the magnificence of their longing for various perfections permeating their concertos and symphonies. This longing in particular mirrored the depths of the desire he felt to overcome his fear. But the strange tonalities of Debussy and Ravel better reflected the imbalance of his personal uncertainties. And the terror remained.

After nearly four years of failure to progress against his anxieties he decided to try to enter medical school and applied to the University of Saskatchewan. He was sick in some way, he felt. *If I have to cure myself, I need the tools to do it*, he reasoned.

A year of basic sciences including biochemistry and physics laid the foundation for his application. He attended his application interview, fear gnawing at his guts, anticipating nervously a humiliating rejection. Instead the two physicians on the interview committee cheerfully commended his

4.0 GPA, chatted about their own youthful interviews (and how nervous *they* had been), and welcomed him aboard.

Thus, he found himself only weeks later donning a white lab coat and working with another hundred or so scrubbed and optimistic youngsters, cutting into human corpses and peering into microscopes, listening to lectures, attending demonstrations, and hitting the books until all hours, memorizing mnemonic chains and esoteric details of human illness and physiology.

One morning he was late for class, only to find that the lecture theater was empty other than with a professor preparing a model for the afternoon's lecture in embryology on the rotation of the gut. The slightly built East Indian doctor looked up at Danny and said, "Good. You can listen to my practice lecture." He gestured to a front seat. Danny sat as indicated and watched in fascination, as using a series of plasticene models, the lecturer demonstrated the rotational folding of the intestines in the developing human fetus. He thought of his own gut folding and smiled in amusement, then recalled with a shiver Cory's punching him, and wondered what that did to the soft tissue under the abdominal wall.

His classmates were a gregarious, cheerful bunch, welcoming the stresses of long hours and demanding curriculum. Most of them also had their eyes on the prize, as well, the six-figure income they could expect once they were licensed and had begun to work. One of the lecturers who took them through the steps of performing an appendectomy joked at the end, "And there, you've made three hundred bucks!"

A Ukrainian youngster at Danny's dissection table joked that, "If you ignore the Jews, the Mormons and the Chinese, there are only three of us left." He would turn up with a new Ukrainian joke every day, laughing at himself with gusto while peeling the external membrane off a kidney or isolating the radial nerve in the forearm. "Why wasn't Christ born in the Ukraine? They couldn't find three wise men and a virgin. How do you tell the bride at a Ukrainian wedding? She's the one with the braided armpits. A Ukrainian was walking down the street with a pig under his arm. 'Where'd you get that?' a cop asked. The pig answered, 'I found him at an auction.' Heh-heh-heh."

Danny's medical schooling was an extraordinary opportunity that should have been exhilarating and deeply pleasurable. But it wasn't. He was still afraid, and he couldn't avoid the fact or evade its consequences. The puzzle of his anxiety continued to roil within him, sometimes ebbing, but occasionally swelling to a feverish and sweaty terror that threatened to undo him completely. Thus, in nearly every spare moment he continued to study psychology's mysteries.

Can a mind understand a mind? Can a brain understand a brain? Can a mind understand a brain? Can a brain understand a mind?

These self-referential questions, amid a tangle of others of similar bent, had been spinning around in Danny's consciousness for more than five years now. He had read *Gestalt Therapy* (the happy therapeutic meanderings of Fritz Perls, lecherous, caftan-clad, bearded, cheerful California therapist/hippy), and selected pieces from the works of Freud (*literary and interesting, but not useful*, Danny had decided).

He had thrilled to the revolutionary revelations of Ronald Laing's *The Divided Self*, and to the political realities exposed in Marcuse's *One-Dimensional Man*, with its observations of the sick-making demands for conformity from society. Laing seemed to admire madness, and to despise conventional society, which he labeled "unsane," especially the "politics of the family" that he deemed responsible for so many of the peculiar symptoms he was preoccupied with treating.

Danny pored through issues (and back issues) of *Psychology Today Magazine* with an intensity bordering on the religious, hoping against hope that some simpleton idea could unlock the key to his misery. No dice. Still, he soldiered on, convinced that somewhere there existed a key to unlock his soul and free him from his terrors.

'Terror' was not an exaggeration. Once during his year at medical school, he had gone to bed in the apartment he shared with two other students (one a chemist and another working toward his accounting degree), anticipating the next morning's anatomy lab, an early morning exploration he usually found fascinating and exhilarating, intellectually, at least. But instead of contemplating the next day's pleasure, he lay in his single bed, curled into himself, shivering with anxiety, brain in hyperdrive, muscles nearly in spasm, heart rattling, wondering whether this night would be the one during which he would have to walk across the quad to the university's teaching hospital and check himself into the psych ward.

Despite his academic successes, relief was not to be found, and after one year he dropped out of the cohort, hoping against hope to find a solution to his anxiety somewhere else. (He understood clearly that the stresses of academic study were not what caused his anxiety; if anything, their preoccupations marginally kept his ghosts at bay.)

He took a series of part-time, two-bit jobs that required little to no creative effort, all in order to enable his reading time. While driving a city bus he kept a book with him at all times in order to read while waiting at turnarounds or during the minimum breaks allowed by the rigid schedules. He actually enjoyed the driving, a virtually reflexive behavior that enabled his mind to be elsewhere, thinking, thinking, always thinking. Even the two hookers (who regularly took his late-night route to wherever was home) were unable to command his interest, and for all the cheesiness of their occupation, they *were* sexy. He blushed furiously when Donna offered to show him her 'titty tattoo,' and he looked away when her partner would bend over the fare box, exposing her pretty cleavage.

"You can look, but don't touch," Donna said, smirking a bit at his discomfiture. "Unless you pay."

"Come on, Donna," Tina said. "This boy's gay." And the two of them sauntered unsteadily on their high heels toward the back seats while Danny burned with humiliation.

Some of the absurd therapy systems on offer were unworthy of investigation, yet he forced himself to consider them, the triumph of hope over a judgment he usually trusted. He scanned through the principles of EST and transactional analysis (*I'm OK, You're Not So Hot*, as the comics characterized it—Danny had not totally lost his sense of humor.)

In a psychology class that he managed to audit (it was scheduled during a convenient break in his split shift driving), he learned of the hierarchy of needs proposed by Abraham Maslow (obvious stuff), and of the unconditional acceptance promoted by Carl Rogers (comforting from a moral perspective, but clinically useless).

Some days were better than others. There were really bright people within his circle of friends. Yet despite the admiration and warmth he felt toward some of them, there was not one whom he trusted enough to unburden his troubles in their presence. To admit his fears would be to reveal a personal failing, he was certain of it. How could they not conclude that he was a lying fraud, that all his putative intelligence was merely an act that covered over the nasty, weak little boy that he really was?

After Cindy, he had been deliberately unwilling to risk himself romantically. When a cute girl from his psych class had audaciously perched herself beside him in the corner cafe and invited him for dinner at her apartment, Bradley (one of his acquaintances) had squinted at Danny meaningfully, and after her departure offered the clichéd wisdom, "She's hot to trot."

Danny did accept her offer of dinner (a forgettable pasta concoction washed down with sparkling water—he had not taken up wine yet), but despite her sweet efforts to make obvious her availability, he didn't even kiss her, a demonstration of juvenile awkwardness that most youngsters lose in their early teens. Instead, he went home and immersed himself in the Zen offerings of Alan Watts. By the next week he was exploring the original koans of *The Mumonkan* (but he couldn't sit still long enough to meditate properly). He became convinced that the Buddhists were right about one thing: life is pain. *However*, he thought, *if experience is all an illusion, my fear is a damned powerful one.*

In the public library, he prowled the psychology section, ignoring the homeless man who snored in one of the window carrels, his head on his arms and his paper-bagged wine upended beside him on the carpeted floor. Here Danny scanned *The Power of Positive Thinking*, but gave it up, thinking *What the hell good would that do?* The head librarian came by to roust out the sleeping man.

"It's against library policy to allow intoxicated people in the library," he said as he firmly helped the man to his feet.

The man looked around blearily and said, "Intoxicated? Intoxicated! Wish I *was* intoxicated." He stumbled off toward the entrance. Danny looked at him with a kind of admiration. *Maybe intoxication is something we all need,* he thought before turning back to his search.

Danny understood that mind-numbing drugs, electro-shock (like in *One Flew Over the Cuckoo's Nest*), and surgical lobotomy were still promoted in many areas of psychotherapy. These were practices that horrified him. He couldn't imagine solving fear by inflicting unhealable physical damage on the organ of his mind.

Following up the intoxication angle, he found that he couldn't even smoke dope properly, (although he tried it a couple of times, with uneven effects, the most significant of which was the realization that when very stoned, he wasn't quite sure whether or not he had shit himself).

Nearly every psychological theory or therapeutic proposal he explored seemed clumsy or ineffectual at best, and dangerous at worst.

Then one day he read about Beatle John Lennon's experimentation with something called 'primal therapy,' an approach to therapeutics recognizing the role of the body as a vehicle for feeling, describing the relief that could occur through the cathartic expression of previously repressed pain from whatever source: physical trauma, abandonment, abuse, humiliation. The ideas electrified him. Associated with this prescribed loosening of one's emotional repressions were the theories of Ida Rolf, a therapist who approached aspects of neurosis through the physical methods of systematic (and nearly violent) massage to free the patients' bodies from their frozen adaptations to pain.

He read everything he could find about the primal therapy approach. He saw snippets of film from therapeutic sessions. True, not everything he found was completely encouraging. The psychologist who first established the treatment some-times appeared as something of a charlatan by trademarking his work, (ostensibly to protect prospective patients from fraudulent practitioners, but more realistically interpreted as a strategy to protect his exaggerated income). This 'doctor of psychology' zoomed around LA in his Porsche, a kind of exuberant revel in his newfound status as a cult celebrity. Still, the clarity of the theory behind his work resonated strongly with Danny.

The so-called "journals of primal therapy" did not draw approval among other psychologists (articles were not peer-reviewed). The theory was written off by most investiga-tors as 'flaky' or 'cultish.' Still, in the writings that explored patient histories, Danny read of how levels of trauma could historically layer into the body's tensions and anxieties, crammed into a physicality of postural distortion and an emotional life marked with irrational fears and enactments.

Those descriptions fit him nearly precisely. Thus, despite the method's questionable bona fides, Danny was intrigued. For once he felt hopeful.

After months of consideration, he determined that he wanted to enter this therapy, somehow. Almost anything would be better than continuing within his straightjacketing anxiety. He wanted to confront the demons within himself, to trust himself and the integrity of his own being, however far into the tangles of thought and physical tension that being might be buried.

Finally, he gave one of the books on primal therapy to his father to read. It was a terribly long shot, he realized. After so many beginnings and dead ends, he couldn't imagine his family helping him in this way. Yet after his uncle had gently refused his financial help but referred him to Dr. Brook instead (a well-meaning gesture), he felt he had nowhere to turn except back to the man who had helped him again and again, the man he had hated and feared as long as he could remember: his father.

Danny's father wrestled with his own demons. *His* own father had been autocratic and abusive, as only a 'paterfamilias' in the Prussian style can be. Parenting methods seem almost as inherited as physical traits. Danny's father was prone to bouts of irrational temper, particularly when he found himself confronted with novel responsibilities he felt unable to manage. It was a situation that came up all too frequently, but with a randomness that meant the family that were in his charge were constantly on their toes, nervously anticipating the next outburst, whenever it might erupt.

Now Danny's father took the cheap paperback and looked at the cover skeptically. *The Primal Scream: The Cure for Neurosis*. It didn't look very promising. Not at all. *This looks like garbage,* he thought. But Danny had seemed so serious and intent that he read it, that he felt obliged at least to scan its contents. His son wasn't stupid. He understood that about him clearly, if not much else.

He went to the kitchen and made a cup of strong coffee. (He ground the beans himself in a manual grinder that he held between his knees, turning a crank vigorously while he watched the beans disappear between the grinder's jaws. It was a metaphor for life, he decided, how the forces that surround us grind us down.) He leaned back against the kitchen counter as the water boiled. Then he poured it carefully into the cone-shaped filter perched over his cup. Almost immediately the deep aroma of coffee filled the room. He would need its heady stimulation, he decided, if he was going to get through this book.

Minutes later he was in his favorite armchair, burrowing into the introduction.

Danny's home town, a prairie community of three or four thousand, embodied most of the features one would encounter then in such towns: a few car dealerships and gas stations, a couple of banks, two hotels (with bars), a bowling alley, two or three small supermarkets, some small-town lawyers, a twenty-bed hospital, an assortment of public schools, and four Chinese restaurants. Half a dozen or so churches raised their steeples, imploring heaven for their faithful adherents. (The

Catholic church had its own adjoining elementary school and a convent, which featured a fine grand piano for the musical edification of the nuns. *They're sure a strange bunch*, Danny had thought when in junior high school.) Four or five grain elevators and an old passenger station flanked the railway line that bisected the municipal area. A swimming pool (outdoor, and therefore open only in summer) was opposite the high school, just a hundred yards or so from the small hockey arena that had been built in the early 1960's to initiate the area's youth into the prairie's ongoing winter obsession: ice hockey. (The only activity that remotely approached its widespread fascination was curling.) A red brick court house, whose structure was made the more imposing by two World War I vintage cannons on its front lawn, faced the street, ready to ward off the foes of prairie propriety. The town was also the home of a trailer manufacturer (seeking and finding here the cheap, non-union labor that enabled its Ontario shareholders to sleep well at night, secure in the payouts of comfortable profits).

It was summer, and for most university students it was time for a summer job. Danny had managed to procure a position on the assembly line, building interior walls and trimming doors and windows for mobile homes and travel trailers. Sided with flashy aluminum, these trashy constructions provided cheap accommodation for working class folk, or trendy holiday vehicles in a rapidly expanding consumer economy. The flash disguised, more or less, their lack of quality, for they were structures that were slapped together with poor insulation, nearly cardboard interior walls, and unreliable plumbing and wiring, not to mention questionable structural integrity, none of which flaws prevented them from selling very well. Where else could you buy your own home for less than $10,000?

Danny's job was utterly depressing, badly paid and dirty, with long hours. He would crawl out of bed at half past six in a stupefied exhaustion, wolf down some toast and fruit for breakfast, make a basic lunch (sandwiches, some fruit or other, and a few cookies), and bicycle the two miles to his job, which began at 7:30 am. Each day was much the same, with two ten-minute coffee breaks and a half hour for lunch, and the laborers worked until 5:30 pm.

At the end of each week he would accept his pay envelope containing $59.25 and take it to the bank, keeping $5.00 aside for his modest weekend activities (perhaps a movie in the musty old cinema on 29th Avenue), and maybe a new paperback. The rest went into his savings. Fortunately, he could live at home where his mother and father would feed him and would not charge him rent.

Two of his hippy acquaintances from high school also worked at the factory, one of them a quiet, lanky, bearded young man with hair down to his shoulders. The older workers called him Jesus, a name he accepted with a resigned sort of grace, as if it were his cross to bear. The other was a lumpy, grumpy youth who kept mostly to himself, but often responded to the arbitrary and ill thought out assignment of work tasks with the comment, "Surely you jest?", while knowing full well that the supervisor was perfectly serious.

Under the summer sun the large Quonset building that housed the assembly line would become insufferably uncomfortable. The workers would all sweat in the 90+ degree heat, while the managers did 'the important work' in a couple of air-conditioned trailers on the other side of the parking lot.

The fundamental injustice of this arrangement was not lost on the employees, who had their own individual methods of compensating for their various miseries. Several of the older men were alcoholics whose levels of chronic, marginal inebriation were just below what would prevent them from barely managing their repetitive tasks. One electrician would crawl under a half-built mobile home, wire his hands up to something on the frame, and fall asleep. He would appear to be busy wiring to any cursory glance by a supervisor. When the bell would ring, signaling that the line was about to move, he would untie himself, wait for the new unit to arrive, and repeat the process. He collected his pay at the end of the week like any other employee, but he made his real money doing electrical work for cash in the evenings, elsewhere in the community.

There was no training of any significant nature provided by the company. Occasionally one of the older workers would be assigned to show one of the newcomers how something was done. No health or safety drills occurred, and one day Danny had to stifle his nausea when a middle-aged 'carpenter' lost his index finger to a table saw. A co-worker belted the victim's arm as a tourniquet, and after the ambulance left, Danny and Jesus were assigned to mop up the blood and clean the saw.

Some employees stole tools or materials. Cans of paint, bags of screws, hand tools, really anything small enough to be concealed in a lunch bucket or deep pocket would disappear with predictable regularity.

About three weeks into the job, Danny noted that the managers had installed a closed-circuit video observation system. Its cameras, mounted overhead, would rotate and swivel, focusing in on various workers at their tasks. One dust-filled afternoon Danny noticed that a camera was pointed at one of his young co-workers, who was occupied stapling cheap paneling onto the frame of an interior wall.

"Teddy!" Danny called to him. When Teddy turned, Danny pointed at the camera. Teddy grinned, turned his staple gun toward the camera high overhead, and fired ten or fifteen staples in its direction. Moments later, with a hum of its small motor, the camera turned away. It was a happy moment in an otherwise dull day.

On another occasion Danny and two other workers were assembling exterior walls. The bottom plate of each wall rested on a steel ledge, angled to prevent the wall from tilting toward the workers. Wall studs were placed at intervals noted on the wall plans and were to be nailed in place from beneath with high-powered nail guns. Danny primed the gun beneath the plate and carefully fired the nail upward. The nail struck a knot in the stud and bent outward. To Danny's shock, the point of the nail, thankfully arrested by friction, was aiming directly at his forehead. *Great,* he thought, *I can enjoy the daily chance to be murdered by a stupid accident for $1.65 an hour. Just great.*

We are the hollow men, we are the stuffed men, headpieces filled with straw... The T.S. Eliot phrases echoed softly in his imagination.

Danny often pondered, if he had to work at such a job for the rest of his life, simply to survive, whether or not he would kill himself. He kept score in his daily meditations on the question, and by summer's end self-murder was slightly in the lead. Fortunately, with the end of summer came the end of the job. Finally, the horror had ended. Danny had saved $328.43 over a summer of misery. Now what?

CHAPTER THREE

Blood is Thicker than Water

Danny's father put down the book and pushed it away from himself, as if it contained something vile, something ugly. He had moved from his armchair to his private study, where he had been reading for two hours, ploughing through the cheap paperback on a form of pop psychology that purported to explain how infant trauma and childhood pains (fear, humiliation, physical punishment) can be repressed unconsciously and kept away from consciousness and expression by physical stress. These stresses were purportedly measurable in everything from body temperature and blood pressure to physical manifestations such as tremors, postural abnormalities, tics, unconscious gestures, phantom pain, stomach ulcers, skin ailments, nail-biting, and various kinds of emotional distress.

He had to admit, he didn't know much of anything about psychology. He knew he had been utterly terrified of his own father—the man's unpredictable temper, the reach of his foot or his fist. He had felt enormous relief upon hearing that his own father had died, but he couldn't imagine Danny feeling that way about him in similar fashion.

He had read some Freud, of course, but despite the elegance of Freud's prose, the theories (as he understood them) seemed fanciful and metaphorical rather than scientific. Of course, he didn't understand much science, either.

This primal theory of emotional flooding his son had handed him, of allowing the body to lead the mind into its nether darkness, scared him. He had always held himself in reserve—socially, maritally, sexually. The idea of openly expressing what might be stewing in the sewers of memory and desire made him very uneasy. Surely it was a roadmap to terrible unhappiness, perhaps even to insanity.

Yet he knew well the pull of depression, the paradoxical attraction of giving oneself over to hopelessness. He knew it was in the family. His own father had committed suicide in a mental hospital, as had an uncle. He had felt his own bouts of long-drawn depression. He knew well the "black dog" of which Winston Churchill had written. Now his son was threatened.

Further, Danny had withdrawn from medical school, a bewildering choice after all the work the youngster had done to achieve entry. He had given no explanation, despite his mother's gentle probing. Then he had confessed to his parents that he no longer believed in God, an admission that distressed his mother enormously and that disappointed but didn't surprise his father.

"Oh, dear," his mother had said to Danny while his father looked stonily on. "You don't really mean that, surely." Danny's heart shrank with pain. He loved his mother, perhaps more than he loved anyone else. To hurt her this way seemed utterly cruel.

Tensing himself, terrified that his father might start yelling (or worse), he nonetheless forced himself to say, "I do mean it, Mom. I just don't believe it. It's just too far-fetched. In fact, I don't understand how *you*, and Dad, believe it. It just doesn't make sense."

He waited for whatever tirade might emerge from his father. But his dad remained silent, his jaw working as if chewing some indigestible piece of gristle, and after a moment he looked away, staring out the window with a far-away expression on his bland features. *Perhaps he doesn't really believe it, either,* Danny suddenly realized.

Now the older man took a final swallow of coffee. *It's cold,* he thought, and set the cup aside. He reached into his shirt pocket and unfolded a piece of worn paper. On it was a letter from his son, typed carefully (with occasional corrections done on liquid paper correction material). It read:

> *Dear Dad*
>
> *I don't know how to ask you this. You have always been generous to me, even when I have, I am sure, disappointed you. And yet, I need to ask your help once more.*
>
> *I have never shared with you or with Mom the degree of fear and unease that seems to plague me. On reflection, it seems that all of my choices and behaviors have been a*

subconscious effort to deal with this affliction. Had I not been so distressed I would have continued in medical school, made you all proud, I suppose. And though I have loved my studies, both there and previously, I have never been able to shake or avoid my nightly terrors and unhappiness. At one point last year, I nearly checked myself into a mental hospital, I felt so desperate.

For many months, I have been investigating various sources of help. I'm sure Mom must have told you of my visit with the psychiatrist, the one Uncle Don arranged for me. Of course, it was of no help other than to reinforce in me the conviction that my family generally love and support me, even when I have disappointed them.

I have finally found a treatment regimen I wish to submit myself to, to participate in. I know you will not find it appealing and may even find it ugly and distasteful. However, its descriptions and theoretical framework speak to me in a way none other has, and I fear it may be my last hope.

At this characterization, his father had felt a shock of interpretive recognition. Was this not how people felt when contemplating suicide?!

Please read this book, as it explains in ways I believe I could not, to find what I wish to do.

The treatment is expensive and is offered in Denver, Colorado. I need your financial help once more if you can see your way to providing it. I know I should not ask, but I cannot see any option.

Your son
Danny

He shoved the letter away and got up from his desk (he had left his armchair after the second chapter, preferring to read in his tiny study, book propped on his desk, because here he could concentrate undisturbed—no one knocked on his study door when it was closed except in emergencies).

He stretched his back. Somehow it had cramped up while he was reading. Then he went to the doorway, opened it, and looked out toward the room where Danny slept. He walked over to it and knocked on the door. There was a rustling inside of someone moving about, and the door opened a few inches.

"Danny?" his father said.

Danny had been sleeping on top of the bed, and he rubbed his left eye with the back of his fist. He really didn't want to see his father much less talk to him. But he answered, "Yes. What is it?"

His father looked at him. "Come into my study," he said. He turned away, and moments later Danny followed him, head down and shoulders slumped.

"Sit down," his father said, slipping into his own chair once more.

Danny stepped over to the wall and sat down on the large chest where he knew his father kept some old books and documents. Once his father had shown him, in "the extremest confidence, you understand," a copy of *Mein Kampf* that he had hidden there since the beginning of World War II. God knew what else might be in there.

"What do you want, Dad?"

His father looked at him, a mystified regard full of disappointment and unease. "I read the book you gave me," he said.

Danny turned away, looked at the floor, said nothing.

"I can't pretend to like what it offers. I think this theory, this therapy might be very dangerous, that it might come between us in ugly ways. It makes me feel uncertain, even a bit angry."

Danny looked up. *Of course, it does. Didn't you know that I was terrified of you all my life? Don't you know that I've come to you as my last hope, even as I can barely stand to be in the room with you?* The thoughts spilled through his mind, a froth of fear and anger and tension.

"Surely you don't want to seek help or treatment from these—these people?" His father laid his hands flat on his desk, as if they were alien appendages that might as easily break concrete with a karate chop as play a piano concerto, or simply fall off his arms. He pried one up again and made an indecipherable gesture.

Danny took a deep breath. "I do."

"But why? Why?"

"I can't explain precisely," Danny admitted. "It just feels right. It's as if it's the only thing that has ever felt quite right in my life." He looked down again.

"You realize what this says about your mother and me," his father said. It was almost an accusation. It was a voice leaden with unease.

Danny's cheek twitched. He didn't really want to hurt his parents, and yet his desperation had driven him to seek this help. This theory of emotional flooding, of allowing the body to release its 'demons,' so to speak, had so profoundly resonated with him that he had decided he must follow it up. And despite his fear that his judgment would be scorned or that he might shock his mother and father, he had felt it only fair that they knew what he was considering. Danny knew that this theory of emotional flooding held as its open premise that various forms of child mistreatment by parents *might* be the origin of much neurotic suffering. Thus, to seek such treatment was tantamount to claiming his parents had abused him in any of a number of ways. And that, too, seemed unreasonable, for although his parents had been strict, within his memory he had never been beaten or similarly mistreated.

"Oh, God, Dad. I can't explain. I don't mean any of what you're thinking. I just need help. That's all."

"You're really determined to do this thing, aren't you? To leave Canada and go to Denver to this, this place."

"Yes. I am." Danny couldn't really say anything else.

They were silent for almost a full minute. At last, his father gave Danny a searching look and said, "All right. I'll help you."

He reached into a drawer of his desk and took out his cheque book.

Danny felt a kind of wild hope.

His father filled out the cheque, tore it out, and handed it to Danny. It was for ten thousand dollars.

Danny looked at it, speechless for a few moments. Then he said, "Thank you, Dad. Thank you."

His father stared at him, as if he might already be regretting a foolish waste of money. But he felt he had to do something. He could scarcely touch his son, and his fears were no longer intellectual, despite the details he had read. And he was out of words. Yet finally he managed to squeeze out, "Be very careful."

"I will," Danny said.

CHAPTER FOUR

Arrival

The Alaska Airlines flight no. 608 from Regina sailed down and settled onto the tarmac of Stapleton Field in Denver at about 4:00 pm on a late October afternoon. The sun was only a few degrees above the jagged Rocky Mountain front range to the west.

After recovering his luggage, Danny headed down an unfamiliar concourse, following the signs to find a taxi. He felt disoriented and a little anxious, and although anxiety was his usual background state, he found himself attributing it to the uncertainties he was feeling about the coming weeks. The new city, new country, and certainly the ambiguous process of therapy all compounded his worries. He would need to get a bank account, locate someplace to live, learn the city's transportation system...the list went on and on, stirring around in his imagination.

As he walked slowly along, suitcase heavy in his left hand, a silky voice to one side said to him, "Hi, stranger. We'd like you to have this book!"

Danny looked to the source of the voice. A tall, bald young man wearing a saffron-colored robe was smiling at him and holding out a large paperback with zodiacal symbols (or something like them) on the cover. *Hare Krishna!* the title proclaimed, and the subtitle stated, *How to Find Peace.* Preoccupied as he was with locating a taxi to his motel, Danny felt a mild annoyance. Yet the stranger seemed so genuinely welcoming and friendly that Danny felt his anxiety diminish a little. The man's orange robe, like some bizarre Hallowe'en costume, was completely at odds with anything Danny had seen before. From under a billowy sleeve, the man thrust the book forward more insistently.

"Perhaps you'd like to join us for a feast?" the man offered.

Behind this weird apparition Danny could see others in similar costume accosting other travelers.

"Fuck off," said a businessman towing a sample case. Another girl in a paisley skirt giggled nervously and shook her head toward the young woman who had approached her, then hastened down the concourse as if fleeing something dangerous.

Further away a group of these robed creatures was dancing to a tambourine and singing: *Hare krishna; krishna krishna...* They hopped and spun in a kind of ecstatic stupidity.

"No—no, thanks," Danny said. At the man's frown, he said, "How much is the book?"

"A suitable donation would be five dollars or so," the man confided, smiling once more, and edging forward.

"I've just got Canadian money," Danny said, "but you can have five bucks."

The man extended the book, which Danny tucked under his arm while he found five dollars in his wallet. The man edged forward, staring greedily toward the contents of the wallet, which Danny pulled back toward his chest in mild alarm. He offered the blue five-dollar bill toward the strange fellow, who took it and examined it curiously, then said to Danny, "Hare Krishna!" In a billow of silk, the man spun toward his companions, holding out the strange-looking blue note like some extraordinary talisman.

I wonder what the hell that goofy saying means, Danny thought, but he didn't bother to ask. Instead, grasping his suitcase firmly, he walked away toward the terminal doors, beyond which he could see a line of Yellow Cabs through the glass. Each cab had *Driver carries only $5 change* prominently displayed on its side.

"Hey, bud," said a driver, who was leaning on his cab. He was a gangly man with dark hair and pasty skin. His clear blue eyes were fixed on Danny. "Those goofball Hare Krishnas buggin' you?" And before Danny could reply, he said, "Ah, you bought a book, huh? I'd ignore those shitheads if I were you."

"Yeah, well, we'll see," Danny replied noncommittally. "Can you take me to the Creekside Motel off South Colorado Boulevard? And how much will it be, roughly?"

"Oh, sure, about fifteen bucks. Gimme your case, I'll put it in the trunk." The driver pushed himself up off the car and reached for the suitcase, hefted it easily, and lugged it around behind the cab. He opened the trunk and swung the case into it. "You got anything else?" he asked.

"No, that's it," Danny said. He climbed into the front seat. Smells of sweat overlain with perfume and pine air freshener assailed him. The driver slid in through the other door, fired up the motor, shifted the car into drive, and the two of them pulled out into the clutch of traffic leading to the airport exit. They turned toward the west, facing the mountains just as the sun was setting, shooting fiery light at them through the front windshield. Below the front range, spangles of city lights were already blinking on. Despite the stink and noise of the traffic it was a scene of obscure beauty. The driver flicked on his meter, and they sped toward a set of traffic lights in the direction of the city.

"I'll take I-25, ok?" the driver suggested.

"Ok," Danny answered. The driver might as well have suggested "rocket ship" or "ground squirrel tunnel," for all the difference it made to Danny's knowledge of the city. For the first five minutes or so he spent his time looking around at the cityscape still visible in the darkening sky. It seemed like a huge place to Danny, lights stretching toward the horizon in all directions, with the rugged, irregular shadow of the mountains looming in the western sky. The driver pulled onto I-70 and raced westward for about ten minutes. Then he slowed for the interchange with I-25, which headed southward, and he sped up again to about 75 mph, weaving through light evening traffic.

"Where 'ya from?" the driver asked. It was a friendly voice, seemingly ingenuous and honest, and Danny warmed to the man, despite his rough speech.

"I'm from Canada—near Saskatoon," he answered.

"No kidding," the driver said. He screwed up his features, probably wondering where a place called 'Saskatoon' might be, Danny realized. "What's it like there? Cold, I bet."

"Not yet. But it won't be long. We usually get some really cold weather, like twenty below zero, toward the middle of November."

"Oh, boy, not for me, not for me," the driver continued. "Too goddamned cold *here*, if you ask me," he went on. Then, "I'm from South Carolina," he said. "Followed a woman here. Go figure. Worst mistake of my life."

He gazed forlornly ahead at the spread of tail lights making their magical light show dance in the lanes ahead. Then, "Nearly there," he said, and signaling carefully, steered them toward an off-ramp. Three minutes later they bumped into the parking lot of a tired-looking motel. *Creekside Motel: Vacancy* the sign blinked at them.

For a moment Danny regretted not asking the driver what the "worst mistake" might have entailed. He imagined the driver trying to protect himself from some nagging woman, improbably buxom, with an acid tongue, and maybe an alcohol problem, and two snot-nosed children (a malnourished girl and a younger boy with scabies) hanging on her skirt. Then he dismissed the image before it developed into a full-blown movie, and instead he focused on the meter, where the driver had swept down the flag with a flourish of his right hand. $13.40 shone from its dial.

Danny pulled out his wallet and said, "I haven't got to a bank yet. Is $20 Canadian enough? I mean, I know it's close." He held out a grimy green note with the Queen's face staring out of it.

"Jeez, I don't know, man. This looks like Monopoly money."

"Just look at it closely," Danny said. "See that? *Bank of Canada. Banque du Canada.* We're bilingual. That means two languages, right? It's like the US Treasury. Look it up," he finally offered lamely.

"Hey, ok, man. I'll just stuff it in the safe and let the bean counters worry about it." He took the twenty, folded it into a small rectangle, and slid it through the vertical slot in a cylinder bolted to the transmission housing. Danny watched his money disappear.

"We're square, then?" Danny asked.

"Sure," the driver said. He climbed out and retrieved Danny's case from the trunk. "Ok. Good luck, man."

"Thanks," Danny said. He watched the cab pull a u-turn in the lot and maneuver back onto the street. "You, too," he added in a verbal afterthought. *Can't be too careful with your woman*, he thought.

Once he had checked in, he sat in the gathering darkness of his room, typically square, occupied by a cheap double bed, a couple of chairs, and a television set standing on an uneven dresser. He stared at the blank screen, replaying in his mind the events of the day.

Damn, he thought. *I left my Hare Krishna book in the cab.* Then, just as quickly, he dismissed his concern. After a few minutes, he got to his feet, closed the drapes (which smelled of some kind of cleanser), ensured that the door was bolted and chained, and lay down on the bed. Fully clothed, he fell into a restless sleep, dreaming of a saffron-robed psychiatrist holding a scalpel, grinning at him. In his dream, he could hear Pink Floyd: *You raise the blade; you make the change; you rearrange me 'til I'm sane.*

Later he woke in a fright of strangeness, heart hammering, until he realized that the banging he was hearing was some sort of cop show shootout on the television in the next room. He thumped his fist on the wall, then wondered if some ruffian next door would come over to his room and shoot *him*. But a moment later the TV volume was reduced. For a few seconds, he stared at the wall, anticipating the TV's return to loudness. But less than two minutes later it went silent altogether.

Danny slipped out of his clothes, folded them, and placed them on a chair. Then he crawled into bed and slept, this time heavily.

CHAPTER FIVE

_____

Sessions

Danny remained more or less isolated for the three days preceding his first therapy session. He even ate in his motel room (junk food, mostly, and bottled juices), except for two weekend breakfasts at a Jewish deli in a nearby strip mall. *Lox, Onions & Eggs* the menu had advertised, a mystery breakfast, since he didn't have any idea what 'lox' was. A weary-looking cook who identified himself as 'Mort' deposited the dish on his table. "Never had lox?" he asked incredulously, with a crooked smile. "You'll like this. It'll change your life." The smoked salmon and cream cheese on a bagel were delicious, as were the scrambled eggs, and after he finished eating both days he lingered over his coffee, always thinking of his upcoming therapy sessions.

When the day of his first appointment finally arrived, Danny showered and walked down to the clinic to await his therapist. He sat on a low bench against the wall. A few dozen feet away a youthful Chicano in blue jeans and a Ché Guevara t-shirt was scrubbing down the wall. On its open surface the remnants of some graffiti still showed as a red smear running at an angle toward the floor. He plunged his sponge into a bucket of soapy water, squeezed out the excess suds, and with a few more practiced swipes, managed to restore the wall to its bland, greyish white.

Leaning back against the wall behind him, Danny closed his eyes and waited. He heard the employee pick up his bucket and walk past and out the door toward the offices that occupied a low building across a driveway. It was there that Danny had deposited his first cheque only three days ago. Two thousand dollars. Just like that.

It was quiet and cool in the waiting room. A couple of minutes later a door to the interior opened and a haggard-looking young woman emerged, followed by another, older woman with grey hair. The older woman clasped the other by the upper arm and said, "Louise, you know you can call me. When it gets bad, call me." Then she released her grip. The younger woman lowered her eyes and nodded. She turned toward Danny with an expression that appeared absolutely haunted. The skin beneath her eyes was dark and puffy, and she moved with an erratic step that might equally have char-acterized a totally spent athlete, or someone utterly defeated by life. She nodded at Danny almost imperceptibly. Then she went outside, closing the door behind her.

Turning to him, the older woman said, "You must be Danny."

Danny looked at her and nodded.

"Dr. Harris will be with you in about ten minutes," she said. "He's a very nice man, very gentle and caring, you'll see."

When he didn't reply, she turned and disappeared inside once more.

Danny wondered just how bad he looked, to merit such reassurance from someone he didn't even know. He felt his stomach clench once more, and a wave of anxiety washed through him. For a moment, the thought he might need to vomit, but the nausea passed as quickly as it had come. He wondered if he would tremble when he stood up. He was nearly at a pitch of nervousness, and he gripped the bench beside him with one hand and rubbed his forehead absently with the other. He thought a moment of the haunted-looking girl. He suddenly realized that she had had a fresh bandage on her left wrist. He tried to push his thoughts of her misery out of his mind.

Minutes later the exterior door opened once more to admit a casually dressed gentleman. He wore an open-necked shirt, khakis and loafers, and he smiled at Danny from beneath his dark-rimmed glasses.

"Are you Danny?" he asked in a low voice.

Danny cleared his throat. "Yes, I am," he replied.

"I'm Dr. Harris," the man said, extending his hand. "But you can call me Mike. I'm way more comfortable with that." When Danny didn't readily shake his hand he withdrew it, an expression of concern flitting across his features.

Danny looked at him. *Be very careful,* echoed in his memory. He didn't get up immediately, but said, "You're a psychiatrist, aren't you?"

Mike looked at him and answered, "Yes."

"How is it you know about this kind of therapy?"

Without pausing or equivocating, Mike said, "I've been undergoing my own therapy." After a second's consideration, he added, "It's changed my life."

Danny climbed to his feet and extended his own hand to shake. Mike clasped it gently, shook once, and let it go. Danny recognized the man's name from the clinic's brochure, and he knew that Mike was meant to be (or at least claimed to be) a medical doctor and a practicing psychiatrist. Danny had just been checking.

Mike had an open, almost easy-going demeanor, and yet there was an element of utter seriousness in his face that inspired Danny's trust, as if it would be almost impossible for the man to lie. Danny felt somewhat reassured by his manner, although he was also deeply anxious.

Mike looked at the young man before him. He could immediately see the tension in the body, and the somewhat locked expression in Danny's jaw and face, the controlled fear. Danny was obviously troubled, and equally obviously was holding it in with near ferocity disguised as an unnatural calm.

"Why don't you come with me?" Dr. Harris suggested, and without waiting for a reply, he opened the door to an interior hallway and motioned Danny to follow him.

Mike led him down a short hallway past several closed doors. They turned right, and after a few steps the doctor opened a doorway on his left. He gestured inside.

The room was very spare. Wall to wall carpet of some thickness covered the floor, and there was a thick mat, almost a mattress, lying along the right-hand wall. The window opposite was covered with heavy curtains, admitting almost no light at all. Beside the mat were several cushions suitable for sitting on cross-legged, and Dr. Harris sank into a half lotus upon one of them. It was an unself-conscious, easy posture. He indicated the mat to Danny and said, "Why don't you lie down, let yourself be comfortable. Let your body dictate your posture."

Danny looked at the mat in the dim light. It appeared clean. He felt frightened and yet determined. He was afraid to trust the man and at the same time wanted nothing more than to unburden himself to him, almost unreservedly. He had come here for this. He glanced sideways at his new confidant, then knelt and reclined on the mat on his back. "Is this ok?" he asked.

"Sure," Mike said. He allowed Danny to settle a moment, then said, "Tell me. What are you feeling? I'm here to help you discover that, get to the bottom of that."

Danny closed his eyes a moment. He felt the familiar fear and anxiety welling up within himself. He wanted to attribute it to Dr. Harris, to the center in which he found himself, to his own stupidity for taking this risk of potentially allowing someone else into a personal interior space where he did not wish to venture himself. Yet paradoxically he wanted nothing else but to dive into it.

He said, "I feel a bit mistrustful. I'm questioning why I should open up to you."

Mike looked at him closely. *Poor sod,* he thought. He looked at the tension in Danny's arms and hands, in the squeezing of the musculature of the face and throat. "That's your mind talking, telling you all kinds of abstract nonsense, trying to rationalize what you're feeling. But it's not what you're feeling. Not really. Your body will tell you what you're feeling—if you allow it to, that is."

Danny suddenly felt a 'whoosh' of breath entering his lungs, and he let forth a deep sob. Tears virtually exploded from his eyes, and he began to cry with an intensity he had never known was possible, his body shaking with the accumulated sadness and tension of decades. Mike watched, his face etched with concentration and sympathy. For a long few minutes he said nothing, as Danny bawled his eyes out, sobbing and whimpering.

"But I'm not...I...I don't know...I," Danny squeezed out between bouts of crying.

After four or five minutes when Danny looked back at Mike, he said, "It's ok. Really, it's ok."

Danny sank back onto his back and practically howled. Mike's reassuring silence simply gave him permission. "That's it. Let it out, let it all out. Let your body do what it needs to do." His words seemed like instructions, and in a sense, they were, but Danny felt them as wildly liberating. He curled onto his side and wept raggedly, as if for the end of the world, for death and pain and all that was wrong, whatever it might be.

Seconds later Danny felt his body seem to contract, to squeeze into itself. His arms and wrists began to spasm, and he felt his head twisting back and forth as if it were being squeezed and jerked by some external force. His legs involuntarily pulled up into an even tighter foetal position, and he howled with abandon, the tears continuing to flow, and the spasms in his body twisted him again and again.

After about thirty-five minutes of repeated contortions, postures he didn't even know to be possible, he began to relax, and the frequency of the spasms diminished until he lay in exhausted silence. Mike simply watched him until he opened his eyes.

After two or three minutes, when it seemed clear that Danny's expressive reactions were finished, at least for the time being, Mike asked softly, "Do you want to tell me what happened?"

Danny was still panting softly from his exertions. Gradually the tears ceased. He sniffed, and Mike offered him some kleenex, into which he blew a copious amount of snot. He looked at Mike and said, "I don't know." Then he laughed a moment and said, "I was hoping you could tell me."

Mike him in the eye sympathetically. "No, I can't do that," he said. "We don't do that here. We see a doctor's external 'diagnosis' of what's going on in a client as an unwarranted imposition. Instead of discovering your self, yourself, we would just be pasting another label on you, covering over your own knowledge (or lack thereof) with our authority. It wouldn't be fair to you."

He leaned back onto his hands with his legs still crossed, looking at Danny. Danny closed his eyes, listening. Mike continued.

"Your body will tell you what you need to know in its own time. If you want to share it then, with me, or with someone else, that's up to you. Sometimes your body will make decisions without you, and that's okay too." He waited a moment, listening to Danny's rapid breathing and to how it was gradually slowing down. "How do you feel now?" he asked.

Danny thought a moment and opened his eyes. "Sore," he said. He felt as if some exterior force had been trying to twist his head off. The muscles of his arms and legs, and of the core of his back had been cramping and enduring intense spasms for the better part of half an hour, maybe more. They ached dully, and yet they were continuing to relax, bit by bit. "But better, in a strange sort of way," he added.

"Do you know why you were crying?" Dr. Harris asked.

"No," Danny said. "I just had to. It was such a relief, like it had been locked inside for half my life."

"Um-hmm," Mike said. "It sure looked like that to me. The 'why' will come later, maybe, when and if you're ready." He stretched his own arms up over his head, as if to loosen away tensions that Danny had somehow transmitted into him.

"Are you okay for a while now?" Mike asked.

Danny thought a moment. "Yeah, I think so," he finally answered.

"Okay," Mike said. "It seems like you've got a lot stored away in there." He smiled at Danny, whose own smile twisted into sorrow briefly once more and he allowed a few more tears to flow. He sobbed a couple of times, and then recovered his composure. Mike just watched.

"I'd like to ask," Mike finally said, "What has been going on in your life that caused you to approach us for help?"

Danny thought, but only a moment. He said, "I feel anxious and afraid, almost all the time." He paused, then said, "I know I must hide it well. I only had one person ever comment on what he thought was my 'nervousness,' and I lied to him about it." He sniffed, reached for a kleenex and blew his nose. Then he said, "When I told a previous doctor, a psychiatrist recommended by my uncle, that I was afraid, he more or less dismissed it."

'Um-hmm."

"I was bullied when I was younger. I'd simply become paralyzed. I couldn't fight back. I'd just take it. It was humiliating, and yet I couldn't overcome my terror."

Mike nodded and said, "When you're feeling afraid, everything makes you afraid, right?"

"Exactly," Danny said. "I can't understand it. And I can't stop it."

"You've done a very brave thing coming here, allowing yourself to collapse into your vulnerability, to admit it, to reveal it as you have."

Danny just grunted.

"I think we're about done here for today," Mike finally said. "This kind of thing, this kind of fear, doesn't go away overnight. There's probably lots more to come. We'll meet here again tomorrow, ok?" Then he said, "The thing to remember is that your body never lies. It will tell you the truth if you let it. Your head will lie to you again and again. Trust your body."

Sitting up, Danny blew his nose once more, and then he nodded. "Yeah, okay," he said.

The two of them got to their feet.

"Stay in the motel for tonight, ok?" Mike said. "It'll be good for you to let some of this experience process in your mind and memory. Just take it easy. Have something light to eat and relax. Keep the television off, and don't read, don't keep escaping into your mind with external stuff. All right?"

"Yeah," Danny said.

"We're going back out into the waiting room now," Mike said. "Just relax there for a few minutes until you feel ready for the outside world once more."

They walked back down the hallway, which smelled faintly of carpet cleaner. In the waiting room Danny sank into a padded chair and closed his eyes. He could still feel the dull ache in his muscles.

"I'll see you again tomorrow at 2:00, ok?" Dr. Harris said.

Danny didn't even open his eyes. He simply nodded, and said, "Yes. Tomorrow."

Dr. Harris opened the exterior door and went out into the dusty sunshine.

The therapeutic sessions were astonishing to Danny. He could scarcely believe how readily he had opened up to Mike. It had been like a dam bursting, one moment a solid wall of concrete, and the next a torrent of release. He didn't quite understand it. To Danny, understanding had always been a verbal structure encasing experience inside an abstract framework. Now the abstract framework had at least to some degree been blown away, leaving a different kind of creeping confidence in its place, a sense that maybe he could simply live in his body after all, without the tension and the shakes, and without fear *all* the time.

Danny and Dr. Harris met four more times over the remainder of the week. Each time much the same thing happened—the spasms, the cathartic release of tears. At one point, Mike asked, "Do you ever see images of things or people during these episodes? Or perhaps hear voices?"

"No," Danny said. "But two nights ago, after our first session, I was lying on the bed in the motel. I felt an enormous loneliness. It was as if my body suddenly shrank, and then I was in my crib in my parents' bedroom, as if I were a baby. I cried and cried, and then, after about ten minutes, my mother came in and picked me up, smiling at me and hugging me to her. I felt the most inexpressible happiness, joy that lasted for the rest of the evening. I sat outside the room on the balcony, watching the sun set over the mountains to the west. Everything—the traffic noise, the color of the sky, the smells of concrete and car exhaust, the sway of the trees beside the parking lot—everything was perfect."

"How did you know it was your parents' bedroom?" Mike asked him.

"I just knew it. Just as surely as I'm lying here. The window above where I was lying... And she was as real to me as you are."

Mike nodded.

CHAPTER SIX

Local Denizens

Madeleine was one of the first people Danny met after his initial week of therapy. She stood looking at him, a tall, pale, skinny young man, brown curls, shadows around his eyes from lack of sleep, sitting there on a plastic chair in the waiting room of the Center. "I'm Madeleine," she said directly to him.

She was a cheerful, motherly type wearing a tie-dyed blouse and a long paisley skirt, a plain, brown-haired woman of about 35 with a reflex smile that made him wonder what was funny. He looked up at her, then away. "And you are...?" she added and smiled some more.

"Danny," he said, at first avoiding her eye, and then meeting her gaze. As if it might be meaningful, he added, "I'm from Canada," in a tone of voice that was half apologetic.

"I'm from Vancouver," she said. She looked at him, sizing him up, it seemed to Danny. "Where in Canada?" And without waiting for an answer she continued, "Do you have a place to live yet?"

"No. I'm still in a motel."

"Gotta get you out of there. You'll go broke," she said, although she really had no idea as to his finances. "Listen," she said confidentially. "I'm going to rent a house from some friends, three or four bedrooms, and I'm looking to sublet. I can let you have a room, $45 a month plus a share of the utilities. It's about ten blocks from here on South Grant Street. Whattaya say?"

"You in therapy?" he asked.

"I have been. I work here now. I'm in training. In a year or two I plan to open a center of my own in Vancouver."

Danny looked at her, thinking. *She seems ok. And the rent's ok.* And as she was from Vancouver, a fellow Canadian, he felt somewhat more trusting than he otherwise might have.

"I'm going to the owners' place for dinner," she continued. "It's just a block from here. Why don't you come along? They'll be cool with it. And I'll lend you my bike to get around for a day or so until you can get your own."

He looked at her speculatively, wondering what these people would be like.

After a few seconds he said, "Okay. Thanks. What's their address? And what time?"

"Walk east from here half a block. They're in those condos that you see to your right from there. They're in number 12. I'm going over at about 6:30. Don't be late."

She smiled and took a deep breath. "I've gotta go get my little boy now from daycare," she said. "See you later." She turned to the door, her skirt swishing around her ample hips. Danny noticed she was wearing hiking boots, giving her a kind of Daisy Mae from *L'il Abner* appearance. She went out into the glaring sunshine and closed the door behind her, leaving the waiting room in cool shadow once more.

Danny looked around. A philodendron drooped where it sat in a small pot on a coffee table covered with cheap magazines—old copies of *Reader's Digest* and *Psychology Today*. Smelling of carpet cleaner and old coffee, the place was quiet and empty. He had nowhere to go, really, but he got to his feet, thinking about his sessions with Dr. Harris. He stretched some of the stiffness from his neck. Then he went out into the sunshine himself, into what seemed almost another world.

The sessions had already become less dramatic, and more predictable. There was still a powerful intensity to his muscular reactions. The twisting contortions left him nearly wrung out. But his conversations with Mike were unrevealing, almost devoid of meaning in any linguistic sense. And his brief excursion into hallucinatory memory was a one-off, apparently. Still, the relief was pronounced, as if some kind of pain were being gradually squeezed out of him like jellied anxiety squished from a tube. The anxiety was diminishing, but slowly, slowly.

A couple of hours later Danny knocked on the door of No. 12. A tall, narrow window lit the inside entry. He could make out a macramé plant hanger behind the grimy glass, and a small, pyramidal crystal hung from a cheap, metal chain beside the doorbell button. Danny pressed the bell and heard a soft buzz from the interior, then steps approaching. For some reason, he thought of "Trespassers Will," and an image of Winnie the Pooh and Piglet flashed through his mind.

The door before him opened to reveal a tall, striking woman with long dark hair and shining eyes, an expression of curious anticipation on her face. Danny was struck by her lovely figure covered by a summer sweater that molded rather than hid her outline, but he tried not to stare, and instead he looked back up into her eyes.

"You must be Danny," she said in a husky voice. Before he could reply she added, "Madeleine's already here, but she phoned earlier to warn us you were coming in case you got here first." She grinned. "Well, not warn, exactly. Come on in." She turned, and he followed her inside. "Don't take your shoes off," she added. "I'm Bathsheba." Danny glanced back at a lady's bike, a rusty, white frame leaning against the side of the stairs he was standing on. He turned again to the door and followed her inside to smells of patchouli and tobacco, hot cooking oil and the sweetish scent of pot.

A radio in the next room was playing a John Denver song. *Rocky Moouuuntain High, Colorado!*

"I just love John Denver, don't you?" she gushed, smiling at him. She took his hand, a gesture that startled him, and led him into a dim living room. On a low table were some covered dishes and a pile of unmatched silverware, the kind you'd find at a thrift store or a garage sale. A scented candle burned on the shelf beside the radio, which she turned down as the announcer came on, yakking about a used car dealer.

She let go of his hand and pointed. "This is my man, David," she said, indicating a scrawny, bearded male lounging on a beanbag chair and smoking a battered pipe. "I call him King David," she added with a musical laugh. "I'm his

63

concubine," she giggled. "Davey, this is Danny, you know, the kid Madeleine told us about."

David took a long puff of what might have been some kind of mild dope or herb-infused tobacco. He removed the stem from his mouth and gestured at Danny with the pipe while he held his breath a moment. Then, breathing out the smoke he grinned and said, "Welcome, man. Have a seat. Smoke?" he asked, offering the pipe.

"Uh, no, thanks," Danny said. Spying a stuffed arm chair a couple of feet to one side, he moved over to it and sat down on its front edge gingerly, elbows on his knees. "Thanks for having me over, though."

Bathsheba sprawled onto the floor beside David, flopping her head onto his lap, the intimate gesture one of comfortable sexuality, and taking the pipe from him, inhaled deeply. David grinned. Danny noticed that David was missing a couple of his front teeth. He wondered if they'd been knocked out in a fight or something.

A toilet flushed somewhere, and a few seconds later Madeleine emerged from a dark hallway that led toward the rear of the apartment. "Hey, Danny," she said amiably. Then, to the couple on the floor she said, "You two smoking again?"

David looked momentarily chastened, but then grinned and said, "A little smoke, a little toke, what's the harm?"

Bathsheba rolled over onto her knees and knee-walked over to the low coffee table that held the food. "Come on, let's eat," she said.

David laid his pipe aside into an amateurish clay ashtray, the kind a ten-year-old might make in art class. He and

Danny got up and moved to the table, where Madeleine and Bathsheba were already seated cross-legged on cushions.

"Smells good, babe," David offered, and she smiled.

There was a big ceramic bowl of brown rice that steamed fragrantly when Bathsheba took the lid off. Another bowl contained an unrecognizable salad of some sort, with chick peas mixed into it. There was hot, fried tofu flavored with a blast of hot cayenne and some soy sauce, surprisingly tasty to Danny, who generally ate hamburger and Kraft dinner when he was on his own.

There was little conversation while they ate, aside from a few contented "yums" from David and murmurs of agreement from Madeleine.

For dessert, they nibbled on dried figs and toasted almonds, and they drank some kind of herbal tea that Danny didn't recognize.

Feeling a little emboldened by these strangers' ready acceptance of his company, Danny finally initiated some enquiries of his own.

"Where are you and Bathsheba from?" he asked David, as he was still a little shy of both the women.

David slid off his cushion and leaned back on his elbow. "I'm from Kentucky, grew up on a farm there." He thought a moment. "I went hitchhiking when I finished high school—no great success there—and traveled around for about a year and a half. Here in Denver I got a job selling diet plans, a kind of direct sales gimmick like Amway or Fuller Brush. That lasted about two months until I realized what bullshit it all was. Then I worked at a Quickie Lube down on Cottonwood, 9 million wheels greased (or so it seemed). Now I'm doing framing down in one of the new suburbs further down I-25. Better money, better job all around."

Throughout this mini-biography Bathsheba stared at him in unabashed admiration, glancing over at Danny every so often as if expecting him to be totally gobsmacked by her 'king's' achievements. Madeleine just smiled dreamily, drinking her tea and watching.

Then Bathsheba said, "I'm from Oklahoma. My grandmother is Cherokee. I came up to Denver to go to college over at DU. I was doing some courses in science and was going to become a nurse, but I kind of got sidetracked when I met David." She took a deep breath, and David smiled at her, as if reveling in the pleasure that his personal magnetism was sufficient to sidetrack a girl like Bathsheba. "Now I'm doing massages out of a shop over on Jackson. David got me into doing massages and I found I'm quite good at it. There's something about skin and muscle, you know?" She chuckled softly, and Madeleine chimed in with a soft snicker of her own.

Danny could only imagine the skin and muscle, among other things beneath Bathsheba's sweater. But he didn't stare.

"She's damn good, you know?" David commented with a contented leer. "Nothin' like a good woman's hands." He nodded toward Bathsheba. "We met in the hot pool up at Chief Idaho's hot springs," he went on, his leer expanding into a proud smirk. "Muscle and skin and hot water!" He chuckled with pleasure. "Later we went skinny dipping!" He put his thumb into his mouth suggestively. Bathsheba frowned a little at his frankness and punched him lightly on the shoulder. He withdrew the thumb with a mock hurt look. Danny smiled faintly and took another almond.

Madeleine asked, "Did you think about the house at all? You want to move in?"

Danny looked up, realizing suddenly that she was talking to him. "Well, I'd need to see it, but it sounds ok. Can I look at it tomorrow?" Then, as an afterthought, he added, "Who else is going to live there?"

"My little boy Darcy, of course. And I've got a friend from New Jersey called Jonas who works downtown in a bank. I know that sounds a little square, but he's cool."

It was the short pronunciation of cool, a kind of 'ok,' rather than the drawn out 'cooool' that suggests one of the wonders of the contemporary world.

"There's an older lady from before who lives in the attic space—her and her dog. And we've got room for two more," she went on. She thought a moment. "Tell you what. I'll let you help me decide on the other two."

That seems fair, Danny thought, and he nodded. "Ok," he finally said.

"We can look at it tomorrow, alright?" Madeleine said. "You in the Creekside Motel? I'll pick you up at about 10:00. I've got a car."

There was no creek beside the motel, something Danny had wondered about when he checked in, but there was a four-lane freeway, I-25, whizzing with traffic below and beside the motel property. *Maybe the creek once ran where the highway is now*, he thought.

"Yeah, I'm in Room 8. Beside the ice machine. 10:00 will be good."

"Oh, yeah, and take my bike. It's the white one outside. It's not great, but..." She shrugged.

"Sure, ok, thanks."

"Keep it in the room, though. There's a lot of stealing around here."

David nodded in affirmation, frowning a little, as if disappointed in a cloudy day or an unfavorable sports score, something you just can't control.

"I better go," Danny said. "And thanks for dinner." He directed his thanks at Bathsheba, who nodded.

Then she said, "Hey, David and I have a little gift for you, just so you know you're welcome here...in Denver, I mean." She got to her feet. "Just wait here," she said, and she slipped down the hallway toward the rear someplace. Madeleine smiled at Danny as if to say, "I told you so."

When Bathsheba returned, she held out a shiny, silver and black bracelet. "Here, give me your hand."

Danny looked at her in surprise, but she said, "Don't worry. I won't bite."

She grasped his wrist lightly, cupped the open bracelet around his wrist, and clicked it shut. She released his hand, smiling at his bewilderment.

Danny looked at the bracelet, a tooled piece featuring some strange, native carvings. "Wow," was all he could say.

"I got it at a native gift ceremony back in Oklahoma a few years back. Some distant relatives. The old guy who gave it to me insisted that someday I should pass it on." She smiled down at David. "I guess today's the day."

She sank into lotus position beside David and took his hand, looking at Danny expectantly.

"Thanks, thanks," Danny finally said. *This is amazing*, he thought to himself. *They don't even know me.*

"But some day you have to pass it on, too, to someone you think might need it, or on some occasion when it occurs to you."

David grinned sleepily and reached for his pipe. "Told ya she's a good woman, didn't I?"

Danny got breathlessly to his feet, nodded his thanks to David, and made his way back to the entrance. He felt a little bit stupid, as though some trick he didn't understand had just been played on him, and yet he also felt a kind of helpless gratitude. Who were these people, and why would they care about him?

He heard the radio suddenly increase in volume, Grace Slick howling out *White Rabbit*, and some muted laughter about something someone said. He went outside, closing the door behind him. He wondered what they were saying about him.

CHAPTER SEVEN

South Grant Street

Danny moved into the South Grant Street house a week later. It was old, a poorly insulated 1930's brick structure that baked in the summer and froze in the winter. The front room, which nobody used, had a couple of bean bag chairs made of faux leather, a sofa with stuffing coming out of one arm, and a tiny color television perched on a liquor box. On the floor was a braided rug, a god-awful orange color. Above the television hung a portrait of the sacred heart of Jesus, left behind by a former tenant, according to Madeleine. The savior gazed mournfully at anyone unfortunate enough to be watching television at the time. People entering through the front door would hasten past toward what, it might be hoped, was someplace friendlier, Jesus watching all the way.

Behind the living room was a smaller dining room in the center of which stood a solid wooden table, painted white over its original grain, disguising the wood species. A collection of matching sturdy chairs surrounded it, as though it were a conference table for indigents. All were variously dented and scratched, and one had a loose leg, so the owners had relegated it to a corner. Any guest luckless enough to need it had to be duly warned. To one side, just outside the bay window, hung an elaborate copper bird-feeder, now stained with droppings. Spider plants strained to eke out a precarious existence in twine macramé hangers just inside the glass. The hardwood floor beneath them, perhaps the only truly quality furnishing in the house, was stained from water that had dripped unnoticed from the plant pots.

Continuing toward the rear one found a homey kitchen. A small, steel tube table with a laminate surface, and two matching chairs with scarlet vinyl seats (one repaired with duct tape) were under a window facing a neglected back yard. Through the window one could see a patchy lawn that stretched toward a gnarled fruit tree, itself half-strangled by a nondescript vine. Against one wall an electric stove and an old GE refrigerator (humming noisily) flanked a counter and sink, whose plumbing looked to be about World War II era. Fortunately, nothing leaked, and everything worked—more or less.

Off the dining room was a large bathroom, the only one in the house. It contained an antique toilet whose flush took a full three minutes to recharge, and a long, deep, claw-footed enamel tub. Even a tall man could recline comfortably within its length. An extra, lockable doorway admitted entrance to the bathroom from the master bedroom, which in turn also connected directly to the kitchen.

Above all these rooms was a long attic chamber accessible by stairway from the front entrance. It was inhabited by an eccentric older woman named Agnes who rarely came down except to collect a cup of tea, and perhaps a piece of toast and cheese, which she would chew slowly, thoughtfully staring out of the back window. She shared the upper space with her dachshund. Anyone sitting in the dining room could hear the tap of its dog nails as it waddled from place to place up there.

In the unheated basement, reached by stairway from the back entrance, were three side bedrooms, really little more than closets, with cheap, loose carpet on the floors. These chambers shared an ugly common room containing two tired-looking armchairs, a coffee table, two stand lamps with tasseled shades (only one worked), and another cheap television set.

It was this basement area that Danny shared with another tenant, a man in his late twenties from Idaho. He called himself Bud. He was a scrawny, vacant-eyed fellow who had done a tour in Viet Nam, where he had seen some horrifying atrocities, and he rarely said more than three or four words to anyone. One evening after consuming most of a jug of wine he poured his heart out to Danny, who listened uncomfortably but sympathetically, especially when Bud described in vivid detail the death of his best friend over there, bleeding out in a rice paddy after a vicious ambush. Tears flowed freely down Bud's cheeks, and he rocked back and forth, hands clasped in front of him muttering, "Fucking Viet Cong. Fucking war."

For the most part, Bud spent his waking hours expressionlessly watching television—game shows in the morning, soaps in the afternoon, cop shows and *Johnny Carson* at night—or thumbing through his collection of *Penthouse* magazines. Sometimes he would motor off in his fifteen-year-old Ford Fairlane to a supermarket, returning with staples like bread, peanut butter, hamburger and milk, all of which he consumed with a lack of enthusiasm comparable to that of his television-watching.

Madeleine was the 'mama bear' of the place, sharing the master bedroom with her five-year-old called Darcy (named after Mr. Darcy in *Pride and Prejudice* she proudly informed Danny one day, as if knowledge of a Jane Austen character were some coup to be celebrated). From time to time she shared her bed (a large mattress on the floor) with Jonas, a muscular waiter from New Jersey who now worked in a bank downtown. On his irregular visits Danny could hear them from below, humping on the mattress which was directly above his basement room, Madeleine's excitement apparent from her repeated, "Oh, God, oh, God, oh, God!" One night when he crept upstairs late for a glass of water, Danny encountered Jonas sitting at the kitchen table with a long-necked bottle of beer in his left hand. He had a bemused expression of satisfaction on his face.

"You must be God," Danny said to him.

Jonas chuckled aloud and said, "Oh, yeah." He swallowed the last of his beer, got up, set the empty on the counter, and returned to Madeleine's room.

Madeleine had a strong interest in Eastern philosophy, everything from the teachings of the fat little Guru Maharaj Ji to the 'wisdom' of Baba Ram Dass (formerly Richard Alpert, a psychology professor at Harvard who, along with Timothy Leary, had experimented quite liberally with LSD in the 1960's). Ram Dass's book *Be Here Now* had created quite a stir only a few years previously.

A lot of these preoccupations seemed naïve to Danny, and he said so. When Madeleine once wistfully confided in him over a rare breakfast of bacon and eggs that her real goal in life was "to know God," he said, "Isn't that a little ambitious, wanting nothing out of life but to know God?" He licked a bit of bacon grease from his fingers.

"No, I mean it," she said, looking at him earnestly.

"So, you think these guys are going to help you to know God," Danny continued. "What do you think they know that you don't?"

She really couldn't explain, but looked at him rather askance, as if even to question her motives and methods was a kind of apostasy.

"I was a Baptist once," she said, eyes far away as if remembering something grand and beautiful.

"Not any more, I take it?" Danny inquired.

"No...no." She didn't elaborate.

One evening several weeks later she asked him to sit with her son, helping him get to sleep while she walked down to 7-11 to pick up some cigarettes. Danny hated the smoking in the house, but she was the landlady. And he didn't mind little Darcy, whose ingenuous attitudes toward life were reflected in his generally good behavior.

"What do you think of those Baba guys?" he asked Danny. He had hoisted his head up to rest his chin on his palm, elbow on the mattress, blue eyes focused on Danny. *The pressure's on,* thought Danny.

"Does your mom talk to you about them?"

"Sort of. She keeps saying, 'Be here now, be here now.' How could I be anywhere else?"

"I like Baba Louie," Danny replied, after a moment's thought. "You know, the little guy with Yogi Bear?"

Darcy giggled. "That was Boo Boo," he said.

"Well, who was Baba Louie?" Danny asked.

"He was with Quick Draw McGraw," Darcy informed him.

Danny put on his best Yogi Bear impersonation. "Hey, Boo Boo, let's go down to Jellystone Park and get some sandwiches from the tourists. That's if we can avoid Ranger Smith." He closed his eyes momentarily, remembering some of the cartoons from his childhood. *Jeez, being corrected on my childhood cartoons by a kid!*

"Well, Bullwinkle, I think we've just about run out of time," he said in Rocket J. Squirrel's falsetto.

"Hmmm," he said as Bullwinkle, tapping on the hourglass somehow fastened to his moose 'wrist,' "mine must be a little slow."

Danny looked down at Darcy, who had slumped down onto his pillow and was already asleep. *Those Baba guys,* Danny thought to himself with a smile.

South Grant was in most ways a pleasant neighborhood. Although it didn't have a decent grocery store, necessitating a bus ride of twenty minutes or so to get food, it had a fine used bookstore called, predictably enough, *South Grant Books*. Doug Battersea, a self-described refugee from the rice fields of northern California, was the owner. He lived in the store, sleeping in a loft that could be reached by a ladder nailed to the wall like a fire escape. It disappeared upward from the end of the *History* section.

The store was rarely locked, and once when Danny walked into the place at about 10:30 one morning there seemed to be no one about.

"Hello!" Danny called. He heard an immediate rustling from above and toward the back. Tousled and unshaven, a head popped up above a railing.

"Oh, shit, I'll be right down," the face said. A minute later Doug emerged from the Napoleonic Wars, toweling his face and hands. Danny introduced himself. "Coffee?" Doug asked.

The two of them shared some espresso that Doug made on a hotplate beside the washroom meant to serve the customers, but which Doug also used for his own daily wash-ups. Danny wondered how many customers got put off by the whiskers in the sink and the stained shower that was behind a curtain beside the toilet.

"I was reading late," Doug said, "*Interview with the Vampire*. You know, Anne Rice? Wow. Creepy. But can she ever write!"

Danny didn't know anything about Anne Rice, but while Doug was making the coffee Danny sidled over to a table and picked up *A Hitchhiker's Guide to the Galaxy*. He thumbed through it absently as Doug busied himself with kettle and cups. Also on the table were *Zen and the Art of Motorcycle Maintenance, Breakfast of Champions, Sophie's Choice,* and *Bury My Heart at Wounded Knee*.

Doug generously allowed his store to be used as a venue for the occasional poetry reading. A number of Denver's wannabe poets were struggling to publish themselves, using one of their group, a fellow who worked at a print shop, to try to save themselves a few bucks on costs. The poets were naively enthusiastic and committed to their work. *Why not?* thought Danny. *Somebody's gotta do it.*

Many of the poems were predictable tosh, of course, but in the same way that if you want to take good photographs, take a lot of them, if you want to write well, write as much and as often as possible. Sooner or later the muse will appear. There were a few golden lines, nuggets that shone up from the sand in the poetic pan.

One poet had written an angry poem about public complacency during Nixon's tenure as president—the bombing of Cambodia, Watergate, and so on. The last couplet was,

> *And the sheep of the earth are fed,*
> *And the wool around the mouth is red.*

The idea of carnivorous sheep living on the blood of others penetrated like a sharp slap!

Danny made the bookstore a regular visit, once a week or so, until bankruptcy forced Doug out. His eviction was a 'damn shame,' (an expression he had picked up since coming to the States), but what could you do? There were only so many books a guy could read, even if he wanted to read more. Besides, South Grant also had a public library, one of the unalloyed goods American public service was still providing.

On a cloudy Thursday, his usual day off, Danny wandered past the shell of the closed bookstore to the nearby branch of the

Denver Public Library. It was a tasteful, one-story brick building set back on a corner lot, a sidewalk running at a 45-degree angle from the street corner, across the brown lawn, and up to its entrance. He pushed open the heavy wooden door (decorated with a big, Gothic brass knocker) and went inside.

A cheerful woman of about 50 greeted him from behind the desk, where she was occupied with some clerical task or other that required stamping and stapling.

"Hello, dear," she said. "Can I help you find something?" She clicked the stapler on a thin sheaf of papers and set it to once side.

Danny thought of the first time he'd ever been in a library. He was about seven years old, and his older brother took him into the library of the small-town where they lived. Danny had been awe-struck. What a bonanza! All those books and you could read any of them. For free!

Now he looked at the librarian sitting relaxed in a faded cardigan as she picked up her rubber stamp. "No, not really. I'd just like to look around," he replied.

She made a gesture of welcome, indicating with a broad sweep of her palm the shelves of books. The place had the familiar, agreeable scents of paper and dust and floor wax. Danny wandered up and down the aisles, appraising the print on the spines, titles both strange and familiar. From a shelf near a side window, he tugged out a copy of *War and Peace*, its gilded cover lettering impressive in the afternoon sunlight.

"I always thought I should read this," he told the librarian when he handed her the dusty volume. She nodded approvingly as she pulled the card.

"It's a great book," she said with the authority of someone who had read it. "Let's see," she said, squinting at the smudged stamp on the card. "The last time this book went out was 1957."

The two of them shared a conspiratorial smile. They were part of a literate élite, interested in the masters!

As she was stamping the card and showing him the due date, a gentleman carrying a small, leather case like a doctor's bag entered.

"Anyone downstairs?" he asked.

She shook her head.

He went to a corner of the room, tugged open another wooden door, and began to descend some stairs.

"What's down there?" Danny asked.

"Oh, he's the piano tuner. VFW members gather here once a month downstairs, and one of them plays *The Star-Spangled Banner* at the beginning of their meeting. The tuner comes every so often to keep the piano in tune. It's a fine old instrument—a Chickering grand!" She looked at Danny. "You play?" she asked, and when he nodded, wondering how much expertise she had in mind within the boundaries of the word 'play,' she said, "Why don't you go down and have a look?"

"Thanks," he said, and picking up Tolstoy, he went to the basement door. From below he could hear the characteristic 'ping, ping, ping, ping' of notes being adjusted; the tuner was already at work.

The basement room was well-lit, spacious, and paneled with some kind of pale wood. In the far corner was the piano, a small grand, black and imposing with the lid up.

The tuner looked up at Danny. "Help me a minute, will you?" he said, and began unfastening the lid hinges. "Hold this," he added, indicating the edge of the heavy curved lid.

Within a couple of minutes, they had the lid disconnected from the case, and together they laid it gently on the floor to one side.

"What are you going to do?" Danny asked.

The tuner was busily uncoiling one of the bass strings. "This pin is loose," he said matter-of-factly. "I'm replacing it with a larger one." Freed, the copper-wound string lay like a golden snake curled to one side. The tuner removed the pin, measured it with a micrometer, and selected another, presumably slightly larger. He inserted the pin's end into the vacant hole and, holding an intervening piece that looked a little like a nail set (to protect the pin's shaped end, the tuner explained), began to drive in the pin with a large mallet.

Danny looked on in awe. He had never imagined that one might repair something as finicky and complex as a piano with a hammer.

"Mind if I watch?" he asked.

"No problem," the tuner said.

About forty-five minutes later he was packing up his tools. After refastening the lid hinges, he left it propped open in that classic, grand piano pose. Danny stood at the keyboard, trying a few random keys. The piano had a beautiful tone, each note clear and bell-like, singing in a long, slow decay.

"I've got another job," the tuner said. "Go ahead and play, though. It's available for anyone to use. Oh, and thanks for the help."

Danny watched the tuner leave. *Jerzy would love this*, he thought. (Jerzy was a musician Danny had met at the center not long after his arrival.) He ran his fingertips over the white surface of the keys. Then he sat down on the piano bench and began to play an old Brahms variation he had once memorized. The beauty of the harmony mesmerized him. He sank into the music, eyes closed, drowning in the joy of its complex patterns.

Later, walking home, he passed the South Grant Cinema. THE FIFTY CENT MOVIES! a sign by the door silently shouted.

Intrigued by the cheapness, Danny stepped closer to an advertising sign beside one of the movie posters. *Only second run, first-class movies!* the sign stated. *Tonight's Double Feature: The Great Escape and Lawrence of Arabia.*

As Danny stood there, one of the front doors opened and a man with a push broom stepped out onto the sidewalk. "Hey, comin' to the movies tonight?" he asked.

"How can you run them so cheaply?" Danny asked.

"With fifty-cent tickets I get a full house. All the films are second run or older, so the rent's cheap," the man answered. He stood leaning on the broom a moment. Then, as if confiding some sneaky secret, he said, "I make out like gangbusters on the concession. People can stow away a lot of popcorn and other goodies in four hours. High mark-up goodies!" He grinned broadly. Then he pointed at the sign, and more seriously he said, "Pretty good films!"

Danny thought of Steve McQueen trying to leap his stolen motorcycle over a fence, fleeing the Gestapo. "Yeah," he agreed.

At Danny's serious expression he opened up even more. "Used to be the only movies that made any money were religious epics like *The Ten Commandments* or motorcycle gang movies. And for a time, I thought about taking everything out of the concession area *except* popcorn. I make 900% on popcorn." He smirked. "But I changed my mind," he said. "You've gotta offer a quality experience."

Danny wondered a moment about the difference between remembering something from your own life and remembering something from a movie. *Not much different,* he thought. *Not really.*

Several months passed (a cold but snowless winter). Danny found that the dramatic nature of his therapeutic sessions began to taper off, although once a week or so he felt an enormous need to repeat the spasms. There would arrive a few minutes of rising anxiety bordering on terror. (Danny started to characterize the feeling as the arousal of a familiar ghost in his spinal cord.) This anxiety seemed to morph into a need to twist and contort, muscular responses that were not voluntary. Rather they were the result of some unconscious demand, as if some great external hands wanted almost to pull him apart. If he could find what he thought of as a safe place to sink into it, he would allow the "ghost" to grip and wring him. It was almost torturous, and yet it was paradoxically also a relief. The insightful image explanations for what was happening never arrived. But with the physical repetitions, he felt himself gradually relaxing into a new and different normality, one that was at the same time unnerving but also liberating. He no longer felt so afraid, although there was a residual wariness to his waking hours, still punctuated by periods of anxiety, that never completely vanished.

After every session he felt wrung out, exhausted, but what he had previously understood as fear he had begun to recognize as a harrowing lack of readiness for something terrible about to happen to his body, something that he could not stop, despite the trepidation that seemed implicit in its mysterious and overpowering approach.

He was now sleeping better, not feeling so drugged and leaden, but instead drifting into relaxation, as if worn out from heavy exercise. From time to time, when the rush of anxiety hit, it felt like stepping off a cliff or falling out of an airplane (not that he knew what these would truly be like). Then he would head for a private space or the center and let his body go 'a bit mad,' as he termed it to himself.

He often wondered when he would discover what it all meant. Some other clients he talked to claimed all kinds of "facts" about the origins of the cathartic reactions to "their pain," as they called it, sudden epiphanies that opened into their consciousness during regressions. Aside from his single experience in the motel, nothing really emerged for Danny. He did continue to feel better, though, with fewer incidences of terror, and greater equanimity and relaxation.

Once a week or so he would attend a group session, where clients were expected to share their therapeutic experiences and insights. Mike asked him more than once as time went on, whether or not he had any clear idea of what was happening to him. Danny could only shake his head.

Sometimes Danny thought other clients were lying about their newfound "understandings," seeking the approval of their therapists and fellow patients. Some that he met, however, were enormously troubled, and he felt a compelled sympathy for their stories. All their troubles were powerful mysteries that deserved attention and respect.

Louise, the girl with the bandaged wrist he had seen on his first day at the center, was periodically suicidal. She had cut her wrist earlier that day and written "FUCK THERAPY" on the waiting room wall with her own blood. She was barely holding herself together, sinking in her sessions into the most regressive and painful places.

Another woman, Carolyn, was from Alabama. She was later to confide in Danny that as a child she had been raped by her father and by one of her elder brothers. She had also been married to an abusive man who had periodically beaten her up. Danny was appalled by her story.

Both these women had magnificent courage, and despite their strangeness, Danny admired their open honesty and their stamina in the face of instability.

But most importantly to Danny, he felt that he was starting to come alive again. Alive! He wasn't ready to leave therapy, but he decided that it was time to find a job. Six months had gone by. His money (*Dad's money,* he reminded himself) wouldn't last forever.

CHAPTER EIGHT

Getting into the Vitamin Business

It was one of those hot, dusty, Denver afternoons. Everywhere was the hustle and noise of the city, the stink of auto exhaust from the freeway and from Colorado Boulevard, the long north-south stretch of commercial mayhem that dominated the southeast part of the city. Its four-lanes of tarry asphalt, clogged with cars and delivery traffic, separated every kind of retail enterprise—donut shops, King Soopers, Macdonald's (still at only 25 million sold), muffler repair shops, a shiny Target store connected to a multiplex theater, and several used car lots. It stretched away to the north to where it would intersect with Colfax Avenue (the long east-west artery aimed straight west at the Rocky Mountains), and even farther north, where it joined the tree-lined parkway that led to Stapleton Field, the international airport.

Under the sunny glare, heat radiated from every surface, and only the tree-lined avenues to the west, where the University of Denver's campus nestled in comparative quiet, and in the somnolent suburban blocks off the main drag, did one get the sense that something natural could live here.

Just off the busy artery, as if uncertain whether it belonged amid the lunatic business carnage on the main drag or in the drift of sleepy housing on its other side, Danny found the place he was looking for: *Healthy Body Natural Foods and Vitamins.* It was a plain rectangular building of faded red brick, perhaps the size of a large, three-car garage. A pair of square picture windows facing the street seemed to shove a glass entry door to one side near the west wall, and an uneven concrete sidewalk dropped away from the store front to three graveled parking stalls intended for the customers. Danny looked at the structure curiously a moment, then stepped up to the door, tugged it open, and entered.

It was dark and cool inside, although some fluorescent tubes in grubby white mounts whined overhead, emitting sufficient illumination to allow him to look around. One of the tubes, pinker than the rest, flickered annoyingly, but Danny looked away, his attention arrested by the long wall of shelves displaying bottles and jars of varying shapes and sizes. He had never imagined there could be so many kinds of vitamin, mineral, and food supplements. An assortment of tincture bottles held naturopathic remedies. There were pint-sized cans of liquid lecithin. The varied arrangements of vitamins and minerals were separated according to company label. From the top shelf a stand-up poster featured a happy looking woman doing curls with a small barbell and smiling at the camera, all above the caption: *Energy for Life! Get Harbor Grove Supplements!*

Danny wondered how you got a grove into a harbor, one of the more oxymoronic commercial pitches he had ever heard.

He turned toward the back of the store where two large, old refrigerators stood side by side. A hand-printed cardboard sign standing on the left one announced that 'organic raw milk products' could be found within. Along two grocery aisles were bags of stone-ground flour beside boxes of rice and couscous, and on a rack near the till were five or six brands of 'healthy' candy bars (only raw sugar--none of that refined stuff) coated with carob instead of chocolate, that unhealthy goop that every informed person knows contains caffeine.

"Can I help you?" a quiet female voice inquired. Danny looked over to notice the 1950's cash register beside a sales counter. On a barstool next to it sat a woman whose long, dark hair was bound in a blue ribbon. She shook a loose strand away from her equally dark eyes and looked at him coolly.

"Hi," Danny replied. He approached the sales counter gingerly and took his hands out of his pockets. (When he was a boy his grandmother had reproached him for slouching with his hands stuffed into his jeans. "It's impolite and gives a bad impression," she had said. It was kind advice, and it had stuck.)

"I'm, uh, looking for a job." He looked at her, an imploring expression on his face.

"A job, huh?" She straightened up on her stool and set down the *Prevention* magazine she had been reading. "Do you know anything about this business?"

"Not really," he admitted. He'd never known much about *any* business. "But I know quite a bit about health and illness. I spent a year in medical school."

"No kidding," she said. It was unclear to Danny whether or not she believed him. The world is full of bullshit artists, that much he knew. He might as easily as not be taken for one of them.

"How come you're not there now? It's the middle of the school year, February... What's your name, anyway?"

Danny hadn't wanted to get into this kind of dialogue where he had to explain himself. He couldn't explain himself to *himself*, so dealing with other people in this way was, in his view, pretty futile. Still, he gave it a game try.

"I'm Dan," he said, trying to lend himself some gravitas. "Dan Long." He thought a moment. "Most people call me Danny," he admitted.

"I'm Pauline," she said. "And the medical school?"

"I quit," he said. "It wasn't the right thing for me."

"How come?" she asked. Now it seemed that she might believe him.

"The medical industry" (and he was proud of that word, its associations with dirt and machinery and noise) "is preoccupied with *sick* people. I think they should be doing more to promote wellness. Maybe kind of like you're doing here."

She looked at him with a new expression of something resembling respect, and she smiled. It was still a cool smile of appraisal, but he could tell she approved.

"And it's all about money," he went on. "Most of my fellow students were more interested in making a bundle than in health."

"Ok. A job it is, then," she said. "But I can only give you twenty hours a week to start. I'll tell you what needs doing.

You do it. Pay's five bucks an hour, no benefits. You got a social security number?"

Danny did some quick calculations. A hundred bucks a week, his rent and utilities were about $65 a month, and he didn't have a car or anything like that. He could manage. Then he frowned. Lowering his head, he said, "A girl I know said I could use hers. If you pay me cash, you can make social security contributions from my pay to Louise Kreuzer. I can introduce you so you can get the details. I'm from Canada," he added. *This Canada disadvantage is getting tiresome*, he thought. He wondered how she might feel about putting one over on the Social Security Administration.

"Whereabouts?" she asked.

"The West," he said noncommittally.

"I've got a crazy Mormon aunt in Cardston in Alberta," she replied.

He didn't want to disparage her aunt, but before he could stop himself he said, "Crazy is right, the religion, I mean, not your aunt, necessarily. I went to university for a while in Lethbridge. Lots of crazy Mormons there." (Danny had done an exchange semester in Lethbridge after his first year in Saskatoon, a way of expanding his experience, he had thought at the time.) He paused, remembering the rumor that a Mormon girl would put out for you if you joined the church, or at least promised to join. He had never tested the rumor, but when one Mormon girl he went out with had confided to him that her goal in life was to get married and have twelve or thirteen children, he had never asked her out again.

"Want some tea?" she asked. "I've got a kettle in the back. We can have some Red Zinger, and I'll tell you my plans for the business." Then as an afterthought she asked, "When can you start?"

"How soon do you need me?"

"Tomorrow? I've got a big shipment of organic produce and dairy products coming in from California."

"Sure. What time?"

"I usually open at 9:00 am."

"I'll be here."

The two of them talked easily for another fifteen minutes or so. Pauline showed him where her husband was going to construct a walk-in cooler, and the corner at the back where they would soon have a juice and sandwich bar.

"Now look," she said on the way back to the front of the store. "Like any business, you've gotta sell stuff for more than you paid for it. And you've gotta sell enough of it to make a decent living. If I have to pay you a hundred bucks a week, your work has to be worth it, that is, whatever it is that I have you doing, it must add at least a hundred bucks a week to our income, preferably more." She lowered her eyes a moment, thinking, and then said, "That's not always easy to figure out. But we'll give it a go. Okay?"

"That's logical enough," Danny said. "I'll do my best."

"Sure, okay."

This is pretty neat, Danny thought. *But that Zinger tea will take some getting used to.*

Walking home later, he was about to cross I-25 on the avenue overpass that led away from the store. A cacophony of engine sounds and the 'whooshing' of vehicles' passing drifted up from below. Preceding Danny in the same direction on the overpass was a young couple, holding hands and dawdling along as if the stink of exhaust and traffic noise were essential constituents of romance.

Danny could scarcely believe his eyes. *Everyone drives in this city*, he thought. *Except maybe me! Now there's actually someone else walking!*

He hurried to catch up to them, and when he did, he said, "Wow! You're the first people I've seen walking anywhere in a long time."

The young man, tall and blonde, broke into a smile and said, "We're from Sweden!" The girl beside him nodded, smiling as well. They might have been twins by their coloring and mannerisms.

"I should have known," Danny said. He left them to their couplehood, however it might be organized or defined, and paced ahead of them toward home. A block or so later when he looked back they were gone.

Danny had been looking backward into his memories for over six months. Now, with the new job he thought he might start doing a little looking forward.

CHAPTER NINE

Intellectual Disneyland

"Darcy and I are going up to Boulder tomorrow. It's a Saturday! Wanna come?" Madeleine looked at Danny over the rim of her tea cup.

Danny had finally settled into the Grant Street house. He had a job at the health food store, but he still felt a little aimless, although he was attending group sessions at the center once or twice a week. And he'd fallen back into his pattern of reading everything he could lay his hands on to do with history, psychology, music, religion, and so on. *A day away from Denver might be just the ticket,* he thought.

"What's in Boulder?" he asked.

"Boulder's the coolest place!" she enthused. "It's set at the foot of the Rockies northwest of here, just a beautiful area. On the mountain side facing out toward the town and the plains to the east is this really cool rock formation called the flatirons (you'll know why when you see them). The town's got the University of Colorado, maybe 25,000 students. The whole place is full of groovy little coffee shops, bookstores, printers, and other alternative businesses. It's like an intellectual Disneyland! It's got the Naropa Institute, an alternative university dedicated to the practices of Tibetan Buddhism—you know, Dharma comes to the West, and so on."

Danny *didn't* know. The whole concept of dharma was unfamiliar to him. But he didn't say anything about that. Sometimes admitting one's ignorance can seem diminishing to a person. He *was* somewhat interested in Buddhism, though.

He thought of his friend Darius back in his early university years. Darius was the son of a Japanese couple who had lost their fishing boat in Vancouver during World War II, when the family was interned for the war's duration in Alberta. (Why they gave their son the name of a Persian king was anyone's guess.) After the war their boat was long gone. Since they'd been interned near Raymond, Darius's parents basically had girded up their loins and worked extremely hard, sacrificed in many ways, in order to start a sugar beet farm. More than twenty years later they were sending their son to university, first in Lethbridge, and then in Saskatoon.

Once Danny had accompanied Darius to the movie *Tora! Tora! Tora!* in the Roxy Theater. It was a World War II epic presenting a Hollywood version of the 'perfidious' Japanese attack on Pearl Harbor. He and Darius had been munching their popcorn, entranced by the apocalyptic vision of a fleet of Japanese fighter bombers approaching over Diamond Head. When the first planes began strafing Hickam Field and dropping their bombs, Darius suddenly stood up, and throwing his hands in the air shouted, "Yaaaaaay!!" Danny had sunk into his seat, wildly embarrassed. A young guy with a typical, military buzzcut glared back at them from a few rows ahead.

Darius sat down abruptly and muttered to Danny, "Well, they deserved it."

Darius was preparing to enter a Buddhist seminary to study the precepts of Zen Buddhism and its koans, and to practice meditation. He had a thin little moustache above a smiling mouth that gave him a mischievous look, as if he could have been one of the L'il Rascals when younger. It was something he amusingly referred to as his Zen smile.

"You'll have to forgive me, but I think that's kind of stupid," Danny pronounced. "Those koans you told me were just dumb, 'one hand clapping,' and 'one finger Zen,' and all that illogical baloney." Darius simply offered his little Zen smile.

It was the most irritating, smug expression Danny had ever seen. Yet despite the irritation he genuinely liked Darius, and underneath the smile's psychological 'pinch' he secretly admitted to himself that his Asian friend might be on to something. He often thought Darius retreated behind this mask because he couldn't refute Danny's characterization of Zen as "nonsense."

"NonZense!" Danny would jest. But seconds later he would be curious about Zen's possibilities, nonetheless.

Once or twice Darius felt compelled to defend himself. Unwilling to have his life's planned course dismissed so easily, Darius had tried to explain to Danny the Buddhist concept of *karma*, a slippery, catch-all category similar to Western ideas of fate.

"Ok, so tell me about this 'karma' you're always talking about."

Darius turned to Danny seriously and said, "We all make decisions in life, right? Suppose I decide to go downtown, or to read a book, or to play tennis. When I do one of those things, I have automatically foregone all my other possibilities for action during that period of time. My decisions and my actions limit what I can do next. For example, if I went downtown I couldn't suddenly be in my living room reading or on the tennis court. That time has gone by, and my options for the future have become diminished. Not by a great deal, perhaps, but a tiny bit. When we add up our decision-making over a lifetime, each decision and action subsequently limits further our future possibilities, much in the same way that in Frost's poem *The Road Not Taken* the poet realized, '... knowing how way leads on to way, I doubted if I should ever come back.' By the time you die, you have no possibilities left." He watched for Danny's reaction, which instead of emerging as another objection, took the immediate form of a quiet thoughtfulness.

Given this explanation, Danny had to admit a certain profundity to karma, and gradually took some interest in Zen and its practices. For his part, Darius changed his mind about Buddhist studies and went to law school. *Go figure*, Danny had thought.

"What'll we do in Boulder?" he asked Madeleine.

"Oh, we'll just look around, maybe do some shopping. There's a people's fair this week in an arena there—should be all kinds of neat stuff on offer."

Danny sipped his tea and thought it over a moment.

"Sure, ok," he said. "How long does it take to get there?"

"It's only thirty or forty minutes away, depending on traffic."

"What about Jonas?"

"He's gotta work."

"Just for the day, right?" Danny asked. When Madeleine nodded, he said, "Yeah, let's go."

Thus, it came about that the next day the three of them were whizzing up the Boulder Turnpike, windows open to the late spring breeze, singing songs from old musicals, and watching the Rockies loom toward them. How'd it go?

La la la di dah di dah dah somthing,
July and August cannot be too hot;
And there's a legal limit to the snow here,
In Camelot!

As they rolled into Boulder, true to Madeleine's description, Danny noted the great slabs of the flatirons fronting the mountains to the west. To their right were the tile-roofed buildings of the campus of the University of Colorado, with the great bowl of the football stadium visible behind them. A few minutes later Madeleine pulled into a parking lot opposite what looked like an indoor hockey rink. Entry doors were decorated with red, white and blue bunting, and a Dixieland jazz band was tuning up beside a hot dog vendor. A tall, scrawny man with a bushy moustache and a Panama hat rattled off a few arpeggios on his clarinet. Then he removed it from his mouth and grinned in satisfaction, as the drummer gave him a little salute on his hi-hat.

"The displays and sales will be in that building," Madeleine said, pointing.

"Can we get hot dogs?" asked Darcy.

"Oh, sure, probably," she said.

"Right there!" Darcy insisted, pointing.

Nodding vaguely and turning to Danny, Madeleine said, "You don't have to stay with us—I mean, there's lots to do, and we'll probably have different interests."

Danny wasn't sure whether she was being considerate or just trying to dump his company. He opted for the former, as she *had* invited him along. And he thought of Darcy, who though a pleasant enough little boy, might prove something of a drag on their explorations.

"Yeah, ok," he said. "Why don't we meet back here at noon? Then get some lunch or something."

"Sure," she said, obviously relieved. To Darcy she said, "Do you have to go to the bathroom?" When he nodded, she took his hand to lead him off. "See you back here at 12:00," she said over her shoulder. Danny watched them go, Darcy tugging on her hand and asking her something that was out of Danny's hearing.

Inside the rink on the concrete surface, Danny lost himself a moment in memories of his childhood hockey games, permitting himself a bit of nostalgia. Within moments, though, he was strolling around the displays, childhood forgotten for the time being. Most of the area was given over to a farmers' market, tables and stalls selling everything from scented soaps to homemade cheeses, live chickens and produce. Further along one aisle was a fortune-teller, a university-aged girl, heavily made up and dressed in gypsy clothing, a Tarot pack on the table in front of her. She gave him a beguiling smile, a flash of white, even teeth and lowered, heavily lashed eyes with dark mascara. He smiled back uncertainly and walked on.

Then he encountered what looked like real fun. Behind a chess board sat a bearded young man wearing an uneven pair of antlers clipped to his skull. A sign beside him said, *play chess with a reindeer, $2, money back if you win or draw.* The reindeer was smoking a cigarillo (that Danny looked at with distaste), and he leaned back on a stool, evaluating the passing folk with a shrewd eye.

"Ok," Danny said, and took a seat. He tugged two bills from his wallet and placed them in the chipped cup beside the board. The 'reindeer' grinned, stubbed out his smoke, and picking up two pawns, juggled them between his palms. He held out two fists.

"Pick white and begin; pick black, and *I* begin."

Danny picked left. The 'reindeer' opened it to reveal a white pawn. He placed the two pawns back into the opposing ranks on the board, sighed, and said, "Your move."

About twelve minutes later Danny was down to his king and two pawns. The 'reindeer' swooped his queen in for the kill. "Checkmate," he said.

Danny shook his head, a bit humbled by his opponent's relentless and successful attack. "Tips from Santa?" he inquired.

The 'reindeer' grinned and offered, "Go again?"

"No, thanks," said Danny. "I know when I'm outmatched." He had been bewildered by the ease and speed with which the 'reindeer' had demolished his simple defense. He hadn't even had the opportunity to castle.

He got to his feet, shook hands with his conqueror, and moved on.

Madeleine had been right about the "intellectual Disneyland" characterization. Danny was particularly fascinated by some of the course offerings displayed on a table promoting the Naropa Institute. He put down his name and a $10.00 deposit beside an upcoming series of lectures on linguistics offered by a professor from MIT. It wasn't Noam Chomsky, but someone who had worked with him. And considerably later in the summer at a local venue, a community center it looked like, John C. Lilly, author of *Mind of the Dolphin* and *The Center of the Cyclone* was to give a lecture. Danny knew he'd be coming back for that. And the week after? Buckminster Fuller. Geodesic domes, dymaxion cars. It was nearly too good to be true.

Later he met Madeleine and Darcy at the appointed time and they went for burgers at a place called, predictably enough, the Boulder Café. Darcy talked on in childish enthusiasm for the contents of some fabulous toy store they had visited. Madeleine simply sat and smiled, listening, and drinking her tea.

All the while Danny was thinking about his own karma, about his decisions. He still encountered episodes of nearly crippling fear and anxiety, and he still 'treated' them with isolated retreats into semi-conscious bouts of spastic physicality marked with depths of sadness and longing that he had scarcely known possible. But the episodes were becoming farther and farther between, and his periods of near equanimity were becoming longer, enabling him to open himself more to the world. It was an extraordinary thing, he had to concede to himself. He didn't understand exactly what the therapy was doing, or why it was to some degree succeeding, but he felt increasingly confident that something useful, something good was happening.

Finally, nibbling down his last French fry, he said to Darcy, "Sounds like it was a pretty cool store!"

Darcy looked at him, an expression suggesting that he knew Danny hadn't really been listening. But then he smiled and said, "Yeah. It sure was."

CHAPTER TEN

Atlantic Avenue

Although South Grant Street was a pleasant neighborhood, after about eight months, staying in the house there became impossible. It was a regrettable development, for Danny had begun to feel somewhat at home. His fellow tenants were predictable and not at all obnoxious. Even the cold basement bedroom he occupied had become a refuge. He had found a World War II vintage, army surplus, down sleeping bag at St. Vincent de Paul, and it was amazingly warm (although it retained a bit of a smell, kind of like old hockey equipment, even after dry cleaning).

But the landlord, Madeleine, developed rheumatoid arthritis, and she decided to take Darcy back to Vancouver with her, where she would receive Canadian, government-insured medical care. She was giving up the lease, and the owner decided to put the house on the market for sale. The other tenants found themselves casting around for new digs.

One afternoon, at work at the store, a semi-familiar face appeared at the juice counter. (Pauline had decided there might be money to be made selling "home-made" sandwiches and freshly squeezed fruit and vegetable juices; one of Danny's regular chores was peeling carrots for the industrial strength juicer they used.)

It was a slim woman with a slight, yet insistent voice. "Are you Danny?" she inquired.

Danny put down the knife he had been using to slice a thick, avocado and Swiss cheese sandwich, and he leaned toward her. "Yes," he said, looking at her open face. She was fine featured, with mousy grey-brown hair, clear blue eyes, and the hint of a shy smile at the corners of her mouth.

"I'm Carolyn. I've been at the center. Madeleine said you might be lookin' for a place to stay."

"Yes, I am."

A lean, well-dressed gentleman seated a few feet away interrupted by clearing his throat. "Can I get another glass of this carrot juice?"

To the new woman Danny said, "Just a minute, ok?" He turned to a small fridge behind him and took out a tall pitcher filled with bright, orange juice. He took it over to the man, who held out his glass to be refilled.

"You might want to go easy on this stuff," Danny said to him. "Vitamin A can get toxic, you know, harm your liver. It's good for you up to a point, but too much can be bad news." He poured another full glassful. The man looked at Danny skeptically and took a drink.

Danny looked more closely at him. *Jesus, I think he's getting jaundiced*, he thought. "You drink this here every day, don't you?" he asked.

"Oh, yeah," the man said with enthusiasm. "It's the best around. I've had some from that store out in Aurora, but it's not nearly as good as this."

"Listen," Danny said in a confidential tone. "Take a look in the mirror when you get home," he said. "Make sure you have plenty of light. If your skin is beginning to look a bit yellowish, you're probably getting too much vitamin A. I wouldn't kid you about something like this. After all, the juice is a high mark-up item, labor intensive."

His customer drained his glass and set it on the counter. He laid ten dollars beside it and got up to leave. He was still looking at Danny critically, but he said, "Yeah, ok, I'll have a look."

Danny turned back to Carolyn. "You have a place?"

She nodded energetically. "It's a three-bedroom bungalow with a full basement. I'm gonna keep the basement. There's another girl, Louise, who wants the master bedroom. You can have the other bedroom for $60 a month, and we all share utilities."

Danny looked at her, taking her measure, in a way. He'd seen her at the center from time to time, but he'd not met her. She seemed immensely troubled, and yet there was a determined and hopeful ingenuousness about her that appealed to him. He had no desire to get too close to this woman, but she seemed plenty capable. A confidence born of necessity?

"Where is this place?"

"It's only a few blocks from here on the other side of the freeway. On Atlantic Avenue at the corner of Holly Street. The church across the alley owns the place. When they get the money together they intend to knock the house down and put in a parking lot for the church. But they assured me that we could have the house for at least a year, maybe two or three."

Danny frowned. It was her last comment that kind of got to him. He had never imagined being in Denver for three or more years. But that wasn't Carolyn's fault. And a church for a landlord. Good grief! Surely there wouldn't be evangelicals banging on the door, offering salvation, would there? He thought not. Brightening his expression, he said, "I'd like to look at it. Do you have it already?"

"Yeah, I do, so I'm kind of eager to get some co-tenants to make the rent go easier. You know what I mean."

"Sure, ok. I get that. Can I come by after work? About 6:00 pm?"

"Yup," she said. "It's 5538. You can't miss it. It's got the dandelion farm in the front yard." She gave a half smile at her own wit.

"Ok," Danny said. "Carolyn, right?"

"Uh-huh."

"See you then," Danny said.

Carolyn turned, looked vaguely around, and then left the shop. Danny watched her climb up into the old brown van she had parked in front. Then he turned back to his work.

Pauline wandered back to the juice bar from the till. "That's that new woman that Louise was talking about," she said. "I think they're going to share a house."

"Louise? You mean the suicidal one?"

"The very same." Pauline scratched the side of her nose, thinking. "What'd this one want?"

"She's looking for a tenant," Danny said thoughtfully.

"Yeah, well, think carefully about it. I mean, she seems ok, like not mean or anything. But, well, you know..." Her voice trailed off, the intended warning clear enough without any speculative embellishments.

After about a fifteen-minute walk from the store, Danny found 5538. *The house isn't that old,* he thought. *She wasn't kidding about the dandelions, though.* He surveyed the field of yellow weeds that, compared to the manicured (and doubtlessly poisoned) lawns up and down the block was a tremendous eyesore. *I'm not into lawn care*, he thought with a certain finality.

He walked up to the cement porch and knocked on the screen door, behind which he could see a spacious and clean hardwood floor with a few throw rugs on it. He heard footsteps from the rear, and Carolyn appeared at the door.

"Come on in," she said. "I'm making soup. You can have a bowl."

She unlatched the screen and let him in. A rich aroma of chicken broth pervaded the atmosphere. Danny smiled appreciatively.

On an armchair near the front picture window sat the young woman who had been in the center the first day of his treatment. She looked up a little anxiously.

"Danny, this is Louise," Carolyn said.

"Hi," Danny said.

Louise raised her left hand a couple of inches in what might have been a wave. "Hello," she said softly.

Louise was faintly pretty, dark-haired and dark-eyed, with a serious expression, almost distracted. She was the suicidal one, all right, Danny reflected.

"If you decide to take it, your room will be down here." Carolyn pointed to a hallway that led off the other side of the living room. Louise looked away as they passed.

It was a more or less standard bedroom, maybe slightly larger (about 14'X12'), with a closet. It, too, had a hardwood floor. Clean and empty, yet a bit musty smelling, as if it had been closed up too long, it echoed as they walked in. Danny approached the window, slid open the curtains to reveal a view of the dandelion farm out front. The bathroom was just around the corner. Everything was simple and functional.

"Louise's room is just there," Carolyn said, pointing to the other doorway off the hall.

She led Danny back through the living room to the opposite end of the house and toward the rear through an open doorway into a bright, spacious kitchen. An extensive set of kitchen cupboards and counter ran around two sides. The kitchen sink was beneath a window overlooking a tiny back yard, beyond which Danny could see the church Carolyn had mentioned. The house was surprisingly quiet given the proximity of Holly Street, across which stood a 7-11 beside a launderette.

"We don't have a washer and dryer, so we've gotta do clothes across the street there. But the launderette's really clean." She looked hopefully at Danny. "Whattaya think?"

"It's a nice place," Danny said. "Everybody does their own food, I guess?"

"Yup. It's a big fridge, though," she said pointing to the Frigidaire at the end of the counter. "Lots of room for everybody's stuff." She looked back toward the living room where Louise sat silently in the growing shadow of early evening, ghostly quiet. "Louise doesn't eat much," Carolyn added. "Sometimes we get together and share a meal, me and Mac and Jody, and Louise. Jody's my little boy. Mac—he's from Canada, too, you know, Toronto—helps me look after him. We could sometimes share a meal if that suits you..."

"Can I get a cat?" Danny suddenly asked. He wasn't sure where the inclination had come from, but he saw a golden tabby pacing across the kitchen toward some pet bowls by the back door, and suddenly he thought having his own pet would be neat. He'd never had a cat or a dog as a child.

"Sure," Carolyn said. She walked over to the animal, which was lapping at some milk she'd left for it. She picked it up and brought it over for Danny's inspection.

"This is My Cat, that's my name for my cat, My Cat." She giggled. "I guess I just felt a bit possessive when I picked him out."

The cat rolled contentedly in her arms and against her breasts. She lifted it up toward her face to nuzzle its face, and in a childish tone she said, "Who's a nice cat, eh. Mmm, mmm, mmm, My Cat, that's who."

The cat squirmed and she set it back down on the floor. It trotted back over to the food dishes and began eating some dry cat food, a box of which was leaned against the wall beside the back door. *Meow Mix!* it said, *the only cat food cats ask for by name!*

Danny smiled. "Yeah, I'd like a cat. I know someone who has a cat with kittens." Then, to the more serious issue, he said, "Ok, I'll take the room. I'll bring over some cash for the rent before the end of the month. Is that all right?"

"Yeah, and there's a damage deposit I had to pay, so for the first month add $20, alright?" Carolyn looked at him.

"Ok," Danny said.

At that moment Louise came into the kitchen and sat down heavily at the table, looking at her hands for no apparent reason. Then she looked over at Danny and Carolyn and asked, "So, are you moving in?"

Danny nodded.

"End of next week," Carolyn added.

"Good," Louise said.

She got up again and left the room.

Danny took a deep breath. For some reason, despite the worries one might have about Louise, this place seemed like the right place to be. He thought a moment of Carlos Casteneda's book *A Separate Reality*, a scene in which Don Juan had challenged Carlos to find his power spot somewhere in Don Juan's yard. Carlos had wandered around, inquisitively bewildered, until he finally sat down and fell asleep under a tree. When Don Juan came back, he nudged Carlos with his toe and said, "Congratulations! You found the spot."

This could be my power spot, Danny thought with a smile. He nearly laughed out loud.

CHAPTER ELEVEN

Vitamins for Sale

"How did you ever get this place, anyway?" Danny asked. Pauline looked up from the big brown carton she had just sliced open to reveal the contents of one of the day's wholesale deliveries.

"Ooh, look at this," she murmured, holding up an elongated cardboard package featuring the smiling face of an Italian chef. "Organic pasta!" She said it reverently, as if she could feel nutritional energy coursing into her body from the cardboard container alone. Danny obediently looked.

"It was a weird day," Pauline said, as she set the pasta on the counter beside where the two of them were kneeling on the lino, tallying the delivery contents to the invoice, and she rummaged further into the big box. "Will and I had just driven in from Cheyenne, you know, up the highway in Wyoming."

Danny nodded.

"We didn't live here then," Pauline went on, pushing her dark hair back from her forehead. "We were just roaming in our camper van. Little Jessie, our daughter, was only ten months old at the time."

"I didn't know you were married," Danny offered, fingering a packet of 'All-Natural Licorice.'

"Naw, we're not," she said. "But we're committed." She said this as a kind of affirmation, nearly Biblical in its assurance. Danny nodded. Looking at Pauline's expression, he thought she could have been Esther or Judith, or more likely Lilith... Pauline did have an earthy kind of sexiness. But Danny kept his distance.

"Anyway," she said, "Will wanted to pick up some lecithin, and a guy down the road at a gas station had given us the name of this place. We drove along the boulevard, found the street he mentioned and turned in."

She took a couple of swallows from the cup of Red Zinger tea she had on the floor beside her. "You're sure you wouldn't like a cup?" she asked, indicating her tea. Danny was surprised she wasn't walking on the ceiling from all the Zinger she drank. He was even more surprised, given that it was caffeine-free. He just didn't care for the 'zing,' whatever it was, but he had to admit it was popular and sold well.

"No, no, that's ok," Danny replied, setting the licorice back.

"Yeah, it was weird," she repeated. "There were two cop cars in front, one of them with its lights flashing. Will almost drove by—you know, you can't really trust the pigs. The draft was still on, but Will had already done a tour. After that he stayed away from home, worked for cash, and kept under the radar. He sure as hell didn't want to go back to Nam. He still has flashbacks once in a while...you know, waking up from a nightmare screaming, sweating, eyes wild? I can usually calm him down, though."

Danny thought of the possible dreams—bamboo forests, rice paddies, helicopter gunships. Then he imagined the police cars out front, the movements of police officers climbing out of their dim interiors, curved aviator sunglasses under their hats, big revolvers on their hips. *The man with no eyes*, he thought to himself, remembering *Cool Hand Luke*.

"We pulled up the van and I told Will I'd go in, for him to stay in the van and watch Jessie. When I stepped into the store the first thing I saw was this fat old man lying dead on his back beside the ice cream cooler. His skin was grey, literally grey! Pukey grey," she remembered. "'Whadda *you* want?' one of the cops asked me. 'Just some lecithin,' I said. I remember the door opening behind me, and two EMT's rolled a stretcher in, and there was this anxious-looking woman came in behind them." Pauline took another sip of tea.

At that very moment, the door opened causing a tiny bell to ring. Danny half expected to see ambulance attendants. Instead, a tall black man wearing a jacket with the word "Nuggets" embroidered in gold thread on its breast looked down at the two of them and asked Pauline, "You got them organic apples yet?" His voice was a beautiful, deep rumble, lazy, Southern, Danny thought.

"Coming tomorrow," Pauline said. She smiled. "Don't worry, we'll get'em juiced up for you, just the way you like'em."

"Remember the beets," he said. "For the iron." He looked around for a couple of seconds, then said, "I'll be back tomorrow."

"Ok," Pauline said. "See you then."

The man stepped back outside.

"That guy's a point guard for the Denver Nuggets," she said, a voice suggesting the importance of the fact. "He gets all his organics here."

Danny nodded, wondering what a point guard or a Denver Nugget was.

His face must have betrayed his curiosity, for Pat added, "He's a pro basketball player, comes from Louisiana, straight out of some slum." She grinned. "Maybe he had a fairy godmother."

"I used to play basketball in high school a bit," Danny said wistfully. He thought of his clumsy dribbling and frowned. *I should have remembered what a point guard was.* Then he asked, "What about the dead guy?"

"Oh, yeah, he was the owner of the store," Pauline replied. "Heart attack. Bam. Some customer found him. But that's not the best part."

Best? Danny thought.

She got to her feet. "Can you pull that over here by the cash register?" She indicated the carton. "I want to sit down for a bit. I'll show you how the register works."

Danny grasped one of the container's folding lids and slid the box over beside the end of the counter. Then he leaned on the counter, looking expectantly at Pauline. She glanced over and smiled.

"The best part," she said, "was that this wasn't really a vitamin store. Oh, sure, it had lots of product. But when the cops looked into the back in the stock room whattaya think they found? A passle of stolen goods, that's what. TV sets, cartons of unregistered cigarettes, all kinds of hot stuff. The whole vitamin business was just a front, probably to launder the cash. He sold the stolen goods out the back." She looked at Danny, a kind of pleased expression, as if running a bandit enterprise was an admirable thing, something slick or clever. Thinking of the popularity of *The Godfather*, Danny smiled back uncertainly. *Americans seem to idolize their criminals*, he thought.

"So how long have you been here?" Danny asked.

"You *are* kind of a snoopy guy, aren't you?" she asked him back. At his abashed expression she said, "Oh, no worries. Just an observation." She took a breath.

"Anyway, no wonder the business is so quiet here. But it's getting better." She smiled, thinking back on the event.

"Remember that woman who came in behind the stretcher guys?" Pauline said. "Turned out she was the owner's daughter. She claimed she didn't know anything about the fencing, and she was in kind of rough shape, her dad dead and all. She was going to school at the time, up in Boulder. Suddenly she was going to be the owner of a vitamin business. She didn't know anything about this stuff." Pauline looked over her shoulder out the front window, quiet a moment.

"What did the cops do?" Danny asked.

"Aw, they were all right, sympathetic really. She was a real cutie, black curly hair, big dark eyes. They fell all over each another trying to be nice to her." Pauline laughed. "Will had finally come to the door with Jessie in the crook of his arm, wondering what was going on. The cops sealed the place off, but not before I got the lecithin. She just said to take it, it was all right. But she gave me her phone number and asked me to call her if we were sticking around for a bit. Then guess what?"

Danny looked at her, genuinely curious. He shrugged.

But just then the bell over the entry door jangled once more. A thin guy with even thinner hair that hung into his eyes walked in carrying a wrapped, paper package. Pauline looked up at him. "Shaaaaaaane," she said, obviously a familiar greeting.

"Hey, Paulina!" he said, riffing on her name. She hopped off the stool and hastened around the counter to give him a long hug.

"Where ya' been, man?" she asked. "Will's been wondering about you—after we left Kansas City and you said you were coming here." She broke off uncertainly, then asked, "Whatcha been doin'?"

"Oh, you know, a little of this, a little of that. What's the password? 'Give me librium or give me meth!'"

"Still doin' that stuff, huh?" she asked.

He shrugged, smiling at her enigmatically. Then he said, "Yeah." He looked down a moment, and then over at the till, and at the electronic scale beside it, a pricey piece of gear Pauline used to measure out powdered vitamins. "Uh, could I use your scale?"

"What have you got *this* time?" Pauline asked.

"Oh, a little snow, a little blow," he said, and he grinned again. "*My* vitamins." Then he looked at Danny.

Pauline straightened and said to him, "This is Danny, our new employee. He's from Canada," a phrase that she often resorted to when trying to account for anything about Danny that might be found unusual or wanting. "He's ok," a phrase meant to mollify any concerns Shane might have about Danny's trustworthiness.

"Hey, man, how's it hangin'?" Shane asked.

Danny just nodded without saying anything, and Shane turned back to Pauline. "Well?" he said. "Oh, yeah, and I need some powdered inositol."

"Cutting it, are you?" Pauline asked. She went over to the vitamin shelves and retrieved a medium sized jar. "Twelve bucks," she said, as she plunked it firmly on the counter beside the scale. He nodded at her. "Yeah, sure, go ahead. Keep one eye on the parking lot, though," she said. "We don't want any unreliable visitors."

Over the next twenty minutes or so, Shane measured out four or five dozen foil packages of blended white powder, placing the closed packets back in the paper bag. While he worked, he listened with Danny to the end of Pauline's tale.

Pauline came back to the stool beside Danny and said, "So, the cops were gone. We called her the next day and she offered me the job of running the place, of turning it into a bona fide health food business." Pauline tapped her temple with a smug expression. "She paid me a decent wage, and I learned the business. I lost some money the first year, but I figured out what to do to avoid repeating that. The next year I borrowed some cash from my Mom in Pennsylvania and some more from a local bank and bought the place." She looked around, as if surveying a little kingdom, which, in a way, she was. "Now, with you here I'm a greedy capitalist employer," she announced, and she laughed lightly.

"Wow, pretty lucky, eh?" Danny said.

"Darn tootin'," she said. "Now I'm *making* money. Not much yet, but we're building. The banker was a riot. He asked why he should lend me anything to buy a health food business that was losing money. I gave him a fresh, organic watermelon and said, 'Try my produce. You buy fruit from King Soopers and the peaches are as hard as baseballs. You bite into one of my peaches and the juice runs down your arm.'" Pauline lifted her bare arm in example and laughed again. "I got the loan," she said. "Now it's two years later, and Will and I have a little house over on Alameda Avenue. Jessie's just turning four. Will's doing carpentry. And life is fun."

"Sure is, ain't it?" said Shane, and Pauline nodded sagely.

Fun, Danny thought. *Yeah, it should be. If I could ever figure it out, it just might be.*

CHAPTER TWELVE

The Church of Perfect Fifths

"I've made my wife a saint," said Jerzy matter-of-factly.

"Really?" Danny asked. "How'd that come about?"

Jerzy grinned. He had a mouthful of teeth like misplaced piano keys (minus the black ones). It was only appropriate. He was a musician. "I've started my own church," he said. "The Church of Perfect Fifths!" He looked at Danny, who appeared a bit puzzled. "You know," Jerzy continued. "The music interval, the perfect fifth! After the octave, the vibration ratios of perfect fifths are the most consonant, the most pleasing to the ear." He grinned again.

Danny looked back at him, a kind of incredulous frown. What could any of this have to do with sainthood?

Jerzy was one of those guys you could never be sure was serious. He lived in a walkup apartment somewhere near Cherry Creek with his wife, a sleepy-looking woman whom he had recently nicknamed PID (for pelvic inflammatory disease), after her recent bout of gonorrhea. It wasn't certain to anyone else whether she got it from him or elsewhere.

Alan W. Lehmann

Clearly it wasn't something that bothered either of them very much. She received a vaguely described disability welfare stipend and spent most of her time reading romance novels and watering her spider plants. *Obvious material for sainthood*, Danny thought, and he grinned.

Jerzy passed many of his days in the library at Denver U., mostly poring through their collection of composers' biographies. And he knew music, and how to play it. One night at a party at their place—there must have been a couple of dozen people there, at least—he had begun improvising on the piano. He opened the piece, utterly sober, a Chopin nocturne, all legato and mournful minor key. Suddenly he got a maniacal expression on his face and he turned the initial motif into a repetitive riff. Using that he launched into a ragtime theme and variations that went on for about eight or nine minutes, ending with a coda in exaggerated largo and a cadence accompanied by the lyrics, "...and that's why I'm so sad."

Never knowing exactly what to expect from Jerzy, who was sipping a Budweiser from a can, gesturing with it, and occasionally slopping a little foam onto the carpet, Danny finally asked, "So what's it all about then?"

Jerzy grinned his piano smile and set the can down on the coffee table. He scratched his leg, a skinny and very hairy stick with a big Birkenstocked bare foot attached. "Mostly about taxes," he said, looking Danny in the eye. "Churches don't get taxed in America."

"Damn," Danny exhaled, appreciating the audacity of the scheme, if little else. He sipped his own beer.

"I can tell by your expression you don't approve," Jerzy said, grinning at Danny sardonically.

"No, no, you're wrong," Danny said. "I mean, it's an outrageous scam, that's for sure, but if a country's stupid enough to let churches collect all kinds of money without taking a fair share for the public purse, then..." His voice trailed off. It was pretty amazing, he thought. *Why don't I ever think of something like this?* he wondered. *How much will he save in taxes?* Sometimes he marveled at the entrepreneurial ideas of the people he met.

He remembered the party. After Jerzy's wild piano-playing, the group had danced themselves into semi-drunken exhaustion to the strains of all kinds of sixties rock: Janis Joplin, the Stones, the Beatles. Then they'd collapsed onto the rug in a group heap that might have resembled a clothed orgy, except no one was moving. Jerzy had put the final track from Keith Jarrett's *Köln Concert* onto the turntable, and the group had fallen into a stupefied doze, grooving on the music, until one by one or couple by couple, they roused themselves enough to untangle from the Twister complex of friendly bodies and say their good-nights. It was a fabulous night. No drugs, aside from beer. Just music, summer sweat, more music, dancing, and hormones.

"Anyhow," Jerzy went on, "we're registered and all with the IRS. I'm licensed to do marriages, too." He eyed Danny speculatively. "Hey, you like classical music, don't you?"

Danny nodded thoughtfully, remembering all kinds of childhood flashes: having to give up Little League baseball because of the violin lessons his father had insisted he take, his grey-haired piano teacher sighing with exasperation as he fumbled at his dominant seventh chords, the trip with his brother to hear the Regina Symphony Orchestra play Ravel's

Bolero. "Yeah, I do," he admitted, strains of Beethoven and Debussy competing in his imagination.

"Listen," Jerzy said. "I'm planning a spring music appreciation weekend. Up at a dude ranch in the Rockies. I've got this buddy there who runs the place. Early in the year the mugs aren't coming from back East yet, and we can get the whole place, including meals—no guarantees as to quality there, but they should be okay—anyway, the whole place for twenty-five bucks apiece for the weekend."

"No kidding?" Danny said. He drained the last swallow of his beer.

"Yeah. I need just 16 people to pay the rent. We'll have music every day, morning, noon and night. And there'll be other stuff, too, horseback riding, that sort of thing."

For a few seconds Danny thought about his therapy. He had been doing pretty well, only suffering serious anxiety about once every two weeks or so. He wondered briefly what he would do if he felt like freaking out a bit up in the mountains. He also considered his financial situation, payday schedule. Finally he brightened. "Sure, count me in," he said.

"I'll let you know," Jerzy said.

About three and a half weeks later Danny found himself (along with three backpacks and some sleeping bags) crammed into the back seat of the jeep of a girl named Veronica, someone else he'd met at the store, a friend of PID's. The vehicle followed a twisting secondary highway up into the mountains behind Boulder. Cool mountain air flowed in through the driver's window, with scents of hay and dust. Sunshine lit up the clumps of pines and the already yellowing spring grass, and in the pastures new hay was already thick, ready for cutting in a week or two. In the other passenger seat up front was a quiet, overweight college student named Bradley, Veronica's boyfriend. The AM radio was playing *Let It Be,* and Bradley was tunelessly humming along and tapping irregularly on his knee with an open palm (*a real irritation,* thought Danny).

"Hey, you missed the sign!" Bradley said, abruptly ceasing his knee slaps.

Veronica pulled the jeep onto the shoulder and brought it to a halt in a crunch of gravel.

"It's just back there," Bradley said, twisting around in his seat and pointing back toward a driveway entry.

There was no traffic to speak of, and Veronica backed the jeep slowly along the shoulder until she could turn into the drive. Sure enough, tacked loosely to a tree trunk beside the open gate was the sign: *Church of Perfect Fifths—Music Weekend.* She pulled into the drive and the jeep rattled across a cattle grate. After about three minutes of driving through an extended aspen wood they pulled into a large, flat yard. Several vehicles were parked haphazardly around the perimeter, and at the far end was a log ranch house with a veranda that stretched along its front wall. From a doggy bed beside the front steps a sleepy-looking golden retriever looked at them as they bumped up to the house.

"Woof," said Bradley with a snort through the jeep's open window. The dog ignored him. Veronica swatted his arm in mock annoyance and turned off the engine.

Jerzy emerged from the front door holding a white mug of coffee that steamed in the mountain air. The three newcomers climbed out of the vehicle. Danny stretched the kinks out of his arms and legs. The music of some Mozart aria drifted out through the open doorway of the house.

"Hey, good to see you guys," Jerzy said. "Bring your stuff in. I'll show you to your dorms. Me and PID have the 'executive suite,' of course." He grinned proprietarily. "Afraid the rest of you guys and girls have to be separate for a couple of nights--just the way the accommodations are. A couple of the girls who registered early have private rooms, but that's it." He gestured inside with the coffee cup. The three of them retrieved their packs and sleeping bags from the jeep and followed him in. PID smiled shyly up at them from the ancient armchair where she was reading, some bodice-ripper called *When He Needs You*. She turned back to the book.

Jerzy turned down the volume a bit on Papagena and looked at them. "Veronica," he said, "you'll be with the other girls down in the back wing. Danny, you and Brad go through that door to your left past the washroom and the sauna. There'll be seven of you down there. The two doors at the far end are the private rooms. Almost everyone's here, and the ones who've made it so far are in the kitchen having some lunch." He pointed through an arched opening in the west wall where there was a large dining table. Beyond the opening Danny could see a brightly lit kitchen and hear the sounds of conversation and crockery.

"You can have some lunch or wander around a bit, if you like," Jerzy added. "Church will begin at 2:00 pm here in the front room with some J.S. Bach!" He smirked proudly.

After a simple lunch of pork and beans and rye bread, the group assembled in the main living area. Jerzy gave a ten-minute biographical tour through the life of Johann Sebastian, and they listened to a variety of pieces from Bach's voluminous output: *Sheep May Safely Graze* on the organ, the theme and several variations from the *Goldberg Variations* played by Glenn Gould, part of one of the cantatas, and two concertos (one for violin, and the other an adaptation of the same piece for keyboard). Jerzy encouraged his informal students to comment on what they'd heard.

"It was sublime," intoned a dark-haired woman named Jeannette. "Simply sublime!"

A long-haired male snorted and said, "Too square, man. Violins! Jeesh."

Jeannette frowned and bit her lip. Another girl said, "You've got to give it a chance. This is great music that has lasted for centuries. Five years from now nobody will know who Meatloaf was."

Meatloaf? Danny wondered.

And so it went. People would eat, go for walks, gather, and listen to music following Jerzy's commentary. The first morning they woke to the strains of a rondo by Mozart. After breakfast was *Afternoon of a Faun* by Debussy.

The second evening after listening to '*Going Home*' from Dvorak's *New World Symphony*, one of the men said, "Hey, how about we use the sauna before bed? A little 'nekkid' fun never hurt anybody." He grinned at his girlfriend, a startlingly pretty girl who was smiling privately at his remark.

Jerzy said, "Yeah, we can use the sauna. As long as we keep it clean. The sauna and showers, I mean." He paused to think. "Anybody who wants to use it should be aware, though. People are going to be nude. So, if you're prudish, this might not be for you."

One of the women, a tall girl with a mass of curly hair and large, squarish glasses looked significant at Danny, who felt suddenly a bit shy. "I'm Penny, and I'm up for it," she said, without taking her eyes off him. "Are you up for it, Dan?" she asked meaningfully. He looked aside, but then got to his feet and surprising even himself, said. "Yeah. Me, too. In for a penny..." he quipped. "Any other takers?" Penny grinned at him.

About 9:30 pm saw a minor parade of youngish music lovers wrapped in towels, heading from their respective dormitories to the sauna, which was situated behind a small dressing room. Within about ten minutes seven people had doffed their towels and entered the cedar-paneled room, which was heated to about 160 degrees or so. Many of them exchanged surreptitious glances at nipples and genitalia, but the enervation produced by the heat dampened any serious arousal. Sweat ran into Danny's eyes. Every so often someone would toss a cup of water onto the hot rocks, generating a flash of steam. During one of these flashes Danny heard the door open and then close quietly, a momentary drift of cool air. When his eyes cleared he felt a minor disappointment to notice that Penny was gone.

The next morning Danny awoke about six a.m. Around him the others were still asleep. It was mountain cool, and he hustled to pull on his jeans and sneakers, and he wrapped his windbreaker over his shoulders.

Once outside he could see the sun just beginning to show past the shoulder of a mountain ridge off to the southeast. Birdsong was spangling the soundscape. He could see the wisps of his own breath, and he slipped the jacket on and zipped it up, setting off toward a low hill beyond the parking area. No one else seemed to be about.

He found a worn trail at the base of the hill and began upwards, zigzagging along the face of the hill as he ascended. For a time, he was in shadow once more, and he hastened upwards, puffing a bit, eager for the sunlight. Finally, he emerged into the dawn dazzle atop the hill and had to cover his eyes from the direct sunlight to see into the meadow just below. He felt a shock of astonishment.

Before him, perhaps sixty yards away, the owner of the ranch was wheeling his horse back and forth in the hay field, ripe grass nearly as high as the horse's belly. Haloed like a saint in the low sunlight, the rider whooped with laughter and wheeled the horse again. This time Danny saw what was in the rider's hand. It was a butterfly net. The man swung it like a polo mallet, swishing it through the top inches of grass. Every so often he would rein in the horse and lift the net towards his face, checking its contents. Then he would wheel the animal again, touch a spur to the its flank, and as they progressed through the hay, swing the net again. Danny stood transfixed a minute or two, watching the strange ballet of horse and rider and net. Then he turned and stepped back over the summit of the hill, back toward the ranch house. He made his way down the trail, whistling *Sheep May Safely Graze* softly to himself. *But perhaps not butterflies*, he thought.

After a morning session featuring the *Brahms Violin Concerto* and some of his work for solo piano, a group of five or six gathered to ride by horseback over a ridge and into the next canyon to look at a huge beaver dam complex on the creek there. Danny had never ridden before, but with the encouragement of the ranch owner, decided to give it a try. Whistling the theme from *The Magnificent Seven,* he arrived at the corral, where the others were already nearly saddled up. Penny was among them, and she gave him a broad smile. "I'm glad you came," she said. She seemed to have picked him out for company, and he felt a little flattered. She looked jaunty and pretty in her tight jeans and boots, a hint of lipstick and makeup.

"Nothing to worry about," the rancher was saying to one of their party. "These horses are so well trained they won't give you any trouble. Pull tight on the reins if you want'em to stop. Slap a rein lightly on the side you want'em to turn to. Nothing to it."

He helped all the riders saddle up, cinching the saddle belt tight. "These rascals often take a deep breath when you're cinching up the saddle. Then later they let it out, and the saddle slides around, dumping the rider. Horses *seem* dumb, but they're not completely stupid." He gave another tug on the cinch under Danny's ride, a dappled grey mare that stamped its hoof in response.

The riders climbed into their saddles and started off in single file along a trail through some pines, heading up along the north-facing ridge. At first Danny felt he had to hang on for dear life, twisting the reins around a white-knuckled fist. But after a time, as the saddle leather creaked, the gentle rhythm of the horse's walk almost put Danny to sleep. The novelty of riding soon wore off. *A piece of cake,* he thought.

The rancher pointed out a pair of hawks circling high overhead.

"Gotta love those guys," he said. "They eliminate a large chunk of the gopher population." He pulled his hat brim lower and added, "If you ever see a horse with a broke leg 'cause he stepped into a gopher hole on the run, you'll know what I mean." He looked grimly ahead, as if at some unseen, looming catastrophe, a giant gopher, maybe.

After an hour or so of riding, Danny's thighs were beginning to feel chafed, but he didn't care. The landscape was fabulous. They had filed up and across another ridge and into a narrow valley at the bottom of which a stream rushed over a rocky bed.

"It's just up here," the rancher called. "Biggest goddamn beaver dam you ever saw."

They rode around a rocky outcrop, and sure enough, there it was. Water gurgled and spurted through a natural flue near the center of the structure, which was at least eight feet high. They wound the horses to the right up and past the end of the dam, which stretched about seventy feet between two rocky outcrops. Atop one of these outcrops a tiny meadow spread toward a copse of cottonwoods. In the pond were two large beaver lodges. Beside one of them a large adult beaver 'thwacked!' his tail before diving beneath the surface.

A chorus of oohs and aahs went up from the gathered riders. The rancher looked them over smugly as if to say *I told you so*.

They dismounted, and the horses immediately began cropping at the tough mountain grass. A few of the riders wandered around, and one ventured to walk out on the dam's upper surface.

"I wouldn't do that if I were you," the rancher called. "That water's damn cold, damn cold," he reiterated, as if his city slicker guests were too stupid to pick up the message the first time. The young man turned and gingerly came back to solid ground. His girlfriend looked at him disapprovingly, and he shrugged and grinned.

A rather attractive woman of about thirty-five with long, absolutely grey hair passed around some gorp in a plastic bag. None of the rest of the group had thought to bring food.

On the way back to the ranch, the sky clouded over. It started to rain, at first softly, and then insistently, and everyone bundled up in jackets. The horses became a bit bad-tempered, and by the time the group was within half a mile of the ranch yard they simply began to run. None of the group save the rancher had the wherewithal to control the beasts, and Danny felt his heart lurch as his horse took off, ignoring Danny's muscular tugs on the reins. The 'piece of cake' had rapidly crumbled. The remaining ride was like a chaotic horse race. Although a few of the group were a bit shaken, no one was injured or even fell off his mount. But it was bone-jarring. One of them lost his hat to a low branch, but he couldn't turn the horse to go back for it. There would be some sharing of adventurous impressions over dinner.

Ride of the Valkyrie was echoing through the common room of the ranch house as in twos and threes the riders stumbled into it. In his bare feet, Jerzy was dancing to the frenetic theme in front of the big stone fireplace. His eyes were closed, as if he were experiencing some ecstatic communion with Wotan. His wife, St. PID, looked up periodically from the armchair where she was reading something called *Autumn in Heat*. She would smile dreamily and then return to her story.

The riders were still chattering about their adventure as they trooped into the dining area, following their noses to the aromas of bacon, beans, and coffee. *Whaya Hoo-Eee! Whaya Hoo-Eee!* sang the Valkyries, and the string section trilled melodramatically. Minutes later came the final cadence with an orchestral 'whap!', and Jerzy, no longer entranced, joined the diners. "Hey, PID!" he called. "Let's eat!" A few seconds later PID slid into a chair beside him and kissed his cheek.

"That music was fabulous!" she gushed.

All Danny could think was of Mark Twain's comment: *Wagner's music is better than it sounds.*

"Wow, man, that sounded like pretty heavy stuff," murmured a somewhat overweight Latino guy who called himself Chiapas Joe. He helped himself to another big spoonful of beans and a slice of bread.

"Just the best," Jerzy replied. After taking a sip of coffee, he said, "Since this is our last night here, why don't we finish off with some Richard Strauss?"

Danielle, a tall, lanky redhead holding a pet lapdog she kept with her wherever she went (*even to the bathroom, I'll bet*, thought Danny) gave the dog a tidbit of bacon. It snapped the morsel from her fingers. Danny expected blood, but apparently Danielle was used to the dog's quickness.

"I don't much like those Viennese waltzes," she offered. "Pretty schmaltzy stuff."

"Wrong Strauss," Jerzy said. "Remember *2001: A Space Odyssey*? Most people only know that crazy theme at the beginning. Stuff they sell cars to. But the rest of the piece is fantastic, based on some ideas by Friedrich Nietzsche, a book called *Also Sprach Zarathustra*. The theme of this piece is meant to represent the riddle of the world, the great puzzle of existence." He tugged a piece of bacon rind from beside a molar, placed it on a saucer, and then went on. "There *is* a small waltz in it, but it's just a bit of charm within Strauss's (or Nietzsche's) wilderness of ideas."

Down the table two guys were singing the theme, "Daaaa-daaaa-daaaa! Da-Da!! Boom, boom, boom, boom, boom, boom. Daaaa-daaaa-daaaa! Da-Da!!" (Back into the major key.) A young woman next to them was giggling.

Danny got up to go to the washroom. When he came out, Penny was waiting beside the doorway. She took his hand.

"Listen," she said. "It's our last night here. Let's pass on the music. Philosophical music, indeed! Anyhow, Nietzsche was fucked." She looked at him and smiled. "And I'd like to be."

Danny felt a jerk of erotic realization. In for a Penny?

"Come on," she said, and she led him down the hallway toward her room, one of the private ones.

Da-Da!! he thought. *Boom, boom, boom, boom, boom, boom!*

CHAPTER THIRTEEN

Survival!

"Listen, it's the most terrifying thing that's happened in *my* life, that's for sure."

Danny felt his ghost tremble a little in his spinal cord at the word 'terrifying,' but the signal passed. He moved over to lean on the counter by the scale.

Terry Borden, one of the store's regulars, sat on one of the stools near the till, a regular perch for him when he came to stock up on chamomile and burdock root, and to exchange gossip with Pauline. Danny didn't know how Pauline and Terry had become acquainted, but he always enjoyed Terry's visits. Terry and Shane shared some digs over by DU, although Terry didn't approve of Shane's drug habits. Those two and Pauline clearly had some history that Danny didn't know about.

Pauline said to him, "Yeah, it was raining pretty heavily here in town. But when the news started coming in about the Big Thompson, like, 'yowsers!' Where were you when it all started to come apart?"

Alan W. Lehmann

"First things first. Got any Haagen-Dazs?" Terry asked.

Pauline sighed. Whenever Terry had a story to tell he accompanied his tale by cadging some treat or other from the store. Danny gave a thin smile, and at Pauline's gesture, he walked over to the ice cream freezer and pulled out a half pint of coffee flavor. He brought it back with a plastic spoon and handed it to Terry.

"Thanks, man," Terry said as he tugged the cover off.

"So, the flood," Pauline prompted.

"Like an act of God," he said prophetically as he savored his first spoonful, waving the empty spoon in the air like a conductor's baton. "You know Brenda and Glenda, right?"

"Yeah, yeah," Pauline said. B and G, as we referred to them, were twin sisters of indeterminate age from somewhere in England. How they had ended up in Denver was anyone's guess. They were a Twiggyesque pair, fond of go-go boots and weed. Neither girl was exactly pretty—large teeth and sleepy-looking eyes with too much make-up—but they weren't ugly, either. They rarely spoke much, and when they did, it was in a British twang that Danny only understood to be 'east end' from once condescending to watch some British soap opera with Louise. According to Shane they could shag like rabbits. Terry and Shane often dated the pair, and it was surprising that they didn't all live together in a kind of 'which one are you again?' game of musical beds. But the girls lived with a Catholic aunt over in North Denver somewhere. Neither Pauline nor Danny ever had the courage to request details.

"Well," Terry went on, "we had decided to go tenting at one of the campgrounds up the Big Thompson. Later hike some trails, maybe. Estes Park was full. You know, the state's centennial birthday bash, and all that. Besides, there are too many tourists there, and you know the prices once you get up into the town."

He paused to wipe some errant ice cream from the side of his mouth.

"We found this campground about half way between Drake and Estes Park town site, something called Seven Pines. We had our tent set up by the time it began to rain, just a drizzle at first. The girls were simply miserable—and you know how whiney they can get—but we had a little camp stove under an awning, and we thought, 'What the fuck, it's a holiday; let's make the best of it.' B and G wanted to take off, though, 'back to civilization' Brenda said."

"Sounds like they had more sense than I usually credit them with," Pauline said.

"Yeah, well, they put on their slickers and went down to the highway, hitchhiked out, caught a bus in Loveland, and came back to Denver. Shane and I decided to stay." He scraped some ice cream from the side of the container, slid it into his mouth, swallowed. "Yum," he said.

"So," he went on, "Shane was doin' a little weed, singin' to himself as he sometimes does, and I was listenin' to the rain on the tent, which seemed to be getting heavier. It must have been around 6:30 pm. It would've still been light, but the clouds were really heavy. It was dark as winter. Just then a State Patrol guy drove into the campground in his jeep and began blowing his horn. He really leaned on it: beep, beep, beep, beep, and then beeeeeeeeeeeeeep! We got out to see what was goin' on. Some other folks got out of campers and tents, too."

"The trooper laid it on the line. 'You guys have gotta get out of here, or at least to much higher ground! It's rainin' real heavy up the canyon and up on the peaks. There's gonna be some serious flooding.'

"A woman from one of the campers said to him, you know the voice, the unhappy school kid one, 'Aw, come on. We just got our tv aerial up!'"

"He looked at her like she was from Mars. 'Come on, lady,' he said, 'I'm here to warn you. This could get really serious.'"

"I grabbed Shane by the sleeve and pointed up the slope to where there was another kind of level shelf, maybe six or seven feet higher. 'Shane,' I argued, 'let's pull the tent up there. If we pull the stakes and grab the corners we won't even have to take it down much. We'll just drag it.'" Terry took a breath.

"Shane was already a bit stupid from the dope, but he did what I told him. The rain was really starting to piss down. It took us about ten minutes to drag the tent up there. The car would have to stay in the lot. We were already soaked, but once in the tent we toweled off pretty good in the light of our flashlights. It was starting to get *really* dark now. We were behind three big pine trees, which cut the wind a bit, but the rain was just pissin' down, now, wild lightnin' flashes, thunder boomin' down the canyon. I squeezed my head out the flaps once to see what I could see. Three or four of the lower campers had pulled up stakes and left, and even the motor home lady and her husband were pulled out and headed toward Drake down the canyon. There weren't very many campers left." He sighed, then said, "I wonder how many of them made it..."

Pauline and Danny just watched Terry, captured now by the logic and suspense of his story.

Terry looked down a moment, gathering his memory.

"By the time we'd got the tent up the patrolman had gone. We could hear the racket of his horn echoing up the canyon. By about 8:30 or so the rain was just a torrent, and it was running down the slope behind the tent, soaking into the canvas and leaking through onto the tent floor. At one point a couple of heavy rocks, one of them almost two feet across, tumbled down the slope past our tent. It thumped onto the ground below and ran across to smash into the parking lot rail. We didn't know what the hell to do now! I was getting pretty scared, and Shane had retreated into that shell of silence he goes into when he gets really stressed or really stoned. I couldn't tell which it was, or if he was just scared out of his wits."

"We huddled in the tent for about another half hour, wet and fuckin' miserable, I can tell you. Finally, I stuck my head out again and aimed the flashlight toward the camp spots below. There was about two feet of water running through the camp. No going out that way now! 'Come on,' I said to Shane. 'We've gotta get higher.' We put on our slickers, and he had a bush hat, I remember. We had to leave the tent. Behind us there was a trail on the slope zig-zagging up toward the canyon top about a hundred feet further up. We humped our way up the slope, slipping on the gravel and mud. It took us about fifteen minutes to get up there. We sat down wheezing on the soaked moss and needles under some big tree. Then we heard it! I tried to see with my flashlight, but there was too much rain."

Terry looked first at Pauline, then at Danny.

"What, what?" Pauline said.

"It started like a distant rumble, a clatter, snapping and crushing sounds, getting louder and louder. Then it was just a roar, the sound of water smashing and scouring through the canyon. It was flash flooding. I'd read about it to do with desert watercourses, but I never thought I'd see it. The water must have been ten or twenty feet high, just roaring along underneath us. I saw a car with its headlights on—I'd never have seen'er otherwise—sailing half submerged, hitting a tree and spinning around it, before gettin' sucked under. I hope there were no people in it."

"Jeezus," Danny said. There was a moment's silence as the two of them absorbed his tale. "How long did it last?"

"The water was smashing through for the better part of forty minutes before it started to go down." He sighed. "We sat up there all night." He stared off into the middle distance, momentarily lost in his memories.

"When the sun came up, we could see that part of our path up the slope had been washed away. Where it remained, we could climb down. For about the last twenty feet we had to slide down the mud and gravel. The campsite was pretty much wrecked, full of mucky rocks and broken trees. The car was gone; I guess my insurance'll take care of that. Water had ripped the shit outta the road, big chunks of the highway just torn away." He paused. Then, as if to sum it all up, he said, "Hell of a mess."

"How's Shane doin'?" Pauline asked.

"Oh, you know him," Terry said. "Probably went through a pound of weed in the last week or so. He's ok." He thought a moment, then said, "We got picked up by a helicopter about 11:00 that morning. It had been cruising up the canyon checking for survivors. When we flew down toward Drake we saw that motor home, smashed into a tree, all bent up. The tv aerial was still up. I don't know if they died or not."

"So now what?" Danny asked.

Terry looked around as if waking up to reality once more. He looked down into his empty ice cream container and frowned. Then he said, "Now I'm gonna get some chamomile tea."

Pauline looked at Danny, who simply shook his head.

Life on the edge, he thought. *An edge here, an edge there.*

CHAPTER FOURTEEN

To New Mexico!

Louise came into the kitchen at about 7:30 pm from wherever she'd been. No one in the house ever knew her schedule, because basically she didn't have one. On any given day, she might lie in bed until four or five in the afternoon, or conversely, she might get up early and take the bus to one of the malls where she would sit in the food court drinking iced teas or wander from store to store, daydreaming about the stylish clothes she couldn't afford to buy.

This evening she had a crafty expression on her face, an uncertain smile, unusual for her, since she was one of the unhappiest people Danny had ever met.

"Hey, Louise, what's happenin'?" asked Carolyn. It was her sympathetic 'Mommy' voice. She put down the bowl she'd been drying beside the kitchen sink and went over to stand behind Danny where he was seated reading the *Rocky Mountain News*. He looked up, as Louise took the seat opposite, plopping her ragged purse onto the Formica table top in front of her. She smiled to show her teeth this time! It was actually a pretty smile, Danny had decided, based on limited exposure. She wasn't a bad-looking young woman. It was just that her depression was visible in everything she did, from her slumping posture to her irregular hygiene and gloomy facial expressions.

"I've got a car," she said breathlessly. At Carolyn's look of incredulity Louise shrugged and frowned once more. "Well, at least you could be happy for me," she said.

"How'd you get a car?" Danny asked. Louise had little to no money, although her younger brother, who worked in construction, helped her out with the rent from time to time.

"You know I used to live in Taos," she said to Carolyn, obviously referring to a conversation or two that Danny hadn't been present for. She shrugged out of her leather jacket, which collapsed behind her over the back of her chair. She shook her wild hair out of her eyes, and at Carolyn's, "Uh-huh," she continued.

"You remember I told you about my ex-boyfriend Randy?" she said.

"The drug dealer?" Carolyn asked.

Danny folded the paper and put it down beside his empty Michelob bottle. *The drug dealer? This should prove interesting*, he thought.

Louise frowned again, looking sideways at Danny, and then down at her nail-bitten fingers. "Yeah," she said. Then, more or less throwing caution to the wind, she explained, "Well, Randy got me the car."

"What'd you get?" Danny asked.

"It's out front," Louise said. "I forget, some Swedish car..." She thought a moment. "Yeah," she said, "a new Volvo."

139

"Jesus!" Danny said. He got up from the table and keeping his ear cocked for the conversation, slipped into the neighboring living room to the front window and looked out. There it was, all right, parked at the curb, a shiny, tan-colored Volvo, sleek and rich-looking.

Back in the kitchen Louise was saying, "Well, he owes me. And I can't get around. Last night I phoned him and said, 'I need a car,' and after a minute or two of talk he said, 'Ok. Go to a dealer and lease one and bring me the papers to sign.' So I did. But now I've gotta take him the papers. He's living in Santa Fé, with his new girlfriend."

Carolyn wiped her hands on the towel she'd been using and sat down on at the table's third side facing the wall. "So how come he owes you?" she asked.

Louise thought a second as she watched Danny come back in and resume his seat. Danny looked at Carolyn and nodded. "What a good-looking car," he said wistfully.

Louise took a deep breath and began her story.

"A few years ago, when we were still together, Randy got caught in Juarez by some Mexican police and put in jail. You know he has a plane, right? He's a crop-duster, and he used to spray fields in the southern part of the state around Las Cruces and up toward San Antonio. But that was just his cover. Most of his money he got from smuggling weed north out of Mexico. He'd fly fifty or a hundred feet off the ground, pretty much under the military radar, and drop off his load to retail dealers here in the States. He'd make about $25 g's a flight." She paused and asked, "Do you have any more beer?"

"Sure," Danny said. Normally he wouldn't be sharing his beer with Louise, who was pretty much a mooch, but this story was too good to miss. He went to the fridge and pulled out two more. "Carolyn?" he asked, but she shook her head. He popped off the caps and brought them back to the table, feeling the condensation already forming on the bottle glass in the summer heat. He set one in front of Louise, who picked it up and took a long pull. He sat down again, shoving the seat back a bit so he could lean back and look while he listened.

Louise began again. "Anyhow, he was off on one of his trips for a couple of days. I was at the apartment in Taos when the phone rang."

"'Louise?' he says to me. The phone was really crackly sounding. I could hardly hear him."

"'You gotta help me, Louise,' he says. 'I'm in Juarez. I'm in jail.' I don't remember what I said. 'What the fuck' or something like that" Louise grinned at Carolyn's discomfiture with the f-word.

"Randy says, 'Listen, just listen, will ya? Go into the bedroom and on the top shelf of the closet there's a sports bag. In it there's a hundred g's. You gotta bring it to Juarez and get me out of here.' Christ, I didn't know he had that kind of money in the apartment. That's the kind of cash that can get you killed."

She sipped her beer again.

"Well, I took a deep breath." Louise smiled crookedly a moment. "I don't mind tellin' you, I thought of just taking the money and, you know, disappearing someplace. But Randy was a decent guy, for the most part." She sighed.

"Everything's quiet for a couple of seconds. Then, as if he's talking to somebody else he says, 'I will, I will! Just give me a second here!' Then he gets louder and he explains, 'Just across the bridge after the border there's a little taco place, it'll be on your right. Pecos Sam's. Come in there with the money. I'll be there with two, maybe three guards. You give them the money, they let me go, and we go back to the States.'"

"So," Louise said, "long and the short of it is that's what happened. I was scared shitless crossing the border, but no one cared to look in the bag. Who knows? Maybe the border guards were in on it." She took another swig.

"I went into this little greasy spoon place that was selling tacos and burritos from behind a counter. Dim electric light hanging from a wire. A slim, good-looking cop with a thin moustache, a Don Diego type if I ever saw one, well, he looked at me from a table and got to his feet, waving me over, his eye on the bag, which I kept a tight grip on. He indicated I should follow him into the back, and we went through a curtain into a room walled with plywood. Across from our door were Randy and two more policemen on an old sofa. They were keeping a careful eye on him. Randy had a black eye and he looked pretty roughed up."

Danny coughed softly and leaned forward. This was better than *The Rockford Files*.

"The cops let him get up—they knew he couldn't go anywhere—and he came over and took the bag from me. He unzipped it, looked inside, and then showed the contents to the man who had escorted me to the back. He rummaged through it a bit, estimating the value, I guess. Then he nodded at the other two, who got up and came over. 'Buenos noches,' he said, bending over to kiss me on the cheek—smug bastard. 'It was nice doing business with you,' he said to Randy. He closed the bag and the three of them left together through a back entrance. Randy just looked at me and shrugged. 'Cost of doing business,' he said."

"Wow," Danny said. "Just about anything could've happened. A hundred grand. Holy shit."

"No kidding," Louise said.

Carolyn just smiled sagely, as if she'd always known that Louise was a bit of a hairball, however nice she could sometimes be. *She must have been a real hell-raiser when she was younger*, Carolyn thought.

"Anyhow, I need to go to Santa Fé. Anybody want to come?" Louise looked at me and Carolyn.

Danny thought of the car, of the potential for adventure, of going to another place he'd never been. "Sure. I'll go," he said.

Louise looked at him doubtfully a moment. "Carolyn?" she said.

"'Thelma and Louise,' huh? No, not me. I've got my little boys to look after." She was speaking about her seven-year-old son, a confused child who tended to daydream, and about her boyfriend Mac, a shy fellow from Toronto via Michigan who had somehow wandered into her life and gotten caught by the tentacles of her sexuality and her personal solidity, the latter something that was difficult to understand given the horrors of her childhood. But Danny guessed you have to develop some solidity to survive all that.

Louise looked back at Danny. "Ok. We can go. Tomorrow?"

Danny thought about his work schedule at the health food store. "How long'll we be gone?" he asked.

"Three days and two nights," she replied. "We'll take I-25 to Raton Pass and then head up over some mountains to Taos Pueblo—you gotta see Taos—and then down a long valley to

Santa Fé. We'll get a motel there; Randy's girlfriend is likely to go ape shit if she sees me. We'll meet Randy someplace downtown while she's off dancing—she's a ballerina, can you believe it? No tits, and he's offered to build her a dance theater." She gazed off wistfully toward the kitchen window, as if remembering better times, certainly times of more money.

Christ, this guy's got a lot of cash, Danny thought. He realized, too, that he felt a little uneasy about sharing a motel room with Louise. Who knew what she might want to get up to? And while he wasn't generally averse to a little touchy-feely (and at this interior admission he thought for a second of Penny), Louise was just too strange a quantity to get very connected to. Still, it would probably be all right.

"Yeah, that should work out," he said. "I've gotta be back for Saturday. That's our big day at the store."

"Sure," she said. "We'll come back Friday, then."

The next day the two of them were cruising south down I-25, Louise at the wheel. It was another brilliant morning, sun glowing out of a burnished sky, the front range of the Rockies rising like uneven battlements off to their right.

"Are you sure you want to be going this fast?" Danny asked, feeling the closed buckle of his seat belt for reassurance. The scenery flashed past, as Louise held the car anywhere between 75 and 85 mph.

"I just can't seem to slow down," she gushed. "It just wants to go, go, go!"

Danny stared off to the southeast where a brown plain seemed to stretch on forever, baking in the late morning sunlight. Ahead and to the right he could see the suburbs of Colorado Springs.

"Better slow down through here," he said, and Louise obediently tapped the brake a few times, bringing them down to about 60. They cruised past the urban area on the freeway. Danny looked down at the city racing past—Taco Bell, Texaco, 7-11—all the shitty service places that seem to stick to highways like flies on flypaper.

"That's Pike's Peak over there," Louise said, pointing off toward the Rockies. Behind the treed slopes of the front mountains a huge rocky peak with snow on the high ridges reclined in a kind of remote majesty. "And further along here is the big air force thingamajig in Cheyenne Mountain."

Even Danny had heard of Cheyenne Mountain, the place where the combined militaries of the US and Canada monitored global air traffic and rocketry in case the Russians decided to bomb North America. It was an eerie idea, that carved into the side of a mountain was a military headquarters secure from even a nuclear bomb, where soldiers would stay alive, for a while at least, while everything outside perished in a blast inferno and its subsequent nuclear winter. He looked momentarily upward toward the glowing sun, as if it were some Soviet rocket streaking directly toward them and their imminent annihilation.

Louise had meanwhile allowed the car to drift up to about 80 m.p.h. Within about three minutes police lights were flashing insistently in the car mirrors. Louise slumped her shoulders, frowned, and pulled to a long, slow stop on the freeway shoulder. "Shit," she said. "Here he comes," she said.

When she opened her window, the state trooper stared down at her through mirrored sunglasses that, along with his sunburned nose, made him look like some kind of alien species.

The man with no eyes again, Danny thought, looking past Louise.

The trooper grinned warily, a silver incisor glinting brightly in the late morning sunshine, and in a surprisingly mellow voice said, "Just pushin' it a little, weren't you, ma'am?" He placed one palm on the grooved sill where the car window had disappeared downward into the door panel and sighed.

"You have to say something," Danny said, nudging her shoulder.

Louise took a deep breath and turned to look up at the officer. She could smell the tic-tacs on his breath. "It's a new car," she said softly, as if the fact were some kind of legitimate excuse for exceeding the limit by 20 m.p.h.

"Well, yeah, I can see that," he said. "And a fine-lookin' vehicle it is, too. I suppose a new car oughtta go fast. But everythin's got its 'oughttas.' Like I oughta remand you for dangerous driving." He turned his head and looked back down the highway, where in response to the flashing lights, no doubt, the traffic was proceeding expeditiously but well within the limit. He turned back to Louise.

"Tell ya what," he said. "You can follow me inta town to the city hall and take a envelope outa the box where I show ya, put $25 in there and deposit it in the fine box, and be on your way with a warning." He paused and looked gravely at the two malefactors before him. "Or, you can stay and face it in court in, oh, about a week."

"Have you got twenty-five bucks?" Louis said in Danny's direction out of the corner of her mouth.

Shit! Danny thought. *I should have known it would come to something like this.* He scratched his head and thought.

"Ok," he said reluctantly.

"Oh, Jeez, I'll give it back to you after we see Randy," Louise said. She turned to the trooper and said, "Lead on, MacDuff."

He straightened and lifted his glasses to look at her more closely. "You bein' smart with me?"

"No, no, no," she answered in a mollifying tone. "No. It's just Shakespeare. It came to mind—kind of out of nowhere." She cast around for some better explanation. "I often quote Shakespeare when I'm nervous." She looked at him, trying to fathom his acceptance of her explanation.

He gave her a critical glance, then said, "Ok. follow me." He turned back to his squad car.

He pulled past the Volvo and continued at a snail's pace down the shoulder for half a mile, the two would-be travelers following. Then he turned into town, and the two-car procession meandered through the downtown area—a mélange of banks, small businesses, supermarkets and parking lots—to where, true to his word, the city hall waited, *Probitas et Felicite* engraved in an arch stone above the main entrance. He got out and pointed to a box attached to the wall beside the door, next to which was also an attached wooden niche containing envelopes. Danny fished two bills out of his wallet, stuffed them into an envelope, and deposited it under the scrutiny of the trooper into the slot in the fine collection box.

Another twenty-five bucks down the toilet, thought Danny.

The trooper grinned beneath his glasses, his silver front tooth glinting in the sunlight. He gave them a 'thumbs up' and turned back to his car. Climbing inside, he fired up the ignition and pulled away.

"Don't say anything, at least not right now," Louise said. Danny looked at her. "Oh, and thanks. I *will* get you your money back." Danny nodded, glumly, she thought, but she supposed with good reason.

Soon they passed the sleepy settlement of Trinidad at the bottom end of the state and were climbing the long, winding approach to Raton Pass, a route that had once been part of the Santa Fé Trail. As they negotiated the switchbacks, they could look back onto the baking plains of southern Colorado. To the northwest they could see the two Spanish Peaks, a pair of mountains the natives had once held to be "the breasts of the Earth."

It's like another planet, thought Danny. The rough, rocky landscape featured tough grasses and low cacti with the occasional small tree that looked vaguely like some kind of olive. He imagined riding through the region on a cow pony, yipping and snapping his reins, pushing a great herd of longhorns ahead of him alongside a dozen other cowpokes. He grinned.

"Everybody thinks Raton means 'rat' in Spanish. It actually means 'mouse.'" Louise smirked at her inside knowledge.

From Raton, a dumpy little town, they turned onto Highway 64 and climbed further into the mountains. On this curvy secondary highway, the Volvo carried them higher and westward past jumbled, worn rocky slopes dotted with juniper and stunted pines, surrounded by the remains of wildflowers from earlier in the year. After an hour or so, they pulled into Taos.

"You've gotta see the pueblo," Louise said emphatically. She maneuvered the Volvo along several side roads with names like Goat Creek Road and Rotten Tree Road, finally arriving at an open parking area. A hundred yards away, across a sandy area spotted with bits of bunch grass, stood the pueblo. It was a startling, impressive sight, a kind of layered set of apartment dwellings constructed of adobe, with flat roofs supported by round, log roof beams.

"These buildings are nearly a thousand years old. At least, settlement has been here that long. Buildings have probably been repaired and rebuilt over time. People still live here," Louise said softly. "You can't take pictures of any of their ceremonies or dances." Her tone was almost reverential.

She and Danny wandered around for a few minutes, staring at the buildings. There was a smell of dust and smoke, and sheep droppings.

Louise was surprisingly knowledgeable about the area. "D. H. Lawrence came here in the 1920's. He and his wife actually owned a ranch somewhere north of here. He was fascinated by Mexico, and then by Taos and by the mountains around here. Here's where he wrote that weird novel *The Plumed Serpent*." Danny remembered references to the book his English prof had made when they had read *The Rainbow* for their course on the modern British novel six or seven years ago. Lawrence was all taken up with blood and sex, he had concluded back then. He thought of Birkin—or was it Gerald—wandering off onto a glacier to freeze to death in *Women in Love*. *Weird is right*, he thought--*all of Lawrence's stuff.*

After twenty minutes or so the two of them returned to the car. They didn't say much, but Louise backed the car around and pulled back onto the road that would lead them to the highway to Santa Fé.

They pulled into Santa Fé at about 8:30 pm. The sun had already set, but there was still a streak of red across the western horizon. Louise turned the car into the parking lot of the Trail Ride Motel, another of those cheap, single story, long bungalows housing a dozen or so rooms. The sign sizzled and blinked as they scrawled their signatures on a card, watched by a suspicious Latino woman, seated on a stool and eating a small burrito.

"Chew have children?"

"No," Louise said. "Just one night. *Two* beds."

"Two beds, huh?" she said, glancing over at Danny suspiciously, as if thinking, *what kind of stupido gringo is this, anyway?*

He was tempted to say, "I'm gay," but he didn't want some loony Latina Catholic toting a shotgun to get the wrong idea.

The room was claustrophobic, and the air conditioning clunked at irregular intervals, but all told, for twelve bucks it would serve.

The next morning, they met Randy at a coffee place on the town's central square, the *zocalo*. Down the street stood the

Eldorado Hotel, a concrete faux adobe construction that mimicked the Taos pueblo and that probably featured $8 highballs in the bar outside the five-star restaurant. Danny found it curious how sentimental nostalgia, often for aspects of life completely outside of people's own life experience, can so readily be turned into cash. He remembered going to Disneyland with his Dad many years ago, standing beside Mickey Mouse while his father snapped a photo, and gazing up Main Street USA. *The whole country could turn into a theme park*, he thought wryly.

Now Randy was stirring his coffee across the table from Louise, glancing every so often with a kind of placid animosity toward Danny.

"This is Danny," Louise explained. "He lives in our communal house. He came along 'cause I need some company to share the driving."

Randy looked back at her. "Uh-huh," he said skeptically, and then, "You got the papers?" he asked. Danny could just imagine Randy thinking, *Looks like I'm paying for a new car for Louise's new boyfriend.*

Louise retrieved a sheaf of official-looking documents from her handbag and passed them across to Randy. He flipped through them, scowling.

"You might have picked a cheaper car," he commented.

Louise ignored his complaint. "There, where those yellow marks are," she pointed.

"Yeah, yeah, bossy," he muttered. "You haven't changed that much, have you?"

She frowned. He tugged a plastic ball point from his shirt pocket, located the right blanks on the pages, and scribbled an illegible signature.

"Remember," he said. "It's just for a year."

"I know," she replied.

He passed the papers back to her.

Suddenly he seemed to brighten up. "Hey, I gotta show you the site of our new theater! It's just a couple of blocks from here. Angel's gonna love it."

Without finishing his coffee (an offensive kind of waste, from Danny's perspective), Randy hustled them to their feet and led them off down a wooden sidewalk promenade. Coming toward them was a Latino in a leather jacket and cowboy boots. He walked straight at Danny, who obligingly stepped aside on the narrow walkway. The man grimaced, as if mildly disappointed, and strode past them. A few steps further on Randy stopped them and turned to Danny.

"That guy," he said, "was looking for a fight. He would've knocked you down if you hadn't moved." Randy looked at Danny for some response.

Danny was a little speechless. He turned to look at the Latino, who was stalking off across the plaza, his back to them.

"It's a macho thing," Randy said. "You see it all the time here, especially from the younger guys. Something to prove, I guess. Still takes me by surprise sometimes."

"Randy's from Philadelphia," Louise said. "You know, city of brotherly love?"

"Sure," Danny said.

After looking over the dusty exterior front of the Avalon Theater (the old sign), they turned and stood uncertainly on the sidewalk for a few moments.

"We can't go in right now," Randy said. "They're renovating. It's gonna cost about 300 g's," he remarked. "I can't wait to surprise Angel."

Presumably she's the ballerina, Danny thought.

"It's time to hit the road," Louise said. "Listen Randy, thanks a lot. I mean, this will really help."

Randy looked momentarily pleased with himself, and he smiled wryly at her. He stepped toward her and gave her a peck on the cheek. "Remember, just for a year."

Louise nodded.

CHAPTER FIFTEEN

Bombs Away!

Danny was humming to himself, mumbling improvised lyrics in a mindless sort of way as he headed north on I-25. Today was the big anti-nuclear demonstration at the Rocky Flats nuclear weapons plant! For years he had been too preoccupied with his own problems to think about nuclear war, although he did remember some of the hysteria surrounding the Cuban Missile Crisis when he was only about thirteen.

One of his mom's brothers, an uncle he truly admired, was also a fierce anti-communist and a not so clandestine supporter of the John Birch Society. Prone to hyperbolic patriotic indignation, it had seemed to Danny that his uncle wouldn't have minded a nuclear war, with his vocal protestations of "better dead than Red," and other such oratorical chowder. If he hadn't been such a decent guy to Danny over the years, Danny would probably have written him off as a nut case.

His uncle had built a fallout shelter in the basement of his new house. He had all kinds of plans for food storage, sheltered ventilation, first aid, probably a bunch of Krugerrands and a machine gun, for all Danny knew. Yet he was a loving father to his own wife and children, committed to their well-being, and to that of the extended family, too. It was another lesson in how complicated people can be—total idiots in some ways and nearly saints in others.

Danny watched the highway stretching out before him, turnpike traffic whizzing along like some choreographed school of fish. Only yesterday his friend Carl had called and implored him to join the downtown protest march and the afternoon event at Rocky Flats, home to Rockwell International, manufacturer of plutonium triggers for hydrogen bombs.

"Ok," had agreed, "but I can't come to the march in the morning—gotta work. I'll come to the protest in the afternoon."

Now he was singing on the freeway. "Firefights and guns, nuclear suns, bombs and jet planes, capital gains, young people dead, Moloch must be fed, Viet Cong song, lah-de-dah-dah-dah." The melody was erratic and made him think of Jerzy and Louise, and PID, and for some reason, Penny. Well, he knew the reason for that...

This month, too, Danny had become another proud owner of a Volvo. True, it wasn't a swizz new one like Louise's, far from it. Danny had bought it for $450 cash from a customer to the store who needed some quick bucks, something to do with a dental bill. The car's body was a mess. It had been rolled *and* rear-ended in two different accidents, resulting in a rippled roof and a rear deck that was shoved in about five inches on the left side. But the motor! It sailed him along, a purring precision engine that made him feel a glow each time he fired up the ignition. Even his mechanic, a Korean American who had gone to Sweden to train to work on Volvos, was impressed, and he'd said so in no uncertain terms in Korean-accented English. (Danny wondered if he had learned Swedish, too.) He wasn't sure how long it would be before Danny would have to replace the U-joints, which clunked ominously each time he put the automatic transmission into drive. But for Danny right now driving the car was just shy of bliss! Perhaps he was easily pleased.

After proceeding for a time toward Boulder on the Denver Boulder Turnpike, he turned onto Highway 129 and headed west for the demonstration's assembly point. Carl had provided directions, and sure enough, off to Danny's left he could see a crowd gathering near where a railway line headed into the big Rockwell International property. He pulled onto a gravel shoulder behind a line of parked vehicles, climbed out of the car and stretched. Then he hustled over to where he could see Carl chatting up a blonde who carried a sign saying *No Nukes is Good Nukes.*

"We've got permission to walk into the property along the rail line until we reach the cement blockade across the tracks," Carl told them. "I guess they don't use the train any more, and beyond that concrete we don't want to go. After all, we don't know what kind of radiation might be buzzing around there. Nobody here has a Geiger counter."

Carl spoke quickly, a kind of breathy voice that, combined with its pacing, lent an air of suppressed excitement to everything he said.

"There are a couple of big name speakers! Helen Caldicott from Physicians for Social Responsibility, and Allen Ginsberg, you know, the crazy, gay beat poet—like, wow!"

In small groups, the protesters began walking into the property. A light wind was blowing down off the Rockies behind them, ruffling the native grasses beside the rail right of way. Someone further ahead was singing *We Shall Overcome*, kind of off topic, but expressing a brave sentiment, nonetheless.

At the designated gathering point the crowd milled around, waiting for the organizers to get the speeches under way. One entrepreneurial character was selling t-shirts from a trailer he had towed behind his bicycle. Danny eyed them skeptically. *Everything's business here,* he thought. *They probably sell t-shirts at executions.*

After what seemed a disorganized ten or twelve minutes, Helen Caldicott called the crowd to attention, using a bullhorn to be heard. "If you love this planet," she said loudly, appealing for attention to the response of some ragged cheers. "If you love this planet, you're going to have to change the priorities of your life." All became quieter.

"Nuclear industry proponents often assert that low doses of radiation produce no ill effects and are therefore safe. But no dose of radiation is safe, however small, including background radiation; exposure is cumulative and adds to an individual's risk of developing cancer. If you inhale a millionth of a gram of plutonium, the surrounding cells receive a very, very high dose. Most of the cells within that area die because plutonium's an alpha emitter. The cells on the periphery remain viable. They mutate, and the regulatory genes are damaged. Years later, that person develops cancer."

She went on in this vein for about 15 minutes, making her listeners more and more uncomfortable, as if they could feel the gamma rays and alpha particles slamming into their bodies, a billion tiny punches leaving their cells black and blue. Finally, to enthused if somewhat scattered applause, she stepped aside and Allen Ginsberg took the bullhorn.

Ginsberg looked wild, half mad, his dark hair and scruffy beard mussed by the stiff breeze, and he spoke with a charismatic urgency that was undeniable. Danny allowed himself to ignore the words and meanings but to bathe in the sense implicit in the sound and feeling. A few phrases stuck with him: "Everybody's heart is broken now... America, I've given you all and now I'm nothing." He hung his head a moment, as if he might burst into tears. The poetry was meditative, *like Buddhism*, Danny thought, a rhythmic, sonic giving up.

When the crowd cheered and Ginsberg said, "Thank you, thank you," they all began to gather around two young men who were filling helium balloons. Carl elbowed up next to Danny, and pointing at a card table someone had unfolded beside the helium tank, said, "See those little cards? They all contain a message that says, 'This balloon comes to you from Rocky Flats Nuclear Weapons plant. Any stray radioactive plutonium on dust in the wind may come this way.'"

That's damn clever, thought Danny.

People were tying the tiny messages of doom onto balloons and releasing them into the gusty breeze, which bore them up and away to the east. Danny wondered how many of them would come down in Denver, and how many would sail on and on, perhaps, over Kansas and Missouri, perhaps to the ends of the earth. Maybe someone climbing Mt.

Everest would catch one, or one would splat onto the pilot's windshield on an airliner far out over the Atlantic. He tied one securely to his balloon, waited for a gust, and tossed it skyward where it swerved dramatically a moment and then rose rapidly, shrinking into the upward distance.

Late that afternoon, after buying a t-shirt (he was always a sucker for t-shirts) and driving back into the city, Danny met Carl for a cheap supper at a Mexican place on Colfax Avenue.

"Best Mexican in the city," Carl breathed as he seated himself before their worn, wooden table. It wobbled when he lowered his elbows onto it. He tugged a napkin from the chrome holder, folded it a couple of times, and wedged it under one of the legs beside him. Testing the table's steadiness, he said, "That's better," and leaned forward once more.

"Did I tell you what happened to me this morning?" he asked, lifting his beer. "At the march?"

Danny had spent the morning working at *Healthy Body*, so he had missed the march through downtown Denver from the gold-domed capitol building down to Larimer Square. "Nope," he said, spooning up some refried beans.

"There were about sixty or seventy of us, a lot of us with signs against the plant. Plenty of cops were watching, both in uniform and plain clothes, usually from parked cars. At one point, I noticed a buzz cut guy in a suit aiming a long-lens camera at me." He took another swallow of beer.

"Jeez," Danny said.

"I went over and asked him if he was taking pictures of us. He grinned and said, 'We have lots of good pictures of *you*, Carl.' Made my spine quiver, I can tell you."

"Jeez," Danny said again, wondering if anyone had been taking such pictures out at Rocky Flats. "What do you think? FBI?"

"Probably," Carl said. He sighed. "Sometimes I don't know about this country, man." Then he said, "How about this burrito, though? Isn't it pure Zen?"

"Oh, yeah," Danny agreed happily. But he kept thinking about the surveillance.

For a time, they ate in silence. Sometimes there are real things to be afraid of in the world. But he and Carl were young and, oddly to Danny, almost fearless, a state that he suddenly found particularly odd, given his initial reason for coming here. *When the fear's in you, it's in you*, he thought. *Just now it isn't in me. Isn't that weird?*

By the time Danny got back to the house he was ready for sleep. *There'll always be tomorrow,* he thought.

As he crawled into bed he could hear Carolyn's stereo softly from the basement, as if from far, far away. Manfred Mann was singing.

Blinded by the light, revved up like a deuce, another runner in the night...

Blinded by the light

As he drifted into sleep he saw recurring nuclear flashes, bits of film from his high school days, children with their arms over their heads crouching under their school desks, buildings being swept away by atomic blasts. *Blinded by the light... Mama always told me not to look into the eyes of the sun...*

CHAPTER SIXTEEN

Bluebird of Happiness

It was one of those fabulous late March days in Denver, spring in the air, hopeful sunshine, not too hot yet, as the summer had been. Better yet, it was a day off work. Danny stretched in bed, listening to the birds in the lilac bushes outside his window, and to the traffic on Holly Street. *What to do, what to do?* he thought to himself as he pulled on a t-shirt, jeans and runners. After relieving himself in the communal bathroom and washing his face, he went into the kitchen.

Carolyn was there, drinking coffee at the table, scanning the *Denver Post Classifieds* for garage sales for the coming weekend. She managed to scratch out a subsistence living driving around to yard sales in her beat-up van, picking out old furniture and knick-knacks, repairing any obvious flaws, and reselling items in a yard sale of her own once a month. She wouldn't get rich, but she was making do.

"This is so flustrating," she said absently at Danny's arrival.

'Flustrating' was another of her neologisms, terms she frequently coined, seemingly out of nowhere. This one was a combination of 'fluster' and 'frustrate,' surprisingly apt as a description of some of Carolyn's travails.

"What is?" Danny asked, pulling a blackened cast iron frying pan out of a lower cupboard.

"There just ain't enough good sales coming up this weekend, or at least ones that are advertised yet. And it's Wednesday. Everybody knows that to get the jump on weekend sales you've got to prepare and map out your route well ahead of time." She sighed and lit a cigarette.

Danny murmured some mollifying phrase, wondering at all the things that supposedly everybody knows, but scarcely paying attention to her really. He was beating up some eggs for an omelet and toasting some of the store's whole grain bread made with stone-ground, organic flour. His mouth watered.

"Is all you ever eat for breakfast those sprout omelets?" Carolyn asked plaintively.

"Yeah, more or less," he said, buttering a couple of slices of toast. "And raw milk cottage cheese. You ever try it? It's to die for."

When the omelet was done, he slid it out of the pan onto a chipped plate and brought it over to the table. Carolyn obligingly tried to wave her smoke away, and when she failed, she stubbed out her cigarette. "Sorry," she said.

"It's ok," Danny said. He knew how addicted Carolyn was to her 'cancer sticks', as she called them. Sometimes her tension levels could become unbelievable, and nicotine seemed to provide some relief, he knew. He ate his breakfast in relative silence, considering the day opening up before him. Carolyn went back to her paper.

"You like bookstores, right?" Carolyn asked.

"Sure," Danny said. He spent hours every week prowling around bookstores, particularly used bookstores like the one on South Grant. And he read like a man starving for print, sometimes six or seven books a week, everything from science fiction to history to poetry.

"Says here there's a new bookstore opening down in Cherry Creek today. Called Bluebird Books. It's got a restaurant, or at least a coffee shop, attached." She closed the newspaper, folded it, and laid it on the table. Louise might want to look at it later. On the visible front page was the headline '**President Carter Visits Denver**' in big bold type.

"I wonder where Carter's going..." he mused aloud, taking a large bite of toast. He chewed vigorously, swallowed, and then to Carolyn, he said, "I might just go down there," Danny said. "Bluebird Books, that is. In fact, I think I will."

Carolyn got to her feet and turning, headed toward the basement stairs, at the bottom of which she kept her tiny suite. "Not before you do your dishes," she reminded him, smiling at him.

They really did like each other. He was kind of like a younger brother to her, but in this case polite and affectionate, not crude and violent like the real *older* brothers she had left behind in Baton Rouge. One of them had raped her when she was only thirteen, a fact Carolyn had confided to Danny during a late-night conversation a few months ago. Danny had been both outraged and terrified by the story. But they hadn't spoken of it for several months.

"I'll clean it all up," Danny said, and before leaving the house, he did.

Elton John's *Rocket Man* was ringing out on the car radio as Danny pulled Maybelline (his nickname for the bashed-up Volvo) into an angle parking slot not far from the Cherry Creek Mall. "*Burnin' out a fuse up here alone...,*" he sang along, mentally half off in orbit someplace.

There it was, a few storefronts down: *Bluebird Books and Café*, neatly printed in what resembled Renaissance script. The exterior front wall was light blue, almost sky-colored, and there was a trellis holding up a potted vine by the front door.

Cool, he thought. He didn't know much about vines, but the fresh growth gave him a vital feeling.

He locked the car and walked down the sidewalk to the store. A small bell jangled as he opened the front door, revealing a long, narrow retail space alive with sunlight from three skylights overhead. A dozen or so customers stood before various displays, one of which highlighted *New Bestsellers*. A hardcover book in a white dustjacket caught his eye: *The Origin of Consciousness in the Breakdown of the Bicameral Mind* by *Julian Jaynes*.

Wow, what a mouthful! he thought, and picked it up.

"That book's amazing!" said a familiar voice softly just behind him. He looked over his shoulder.

"Penny!" he said.

"The one and only," she said back, and grinned. "How're *you* doin', soldier?"

Danny felt a little embarrassed, mostly because after their encounter up at the dude ranch he had never made any move to call her. She had been exciting as hell that night, but he had things on his plate.

"You know I'm sorry I..." he began, but she said, "Tut, tut. None of that now. Besides, I'm married."

"Whoa," Danny muttered, a kind of incredulity in his tone. "Married?"

"You know," she went on, "when a man and a woman get a license and stand in front of a priest and commit to one another?"

"When?" Danny said, genuinely pleased for her, and relieved for himself.

"Oh, about five years ago," she said, and she grinned her foxy grin once more.

Oh, wow, Danny thought. *I was shagging a married woman.*

"Not to worry," she went on quietly. "We have an 'open marriage.' He fucks around from time to time, and so do I."

Danny didn't know what to say. Penny grinned at his discomfiture.

"Now," she said, "about the book. I work here. You should get it."

He grinned wryly back at her. "You on commission? I suppose it's the least I could do," he replied.

"Do you feel like some tea?" she asked. "We're a café, too, you know."

"No, I don't think so. How much is the book?"

"Only $22.95."

Danny groaned inwardly. On his wages, it was a lot of money. But he said, "Ok. I think I'll look around a bit more, too."

"Sure."

Penny drifted away and struck up a conversation with another customer. Danny scanned a few more titles, but he kept getting distracted by the memory of her freckled breasts by candle light, and of panting in the dark.

Soon enough, though, he had paid his bill and left the shop. Down the street he could see the neon sign of Rick's Café, a riff on *Casablanca*. Normally he might have stopped in there for a sandwich, but something was going on. Several large, black limos with American flags on the fenders were idling in front, and even from nearly a block away he could see what must have been several law enforcement figures surrounding the cars and talking into walky-talkies.

Holy shit! It's President Carter, he thought. Then, to a couple of young blacks walking his way, he asked, "Is that Carter down there?"

One of them, a big guy with dreadlocks, turned to him and said, "Sure is. We was about to have some lunch when they all pulled up and the owner hustled over an' ushered us out. Don't much like bein' denied service. We got civil rights," he said and frowned. Then he added, "Carter's a pretty good guy, though. Any president who can admit to committing adultery in his heart's gotta be all right." His deep bass voice was musical, reassuring, almost forgiving.

Just in his heart? Danny thought, and Penny flashed to mind once more.

The other fellow snickered and said, "A waiter told me Carter doesn't even know what alfalfa sprouts are! What a laugh. Suppose he wanted peanuts?"

"Come on," the first one said, and the two continued down the walk, one of them gesturing to emphasize something he was saying, just out of Danny's hearing. He curiously watched them go, a couple of nearly alien beings, they seemed to him. For a second, he had an overwhelming sense of his personal solitude, almost a loneliness, one person within this great mixing bowl of a city. But almost immediately the loneliness passed.

Danny clutched his new book and after checking out the traffic, jaywalked over to a small park. There on a slatted bench he opened it and began reading.

INTRODUCTION: The Problem of Consciousness were the first words he saw. *O, what a world of unseen visions and heard silences, this insubstantial country of the mind! . . . This consciousness that is myself of selves, that is everything, and yet nothing at all—what is it? And where did it come from? And why?*

Danny nearly trembled as he read. *Problem? No kidding,* he thought.

CHAPTER SEVENTEEN

Junkyard Dogs

Danny glanced at his watch: 9:48 pm. The cab business was slowing down fairly early, considering it was a Friday night. He had been parked at the edge of the Safeway lot for just over five minutes, the motor of his Yellow Cab shut off, the cooling hood audibly ticking. The radio crackled and scratched with the occasional dispatch message bursting through in just sufficient volume for him to know the pick-up was too far away to bother bidding on it.

He had been driving a taxi weekends for about three months now. He'd had to give up Saturday work at the store, but Pauline didn't mind, and he still put in two days for her during the week.

Driving cab weekends was a pretty good gig, especially if you valued your time more than money. You picked up a car at 6:00 pm on Friday evening and could use it all weekend until 6:00 am Monday morning, all for the price of one day's cab rental. Nobody cared how much you worked. Some drivers drove straight through, although they might pick up a couple of hours sleep here or there when exhaustion set in. Even getting regular sleep, on a good weekend you could make a couple of hundred bucks, especially if you got a trip from the airport to Aspen or Vail, or someplace else out of town.

He thought a moment about his training into the exotic world of taxi-driving.

The instructor, an obese black man wearing a Broncos cap and sporting gold fillings that glittered when he grinned, was an experienced driver who had smashed up his cab when he took an exit ramp off I-70 at too high a speed. He had a broken leg to show for his skills. His name, or perhaps nickname, was Bonzo. Yellow Cab had agreed to pay him minimum wage to train new drivers while his leg healed.

"This is a bell," he had said in a meaningful voice, basso profundo, one almost oracular in significance, a James Earl Jones/Darth Vader ring to it. He held up a miniature piece of paper for their inspection. On it was some cribbed handwriting, a few numbers and an address. "When a dispatcher is handed one of these, he'll read out the pick-up address by its cross streets and start counting down from a random number anywhere from zero to nine. When he says the number that matches the last digit of your cab number, you're eligible to bid on the pick-up by calling in your cab's numerical ID. If you're first to call in, you get the trip."

The three of them listening, new drivers all, looked at one another speculatively.

"Ok," he said. "Bob, your cab is number 177, Lance, 231, Danny, 254. I'm going to pick up a bell and start a countdown. When you think you're eligible to bid, squeeze that send button on your radio mike and say your number. Got it?"

Danny looked at the Motorola microphone in his hand, positioned his thumb on the switch, and nodded.

"Yup," said Lance.

"Ok. Here goes." Bonzo picked up a bell and looked at it. "Porter Hospital. Three, two, one, zero..."

"231!" shouted Lance, and he took a breath like a happy hiccup.

"Bingo," Bonzo said, nodding with approval, as if Lance had just won a Nobel Prize. "Bingo," he said again, and then as if the meaning behind the word was insecure, he grinned his glittery grin and added, "Good. You'd have got the trip. Let's try again." Lance beamed and held his microphone at the ready. Bonzo picked up another bell.

"Thirteenth and Alameda," he said. "Six, five, four," and "254!" Danny snapped.

"Did you squeeze your mike?" Bonzo asked severely.

"Oh, yeah," Danny said smugly.

"Now I'd tell you the exact address and the name of the client, in this case 'Sandra at the kitchen entrance.' Ok, ok, you guys got it?" Bonzo looked particularly at Bob, who was scratching the back of his neck, still looking puzzled, but nodding along with the other two. There was a minor chorus of assent.

"Ok, go get a car." And so it had begun.

Danny yawned and looked at the thinning traffic. At just that moment his radio crackled. "Oxford Hotel, five, four..."

Danny reflexively thumbed his radio and called, "254."

"254, pick up Sid at the front entrance."

"Roger," Danny said.

Wow, the Oxford Hotel, Danny thought. He remembered Pauline's telling him about the place once, in a voice filled with girlish enthusiasm.

"Yeah, what a place," she had said. "It's down by the river and the railroad, one of the first great hotels built in the city. Bat Masterson shot a man there once, or so the rumor goes. You can still see a bullet hole in the wainscot in the lobby, maybe *the* bullet. A distant friend of mine bought the place about a year ago for just $80,000—it's pretty run down. But it's got a marble staircase and oak trim..." Her voice trailed off. Then she said, "My friend lives in a small room behind the desk. He works probably eighteen hours a day doing one thing or another. A lot of indigent old men live there, and he's got some contracts with human services to pay rent for these old guys. He saves pretty hard, and he's in the process of slowly fixing the place up. Who knows, maybe it'll be a great hotel again one day."

Remembering the details, she'd been gazing out the window behind the till at the store, watching a thin drizzle fall out of a grey sky (unfamiliar weather for most of the year).

Now Danny cranked the motor, glanced both ways, and pulled out of the Safeway lot, heading west on Colfax for downtown.

Five minutes later he pulled up at the dim entry of the Oxford. A thin, scruffily dressed young man, maybe just over twenty years old, detached himself from the wall where he had been leaning in the shadows and approached the car. Danny stretched over and cranked open the passenger window.

"Sid?" he asked.

"Yup," the man replied, and he tugged open the door and settled himself into the front seat. He removed a Yankees ball cap and ran his right hand through his limp hair. He sighed.

"I need a little help," Sid said. He stared at Danny a moment. "You know where the Keebler factory is just off I-70?"

Danny's imagination flashed a bunch of Keebler baking elves in a tree holding trays of cookies, an ad for Monday Night Football. "The cookie place? Sure," he said. "Couple of miles east, right?"

A person couldn't miss the Keebler factory. It was right next to the rendering plant. You'd be driving down I-70, enter a cloud of sugary, vanilla scented air reminiscent of cotton candy or ice cream, and then suddenly those aromas would be replaced by the foulest of stenches, rotting meat and melting beef fat. Yuch!

"Just a ways down the street behind the cookie place is a junk yard called Gooney's Wreckers. That's where I need to go. I've got to pick up some stuff and bring it back here to the hotel. Can you help me?"

Danny looked at the man. *He's even younger than I am*, he thought. "What's your name again? Sid?" His memory had gone blank for a moment. *He doesn't look dangerous*, he thought.

"Yeah," Sid said.

"Ok, sure," Danny said. "But I'll have to leave the meter running."

Sid frowned, but then nodded. "All right. Let's go."

Danny pulled the cab away, and after a few turns pulled them up onto I-70, headed east.

Sid sat with his arms folded and hummed quietly to himself, a sort of tuneless murmur. Danny caught the smells of tobacco and garlic. "You see the Broncos game Sunday?" Sid asked.

"Nope," Danny replied. "I work Sundays. I tend to watch Monday Night Football with the rest of the people in my house, though." He snickered, remembering something. "One of the women in the house has a cat she calls 'My Cat.' Monday nights she gets him and puts a doll's football helmet on him. Turns him into a real fierce-looking little guy." He chuckled again.

"My Cat? Boy, that's original," Sid said. "A left tackle with claws! Uh-*uh*! Yowee!"

Danny couldn't tell whether or not he was serious.

"Turn off up here at Exit 28 and hang a left at the bottom to go under the freeway."

"Ok," Danny said.

After a couple of minutes of following Sid's instructions ("turn left here, go down to that warehouse on the corner, turn right and follow on to the stop sign, after that on the right you'll see the gate and the sign") they pulled up to a chain link fence with a padlocked gate and the welcoming sign *Gooney's Wreckers--KEEP OUT,* in unambiguous capitals. Sid climbed out of the car, hawked and spat to one side, and then leaned back in to say, "Come on with me if you're gonna help."

Danny watched him go to the gate and unlock the padlock. When he joined Sid, the gate was already swung partly open.

"Hurry up," Sid said. "We don't wanna let the dogs out."

Dogs? Danny felt a prickle on the back of his neck.

The two of them slipped inside and Sid shut the gate behind them, leaving it unlocked. "Come on," he said. They began walking across a sizable open space, packed earth, toward some low trailers. There was very little light—a reflected glow from the streetlight down the road, and a sliver of moon. To their right was a huge pile of wrecked cars stacked three high. *Jeez, I hope that pile's stable*, Danny thought.

"Reason we're here is my family threw me out. I won't bother you with the details," Sid said. "But I need to get my stuff. I've still got a key. They'll all be down at the bar."

Danny looked to one side a few yards to where two pairs of red eyes glared at them from under a shed that was sitting on an uneven foundation of used tires. He heard a distinct growl. He shivered. *Like the wolves in <u>Dracula</u>*, he thought.

"Don't worry about them," Sid said. "They know me. Hey you mutts, cool it!" he shouted in the direction of the dogs. The growling stopped. One of them gave half a whine.

Danny and Sid approached a pair of Atco trailers linked together to make one long building. It glowed a muted white in the dim light. Sid inserted a key in the door lock of the left one and opened it. "You wait here," he said. He disappeared inside and closed the door.

Danny looked back toward the shed where the dogs were, unsure of his safety. Beside the low step leading into the trailer was a short spade leaning crookedly against the wall. Danny picked it up, unsure how he'd use it if he had to, but determined to have some kind of weapon in the event the dogs lost their patience. It was dark and quiet, although the white noise of the city hummed around him.

A minute or so later the doorway swung suddenly open, spilling light into the yard. Sid kept the door open with his foot and held out a cardboard box. "Take this, will ya?" he said. Danny set down the spade and took the box, which held some rumpled clothes. Sid disappeared inside once more, only to reappear seconds later with another box, this one with the lid folded shut. He came outside, allowing the spring-loaded door to swing shut behind him.

"I left'em a 'fuck you' note," he said, without explanation. "Let's go."

They made their way back across the yard to the gate where the chain link glimmered faintly. The gate hinges squealed as it swung open, and one of the dogs emitted a throaty growl. Danny hustled through. Once they were outside Sid swung it shut and refastened the padlock. They deposited the two boxes in the back seat. It was only when the gate was secure that Danny noticed his heart had been racing, but that he was beginning to calm down.

In the cab, he realized that he'd forgotten to set the meter. *Shit*, he thought to himself. He swung the flag down and the meter began to tick.

Sid grinned. "Oxford Hotel, Jeeves," he said, and snickered.

Back at the hotel they parked in the taxi stand and collected the boxes from the rear seat. In the lobby, a sleepy-looking clerk looked up from his paperback novel, glanced at them and nodded at Sid. Danny followed Sid to the marble staircase.

They climbed two flights on the main stair, then walked down a short hallway covered with a threadbare runner to where another, narrow stairway ascended off to the right. At the top was another narrow hallway flanked by two sets of rooms. "The second one on the left is mine," Sid said. "You can just put the box there." He indicated a spot beside the doorway with his scuffed boot. "What do I owe you?"

Danny deposited the box on the thin rug, thinking about the unmetered part of the trip. "Say $20?" he finally offered.

Sid fished in the pocket of his stained jeans and tugged out some crumpled bills. He counted out three fives and four ones. "All I got," he said. He handed them to Danny.

"Ok," Danny said. He took the greasy money, folded it, and put it in his back pocket. He looked at Sid, who was staring down at the rug, scuffing his worn runner in an irregular rhythm against the faded surface. Danny took a breath and then took the money from his pocket once more. He peeled off a five and extended it to Sid, who held his foot still for a moment and looked up at him.

"Take it," Danny said. "It's ok."

CHAPTER EIGHTEEN

Inshallah

The taxi line at Stapleton International Airport stretched out ahead of and behind Danny, a segmented worm of yellow vehicles, whose head (the lead taxi) would periodically 'devour' a human meal, separate from the worm, and race off toward who knew where. Then the long worm's tail would crawl forward along its predetermined path, only to repeat the process.

The chaotic racket of airport traffic—the roar of planes landing and taking off, the irregular whine and grumble of buses and cars, shouted instructions and conversations—and the stench of jet fuel and vehicle exhaust made waiting in the line for a fare a seemingly interminable misery. Yet Danny knew that here was where the jackpot trips could often begin to far-off suburban hotels and industrial parks, or even up into the mountains to one resort or another. It beat bumping around Capitol Hill carrying the food stamp inhabitants from the projects and nearby residential hotels to the supermarkets for cheap wine and frozen tv dinners. He sighed and shifted uncomfortably behind the wheel of his cab, then slipped it into gear and moved forward another cab-length as another worm head detached itself with a blat of its horn about sixty yards ahead.

Danny had been driving cab for nearly a year now. Sometimes he wondered what he was doing in Denver. Whatever it was, it wasn't getting rich quick, although he was managing to save a hundred dollars or so a month. It was a make-do job. But despite its low pay and its repetitive sameness (drive, pick up, drive, drop off, wait, drive) Danny had found himself fascinated by the eternal variety of the clientele, the weird diversity of people who, for one reason or another, took taxis. *It's an education of its own*, he often thought.

He mulled over the strangeness he noted to be inherent in working in service industries. The driver or the maid or the waiter becomes, at least for a time, a thing, a fragment of humanity delivering what is desired—a delivery, a ride, a clean room, or fine meal—on schedule and to standard. He or she becomes a function, not a person, and although discerning clients can draw the human out of the role, most clients are not discerning. The barber becomes his clippers, not Mr. Grey, the prostitute some flesh and orifices, not Joanne. Many clients prefer things this way. Ultimately, of course, greasing the wheels of their interaction, is money.

From his taxi experience Danny well understood that such human reduction can be demeaning. Losing personhood to an economic role is a kind of diminishment. True, many people take pride in the fluidity and ease of their self-efface-ment. They embrace the shininess of their talent and mastery, and are content to bask in the warm glow of the client's cash. "Will there be anything else, sir? Madam?"

He had learned, too, that this retreat into a specific social position defined by its servile nature allows the person to hide within the mask of the role, to seem literally to shrink out of sight. *This client doesn't know ME,* the server might say to himself. *And he certainly doesn't care about me. And fair enough, I don't really care about him, either, just about his money. I will play act at being the agreeable bartender, sympathizing with every drinker's woes. I'll be the hygienic maid, polishing the bathroom sink to surgical cleanliness, the attentive masseuse, guaranteeing a happy ending. I will smile and fawn, effusing concern and demonstrating the lengths to which I will go to please my client.*

From such a position of social camouflage one can almost literally disappear. At most you are a fly on the wall, a being of such insignificance that paradoxically the most intimate of confidences might be revealed in your presence, as if you are no one. After all, you are a fly, just a fly. (Of course, you don't wish to be swatted.)

On frequent occasions in the cab Danny felt himself shrinking into this insecthood, like Gregor Samsa, only without the sympathy of the Samsa family. Sometimes he thought about this phenomenon, mostly abstractly, but occasionally smacked into a sensory present due to some unanticipated, shocking kindness or nastiness, or even just a mystery. Like today, for instance.

It was a sunny afternoon, and he had worked his way up to third in line for a fare at Stapleton Field. He sat in the baking cab, picking nervously at some loose vinyl on the edge of the bench seat beside him, wondering idly what kind of fare he'd get. The front cab pulled away with what appeared to be a mother and daughter, the latter a Russian doll simulacrum who had climbed into the vehicle beside the older and taller woman, presumably her mother. Fancy luggage. *Probably headed for the Brown Palace or its ilk*, Danny thought. Then two young men in baseball uniforms and lugging sports bags accosted the remaining cab. Cracking their gum, they tossed their gear nonchalantly into the trunk and slid into their seats. It pulled away. He was up next.

After a four or five-minute interval of impatient waiting, Danny watched as a middle-aged man of about fifty, carrying a small, black leather attaché case, approached. The man stopped a moment, looking slightly distastefully at the old taxi with Danny at the wheel. Then he turned back toward the terminal, where a porter was carrying two rather heavy suitcases. On seeing the porter, the man turned once more and snapped his fingers toward Danny, apparently expecting some kind of quick action.

Danny hopped out of the cab and popped the trunk. The exhausted-looking porter deposited the cases carefully into the cavity and Danny clunked it shut. The client, some sort of salesperson, Danny judged, gave the porter a bill, a gesture the porter acknowledged with a polite, "Thank *you*, sir," before heading back to the terminal.

"Where to, sir?" Danny asked the cases' owner.

"I'd like to go to the Marriot Hotel, the one down S. Monaco Parkway from here."

Whoopee! Danny thought. *A decent fare, at last.* "Yes, sir, no problem. It's about fifteen to twenty minutes away, depending on traffic."

The man gave Danny a piercing look, as if sizing up the youngster's honesty. Then he softened his expression. "Ok," he said, adding, "I'll ride up front."

Once they were clear of the airport's traffic crush and onto the parkway, the man fished in his pocket, withdrew a silver toothpick, and began needling between two of his lower front teeth. "Damn airline salad!" he grunted. "Goddamn stringy celery."

"The airlines are rarely known for their fine dining," Danny offered agreeably. His customer turned to look at him and said, "Just drive."

What the fuck does he want to sit up front for if he doesn't want to talk? Danny wondered. He sped the cab up marginally and focused on the road. But then his customer surprised him.

"What's your name?" the man asked.

Danny glanced sideways momentarily, then back at the roadway. "Dan," he said, giving himself a little more masculine confidence than he normally felt.

"See this attaché case?" the man said, tapping the leather case in his lap with a big finger. "It's just big enough to pack an Uzi."

Danny felt a slight prickle on the back of his neck.

"Suppose," the man said, almost amiably this time, "suppose there really isn't a Marriot Hotel at all down this road. Suppose I were directing you someplace else entirely, some dilapidated apartment building where, on the pretext of getting you to help with my cases, I took you in to shoot you?"

Danny felt the man's eyes boring into him. He took a deep breath.

"Just suppose," the man said again. A long ten or twelve seconds seemed to slide down the sweat between Danny's shoulder blades. He glanced at the man, who smiled enigmatically and asked, "How do you know I'm not a killer?"

Danny slowed down about 10 mph and looked over at his passenger. Finally (and deliberately), he said, "How do *you* know I'm taking you where you asked?"

"Hah!" snorted the man. He drummed his fingers impatiently on the case a moment. In a softer voice he said, "Hah!" once more.

An impatient driver behind them honked, and Danny sped up once more. They rode on in silence for another four or five minutes until Danny saw the exit sign with the Marriot Hotel looming up beyond and beside it. He pulled into the hotel's check-in access and flipped the meter. "That'll be $14.80," he said. He stared deliberately at the shiny glass hotel doors under the crisp awning, and at the potted dracaena beside them. Then he turned to his passenger, who looked back at him a moment, then asked, "The cases?"

"There's a bellboy," Danny said, indicating a youngster in a uniform descending the wide concrete step from the entry. But he got out and went around to open the trunk.

The customer climbed out himself, and approaching the trunk from the passenger side, and pulled a bill from his wallet. One at a time, Danny deposited the heavy cases on the drive beside the bellboy.

"Here," the man said, extending a $20 bill. "Keep it," he said.

Danny nodded, slipped it into his pocket, and hurriedly closed the trunk, moving to get away from the taxi's exhaust.

Indicating Danny with his thumb, the man said to the bellboy (who was hoisting the two cases and turning toward the entrance), "This guy's a pretty sharp driver."

The bellboy grimaced at the cases' weight. Then he and the salesman headed toward the glass doors.

Danny climbed back behind the wheel and turned to watch them go. Through the open driver's side window, he could hear the man saying to the bellhop, "See this attaché case? It's just big enough..." Danny shivered. He put the car into gear, stepped on the gas and steered back out of the lot toward the parkway.

As it was a weekend, driving hours were long. It was now nearly 8:00 pm, and Danny was parked on a residential street in the capitol area awaiting the next bell. It wasn't likely to be too long in coming; weekends tended to be busy and fruitful. The radio muttered and fretted, but one bell after another was being distributed in distant areas of the city.

The street was quiet and would have been shady, for large elms lined the street on both sides, but the sun had already sunk behind the western mountains, leaving only an orange-pink glow in the fading western sky to mark its passage. The coolness of the evening was welcome, and Danny lounged, elbow on the open window, the lyrics of *American Pie* drifting through his imagination. *Singin' this'll be the day that I die, this'll be the day that I die.*

Set back from the sidewalk across the street stood a three-story walk-up apartment, *Shady Lane Suites*. It was a cheap place, with reflective white siding instead of air conditioning. Danny could tell the apartments were small from how closely adjacent the balconies were. A careful cat burglar could have climbed from one to the next with barely a thought for caution.

A movement on one of the balconies caught Danny's eye. A large American flag hung from the rail. *Probably some army guy*, thought Danny. A deck door slid open, and a young couple, perhaps in their thirties, stepped out into the dimming evening. They were backlit from the interior, creating a halo effect behind them.

Next to invisible in the shadow beneath the trees, Danny watched curiously.

The girl was slim and pretty, a froth of brown curls surrounding dark eyes and a cheerful smile. She moved to one side and leaned her back on the side railing of the balcony, facing her partner. By his buzz cut he was obviously a marine or a GI, thickly built, strong, not fat, with bulky arms and shoulders and the neck of a body-builder. He looked around for a moment and he and the girl exchanged a few words, inaudible to Danny. She appeared to laugh a little. Then he bent forward to pick something off the floor of the balcony.

When the man straightened up it was apparent that he was holding a considerable weight. Sure enough, he began to do curls with a heavily weighted barbell, probably 150 lbs. or more. He didn't appear to strain at all, and he did ten reps, only slowing his rhythm for the last two. Then he set the weights down and straightened up again, turning to look at the girl, who gazed at him adoringly. She reached out to stroke his bicep, and then stepped forward to give him a kiss on the cheek. He grinned benignly at her as if the kiss was his due, and when she stepped back, he bent forward to begin another set of reps.

Just then the radio muttered, "13th and Logan, 5, 4..."

"254," Danny said softly into his mike, and the dispatcher replied, "254, pick up Hamid at the *Capitol Hill Apartments* there ASAP. That's 13th and Logan."

"Roger," Danny said, and started the cab. He took a last look up at the balcony, where the weightlifter was lifting the barbell over his head now, a maneuver that appeared dangerous, given the small size of the balcony. Danny imagined the man losing control and dropping the weights over the rail, down onto some unsuspecting schmuck below. *Good luck, buddy,* Danny said to the imagined victim, and pulled the cab out into the street.

The name Hamid was Persian, or maybe Arabic, he thought as he drove. Some wild stuff had been going down in Iran, recently. He remembered from the nightly news he, Louise and Carolyn would watch together after supper most nights. Some religious guy called Ayatollah Khomeini had returned to Iran, and a huge crowd of protesters that hated America had invaded the US embassy and taken hostages there. Further, he knew that some Iranian pilots were stationed in Denver, about thirty of them, training at Andrews Air Force Base. The American trainees didn't like these 'semi-gook' foreigners because they got paid about five times what the Americans got—the Shah hadn't stinted on pay for his military. These young Iranian guys lived in town, too, not on the base. When they weren't training they would frequent the clubs and strip joints on Colfax Avenue, dropping wads of cash on girls, and on hash when they could find it. The air force boys couldn't compete.

Danny turned off Colfax and drove slowly down Logan, looking for the *Capitol Hill Apartments*. There it was. And it had a drive-through entrance.

He pulled into the drive and stopped the car in front of the lit-up glass doors, turning off the engine. All was silent, save the hot metal ticking. A minute or two later a swarthy young man wearing a brown bomber jacket and carrying one small and one larger suitcase entered the lobby, saw Danny's car, and shouldered his way through the door into the drive. He opened the front passenger door of the cab.

"Hamid?" Danny asked. Long ago he had learned that sometimes you can get the wrong client, and the person you left behind can become pretty pissed off.

"Yes, yes," the young man said. "I am Hamid." He laid the larger case flat on the rear seat. Then he climbed into the front and placed the smaller case on his lap, closing the door beside him.

"Where you from, Hamid?" Danny asked before putting the car into gear.

"I am from Tehran," the man replied, looking directly at Danny. "You know Tehran?"

"Yes. Well, no, I've never been there. But I know it's in Iran, the capital, right? Wow. Long way from home," Danny said. "Lots goin' on there, these days," he added noncommittally. Then he said, "Where can I take you?"

Hamid stared at him a moment. But instead of giving Danny his destination, he said, "Aha. You watch the news. Do not believe all you see." It was a tone that sounded more like admonishment than friendly advice. He waited for Danny's reaction.

Danny looked at the swarthy stranger and said, "Are you one of the Shah's pilots? So, what's your take on the Ayatollah, then?"

"Take?" Hamid said. Then he said, "What do I think? Well, I am *not* one of the *Shah's* pilots. I fly for my country, though. As for current events, I think things will get very much better soon. Much better."

He said it with a finality that seemed to brook no argument, as if he had said, *It is evening, and it is getting dark*, which it was.

He looked at Danny as if to watch for some kind of outburst or protest about the embassy. At Danny's lack of reaction, he straightened, seemingly satisfied.

"Let me show you something," Hamid said. He unsnapped the clasps on the small case he held on his lap and lifted the lid. Under some tissue paper inside lay a large, heavy book, bound in rich, oiled leather with shining tooled brass on the corners of the cover. He bent forward and lifted it out carefully, brushing some tissue paper that adhered to its back down into the case. Tilting the volume so that it was vertical, he opened the cover, leaning the book toward Danny.

It was the most beautiful book Danny had ever seen. It seemed to exhale the light scent of lilac or some exotic flower. The title page featured a single word in an exotic script. Danny looked questioningly up at Hamid.

Alan W. Lehmann

"It is my Koran," Hamid said proudly. He stroked the title page lightly with a kind of reverence. "Do you wish to hold it?" he offered. "You must be very careful."

"No," Danny said. He thought of the KFC grease that might remain on his fingertips from a hasty supper an hour or so ago. "But I'd like to look."

Hamid straightened once more, and holding the large volume as if it were some fragile work of art (which in a way, it was), he turned one of the thin pages.

Danny couldn't make any sense of the text, or even recognize any of the letters. It looked like something from the illustrations in his childhood copy of *1,001 Nights*. He stared entranced for a few seconds. "It's very beautiful," he finally breathed.

Hamid closed his eyes reverently and smiled with approval. "Yes, very beautiful," he affirmed. After a moment, he closed the book and carefully replaced it in the case, shutting the clasps. He looked at Danny once more.

"Now take me to Stapleton airport," he said. "Please. It is time for me to go home."

"Ok," Danny said. He put the car into gear and they rolled out into the street.

Hamid was quiet as they cruised east on Colfax Avenue to Quebec Street, and then north toward the connecting road that would take them directly to the airport. Finally, he spoke again, almost as if he were speaking to the street lights that approached hypnotically, only to disappear behind them.

"You are not American," he said.

Danny glanced at him. "No, I'm not. I'm from Canada."

"Ah," said Hamid. Then, "If you will permit me, why are *you* here?"

It was a question whose answer was so loaded with complexity that it seemed almost pointless to try to answer. Danny imagined a few possible answers. *I'm here because I'm crazy? I'm here to experience the belly of the beast? I'm here because I have to be somewhere?* After a breath or two he said, "Does anyone really know why he is anywhere?"

It sounded flip or glib, but Hamid seemed to accept this non-explanation as something nearly profound. "Inshallah," he murmured. "It is inshallah. As God wills it."

"Maybe that's it," Danny said.

He pulled the car up at Departures and made to get out to help with the case.

"No," said Hamid. "You stay here, my friend." He handed Danny $20 (the fare was only $11.60), then $10 more. "I will not need this," he said, referring to the cash. He climbed out of the car, retrieved his bag from the back, and then, before disappearing into the airport, said once more to Danny, "Inshallah. Remember."

Danny said, "Thanks very much. Thanks."

Hamid touched the side of his aquiline nose with an index finger, all the while looking Danny in the eye. Then he turned with his cases and pushed through the glass doors and into the airport.

CHAPTER NINETEEN

Disillusionment

"I can't do that crazy cab-driving job anymore."

Heath Franklin, one of Danny's closer acquaintances in Denver, delivered this line with an air of depressed resignation. Danny looked at him with concern.

Heath had arrived in Denver a couple of months after Danny, for much the same reasons. But his path through the maze of therapy and life had taken a distinctly different route.

Heath was from South Australia, a little town an hour or so from Melbourne. He had spent several years at sea, working as a radio man for a small shipping company on general cargo vessels, sailing frozen mutton and loads of coal to Taiwan, and returning to Sydney and Melbourne with electronics and other manufactured goods. It had been something of a lonely existence, and apparently Heath had found some of the ships' officers of the company abusive and barely competent.

"What does a young man know when he first takes on a job like that?" he had asked rhetorically over an evening pot of tea. "You get sucked in by the romance of travel and exotic locations, and then you find that people are the same assholes nearly everywhere. On ship it was worse, because you had nowhere to go."

Heath suffered bouts of anxiety, a familiar complaint among clients at the Denver center. Worried that he might be deported when his visa expired, he had courted and romanced Sherry, a local woman who was originally from west Texas, in the panhandle someplace. She had agreed to marry him for $2,000. (Ah, romance!) Heath duly applied for and received a green card that permitted him to work. They would live together until he could gain legal status that allowed him to stay in the States.

Sherry was crafty and pragmatic, and not averse even to loving him a little bit, despite the fundamentally commercial nature of their relationship. After all, Heath was a good-looking guy, not to mention pretty sensitive and kind. But she enjoyed her independence and didn't want "to be pinned down too hard" (her words), a notion that seemed rather paradoxical, because she was extremely possessive. To her, Heath was bought and paid for in a perverse sort of way (even if it was his money that had sealed the transaction). She could be a hard woman, too, Danny knew. He'd become something of a confidant to Heath, who had once mentioned, in tears, that Sherry had hit him on more than one occasion when he had seemed, to her, to have a roving eye. Heath simply didn't have it in him to hit her back, an attitude Danny knew all too well. To Danny the whole arrangement seemed a bit desperate, maybe even nuts. But that was why Heath was here, wasn't it?

"Come on, Heath," Danny said. "You've been driving cab for months now. You're making a living. Things haven't been too bad at home, have they?" He wondered how much Heath's muddled living arrangements were having an impact on his work life.

Heath looked across the table at Danny, an irritated expression on his face. Then he sighed and relaxed his grimace. "No, no. Sherry's fine. I mean, generally everything's going to plan in our 'arrangement.' It's the driving job. I've had some really unpleasant experiences. Like A-One unpleasant. Ugly. Scary. Nasty."

"Tell me," Danny said.

"Well, like for instance, three weeks ago. Broad daylight in one of the grubbier areas near downtown. I picked up this anxious-looking fat guy near Five Points. He sat directly behind me in the cab, mumbling a little, incoherently. Phrases like, 'Whattaya think, then, huh?' 'Gotta gimme something.' Supposedly I was taking him to an address out on Federal Boulevard. I stopped at a red light and suddenly he says, 'You better pull into that alley up there on the right and give me a blow job.' 'I'm not giving you any blow job,' I said. 'Oh yeah?' he said, and then I felt this cold circle pressure like a gun barrel on the back of my neck. 'Oh, fuck,' I thought."

"Jeez, what happened?" Danny asked in surprise.

"I reacted almost without thinking. I bent forward and opened the car door in one motion. I jumped out and started to run. I heard him swearing behind me, but I was shit-scared, believe me, and when I'm scared I can run like hell."

He paused and poured each of them more tea. *Does everybody drink this damn Red Zinger stuff?* Danny asked himself.

"Thanks," he said, but he left the mug on the table. "So—then what?"

"Well, I ran like my life depended on it, which in a sense, it did. I hightailed it around the block, leaving him behind. When I came back around the fourth corner I could see my car, with traffic lined up behind it, horns beeping like mad. One angry driver was getting out of his car, and all I could think was, 'Oh, shit, *another* guy with a gun, probably!' But he saw me coming, gave me the finger, and got back into his car. I climbed back into my cab and drove away. I could see the guy chasing me coming around the last corner in the rear-view mirror as I pulled out. The drivers behind my cab were pissed, I can tell you."

"Still, you got away!"

"Sure. The guy was waving an empty coke bottle at me. I guess that's what I thought was the gun. But Jesus, how would you know? The guy was transparently nuts, and I was really, really scared." He sat mulling the scene in his memory. Then, changing the subject for a moment, he brightened and asked, "How about a beer and some pretzels?".

Ah, my drug of choice, Danny thought. "Sure, thanks," he said, and he pushed the mug of cooling Zinger off to one side.

Heath shook some pretzels from a plastic bag into a cereal bowl and parked it between them. From the humming fridge in the corner, he retrieved a couple of Budweisers, snapped the tops off using a counter-mounted bottle opener, and came back to the table, settling into his chair once more. "This Bud's for you," he said, setting one in front of Danny.

Danny thought a moment. "Thanks," he said, and lifted the beer. Before taking a sip, he offered, "I can see that could have been pretty nerve-wracking. But as a one-off, I don't think it's worth giving up your job for."

"That's what Sherry said," Heath replied. "But it's not a one-off. I haven't told her about the other ones."

"Really?" Danny said. "Like what?"

"Two weeks ago, I was driving really late. I got a bell for a night club over north of City Park. It was about 2:30 am, and I was ready to call it a night. But some of those super late club fares can be pretty lucrative. You know, drunks who just hand you a roll, or who tip generously when they're feeling tipsy."

He grinned at his pun, and Danny snickered.

"Anyway, I pulled into the parking lot of the place, totally empty, sign lights off, and I was just going to take off again and head for home when this guy came running from behind the building. 'Open the door!' he was yelling. 'Open the door!' Twenty feet behind him in full chase was this mean looking fucker with a knife in his right hand. Suddenly I was shit scared! I swung open the back door on the passenger side, some maneuver, I can tell you. The running guy dived, literally dived, head first onto the back seat, one leg still extended out the open door. 'Drive!' he yelled. As I was putting the car into gear the guy chasing him stabbed him in the back of the thigh. I started to pull away and my passenger kicked back with his other leg hitting the knifer in the face, knocking him backward, and giving just enough time for us to get away. I took off, tires screeching, and the back door was swinging wildly. Half a block away I slowed down so he could pull the door shut. He was bleeding all over the back seat. 'General Hospital,' he said, and he passed out. Shock, I guess."

Danny had been swilling his beer steadily all through this shocker of a tale, and he lifted the bottle, looking to see what he had left. "Jeezus!" he muttered and drained the rest of the bottle. It wasn't clear whether his expletive was about the events or about how fast the beer had disappeared.

"I didn't even get paid for that trip," Heath said morosely. "I expect the guy's ok, though. The orderlies had him on a gurney within a minute of our arrival at emergency, but I never saw him again, and the hospital wasn't going to pay me." He eyed Danny's empty bottle speculatively, but he didn't offer another one, to Danny's disappointment.

"Last Friday was just the topper," Heath finally said.

"What happened?"

"It was another club fare. You know that strip club on Colfax and Madison?"

"Sure," Danny said.

"About 11:00 pm I got a call there. I swung into the parking lot and up to the entrance door. Standing there, small handbag in her hands in front of her, was one of the most beautiful women I've ever seen. Long, black hair, short skirt, legs up to here--you know what I mean. She gave me a smile that would melt an iceberg, and she climbed right in beside me. 'Glasbury Towers,' she said, and stretched out those beautiful legs. I wondered how I was going to drive with a hard-on, but I managed to get us going."

Danny pictured the Glasbury, a kind of ultramodern apartment building, twenty stories or so looking down along Cherry Creek. *High rent district*, he thought.

"It was pretty dark," Heath said. "As we approached the building, this girl put her hand on my arm and in this sexy, husky voice said, 'Don't drive into the entrance area. Pull up and stop behind that sports car.' She pointed to a little European convertible about forty yards from the apartment entrance. Anyhow, I did as she asked. 'Can I walk you up to the entry?' I asked her. But she didn't answer. Instead, she slid over closer to me, put her hand on my thigh, and whispered in my ear, 'You're a pretty good-looking guy, you know that?'"

Heath paused to take a drink. Danny was all ears.

"Anyhow, she grabbed my head with both hands and started kissing me, tongue halfway down my throat, and I was likin' it. She ran her fingers across the bulge in my pants and kind of sighed. Then she said, 'You want me to blow you?' She rubbed my cock through my pants again and smiled. Now, here's the kicker. She hoisted her skirt up, showing me the biggest dick I've ever seen and asked, 'Or would you rather blow me?'"

"Holy fuck!" Danny said. "What'd you do?"

"Whattaya mean, what did I do? I got the fuck out of there, that's what. I think I elbowed her...him...in the head, yelling, 'Get out, get out, get out,' or something like it. And he got out. Jesus, it scared the shit out of me! It was worse than the stabbing, no kidding. I drove around for about half an hour, just trying to figure out what the hell had happened. Then I clocked off and came home."

"Does Sherry know?" Danny asked.

"No, Christ, I couldn't tell her," Heath said. "Shit, I'm not sure I should have told *you*." He sat back and drained his beer.

"Huh!" Danny said. He stared at his friend. He had to admit to himself, these experiences his friend had recounted were dangerous and bizarre. He'd had a few strange ones himself, but not like this, not yet.

"I don't have any advice for you, man," Danny finally said. "I don't blame you for being upset. But if you quit, you're going to have to tell Sherry something sooner or later."

"Yeah, I know," Heath said morosely. He stared at his empty beer bottle.

CHAPTER TWENTY

The Animal Circus

D anny didn't *really* think his first cat was a magician. He was simply so taken with Carlos Casteneda's portray-als of Don Juan Matus and his brujo friend, Don Genaro in *Journey to Ixtlan*, that he decided to name the little animal after the latter. Danny would play around with pronouncing the Mexican 'g' sound. "Heenaro, Henaro," he'd repeat and smile to himself.

Genaro was a shy little being, affectionate when he was comfortable (especially after eating), but leery of strangers. Danny would be walking home the last few dozen paces of his way to the Atlantic Avenue digs, and suddenly he'd find himself hurrying a little. Sure enough, there would be Genaro, lying on the front window sill, watching for his arrival.

Danny would swing open the door, and Genaro would stretch, eye Danny speculatively, leap softly to the wide arm of the stuffed armchair by the door, and look up expectantly, waiting for his late afternoon cuddle. In his turn, Danny would eye Genaro suspiciously (in a kind of mockery that somehow he imagined that little cat brain could understand), and then mutter, "Oh, all right, since you've been so patient," and lift the feline up into the crook of his arm where he'd nuzzle the little beast and tickle under its chin until its regular purr of pleasure would be emitted at a volume surprising for such a small cat. Then Danny would set Genaro down and head for the kitchen for their evening repast, Genaro trotting gamely along behind him, anticipating the whine of the electric can opener and the rattle of the cat food box.

Today was only marginally different, at least at first. When Danny opened the door, Genaro looked sleepily at him from the window sill. But he didn't get up right away.

"Hey, buddy," Danny said. "What's up? No energy today? Been outside hunting bad guys?"

He walked over to the window and picked Genaro up under the front legs, drawing him up toward his face.

"Who's a sleepy kitty?" he said, flopping the cat onto its back in the crook of his arm.

Genaro yawned at him and squirmed around so that Danny set him down onto his feet.

"Come on, let's get something to eat," Danny said, and headed into the kitchen, Genaro trailing along behind. Tugging open a lower cupboard, Danny pulled out a can of expensive cat food, something special. "How about some of the good stuff tonight?" he said, and fitting it into the electric can opener, pressed the switch. The device emitted a whine, the can rotated in his hand, and four or five seconds later a magnet tugged off its lid, allowing the scent of tuna to spread into the room.

Of course, at the sound and then the aroma, the other animals arrived lickety-split. Carolyn's little dog, fondly referred to by Danny as "the living dust mop," and My Cat trotted into the room. The dog stationed himself on his haunches beside Danny's leg and whined pitiably. My Cat paced around the kitchen, meowing noisily. Genaro, who was used to being first to the food (he had established the feeding order with threatening hisses and a few well-aimed swipes of his claws several months ago), sat patiently at the food dishes.

As Danny began to move across the floor to scoop out some food, the dog jumped upward toward the hand with the can in it.

"Get down, you little mutt!" Danny said, giving it a light 'whap' on the nose with a spoon. The dog gave an offended little "woof" and slunk over near the food dishes, where he collapsed onto his outsized little belly, panting eagerly. My Cat emitted another moan and took up another position to the side and just to the rear of Genaro.

"Ok, you guys, ready?" Danny said. He leaned over the three food dishes, spooning out the tuna into three more or less equal quantities. Then he backed away.

The three animals hustled to their respective plates. For two or three minutes, all that could be heard was the rapid motion of the three animals' eating.

The dog finished first (typically), having bolted most of his portion in three or four large mouthfuls. He looked over at Danny as if to say, "Is that all? Aw, come on..."

When Genaro was finished, he stretched, and then wandered back into the living room. My Cat trotted down the basement stairs to Carolyn's suite. The dog moved from plate to plate, licking away any remaining flavor. Then he moved over to the door mat at the back door, arranged himself comfortably, and went to sleep.

Danny made himself some toast and peanut butter (organic, of course) for a light supper. Then he headed into the living room to reread part of Julian Jaynes' book on consciousness. Jaynes had made some startling observations. One was his assertion that humans don't need to be conscious to think! How extraordinary! Yet the evidence was pretty clear. Another section was an extensive analysis of the workings of metaphor.

He collected the book from the coffee table where he had left it and lay back on the weathered sofa to read. But just in the corner of his eye, he noticed Genaro lying on all fours on the carpet, a posture reminiscent of the Egyptian sphynx. Genaro was barely awake, eyes blinking sleepily, and then— plop, his little head dropped forward onto the carpet, right on the chin.

What the...? thought Danny. He shut his book, got up, and went over to Genaro. Down on his knees, Danny stroked his little cat's back, and said, "Hey, what's the matter, little guy?"

Genaro didn't even look up.

"Shit!" Danny said. He got up and went into the kitchen to use the phone. He drew a fat phone book out of a drawer and flipped through the Yellow Pages to Veterinarians. After scanning the names for a minute or so he located one in the neighborhood. He picked up the phone and dialed quickly.

"Hello?" he said. "Yes. I have a sick cat on my hands. Are you still open? Yes? Ok. I'll be right over."

He went to the closet in his room and found an empty shoe box. He took an old towel and lined the box. Back in the living room, he tenderly picked up Genaro and laid him into the box. He checked his wallet and keys, and Genaro under his arm, went out to the car.

Ten minutes later he was showing Genaro to a grey-haired gentleman wearing gold-rimmed glasses and sporting a white coat. *Typical doctor costume*, Danny thought. *I wonder if he does psychiatry in his spare time.*

"Not very responsive, is he?" the vet said, probing Genaro's abdomen. "Let me take him into the back to check him out more carefully. You can wait here." He indicated some standard issue office chairs surrounding a coffee table.

"There's coffee in the corner, if you like." The vet pointed to a carafe and some paper cups on a white counter across the room.

"Ok," Danny said. "Thanks."

He sat impatiently for about twenty minutes, sifting through the popular magazines on the table, glancing through one or two hurriedly before tossing them back down onto the stack. He yawned and drummed his fingers on the chair arm.

When the vet returned, he carried the nearly limp Genaro gently in his gloved hands.

"I have some bad news, I'm afraid," he said to Danny, who looked up, face giving nothing away. "Your little cat here has cancer."

He laid Genaro on the table, and with his finger indicated a lump under the skin of Genaro's abdomen. "See this little bump here? It's mostly hidden by fur. You likely wouldn't have noticed it. It's a tumor. There's another one just under the hip joint of his rear left leg, and another under his shoulder blade. The cancer is all through him. Here, feel." He pointed to a tiny lump, not much bigger than a mosquito bite.

Danny felt his gut clench, but he reached down and touched it, running his finger lightly over it as if by stroking it he could make Genaro recover.

"What can you do?" he asked.

"I'm afraid I can't do much of anything. He's too far gone." The vet looked kindly at Danny. "About the most humane thing we can do for him is put him down...a shot that puts him to sleep, without pain. Otherwise the cancer is going to cause him a lot of pain—a lot."

Danny's head spun a moment, ideas of death and loss slipping through his mind, images of the pleasures of the cat's more or less mute company, a little being that asked for next to nothing but food and a little loving, followed by images of his absence.

"Are you sure?" he finally said. He swallowed.

"It's a cancer caused by a virus. It's often transferred into the kittens in the womb of their mother. Sometimes the kitten has developed enough immunity to fight the cancer off. Other kittens may last into their development of up to a year or two before succumbing to the disease. Your little cat is one of those."

Danny looked down at Genaro.

"It's hard, you know, just to write the little guy off. Doesn't he deserve the chance to fight it off?"

"Well, it's up to you. But in my experience, the kindest thing to do will be to help him on his way." The vet sighed.

"It's not easy. I can tell that you love your cat." He looked at Danny.

Danny swallowed again. He took a deep breath and said, "Ok. Do it."

The vet patted Danny's shoulder. "It'll be ten dollars for the shot. Otherwise, I won't charge anything."

Danny just shrugged, then nodded. He looked down again at Genaro, whose eyes were closed. He appeared inert, almost dead already. "Good-bye, little buddy," Danny said. The vet picked Genaro up and went back into the larger, fluorescent-lit room that doubled as a lab and an OR.

Danny sat still a moment. Then he went back into the receptionist's office, where he handed a ten-dollar bill to the young woman behind the desk.

"This is for...?" she asked.

"He'll tell you," Danny said. He turned and went out into the late evening sunshine. He sat in the car and cried.

A couple of weeks later he was playing bridge with some friends from Virginia, Dick (a finishing carpenter) and Janet (his lanky, blonde wife). Laying down the dummy, she turned to Danny and said, "We heard you lost your cat." She waited for his response, then, getting none, said, "That's really tough. We get so attached to them, don't we?"

A wash of empty sadness rushed through Danny, but he didn't say anything, only nodded, preferring to focus on the pair of tenaces on the board.

But Janet continued, "You know, our grey cat Samantha just had a litter of kittens. In a week or two they'll be ready to part from their mother. We could let you have one, if you like."

Danny looked up at her. It was an obvious kindness, truly well-meant and thoughtful. She smiled at him, a hint of rueful condolence along with some affection. They'd all been playing bridge together for several months after meeting at the center one evening.

Dick smiled at him, too. In his Virginia drawl, he added, "They're all pretty small and snoozy right now, and their momma's pretty possessive. But we sure can't keep'em all. You wanna see'em? After the game?"

"Sure. Okay," Danny replied.

Half an hour later the four of them were clustered around a closet door in a second bedroom of Dick's rental house. In a cardboard box lay a grey mother cat surrounded by five tiny kittens that were crawling over one another and on their mother's flank, mewing insistently in their squeaky kitten voices.

"Hey, Samantha," Dick murmured, "how's momma doin'?"

The grey cat squinted up at her audience and yawned.

For some reason, a tiny grey kitten with white socks caught Danny's interest.

"Can I pick one up?" he asked.

"Sure," Dick said.

Danny pinched the kitten gently by its ruff and lifted it out of the box. It barely fit in the palm of his hand. Its eyes were open, but hadn't been open long. He nuzzled the little being, breathing lightly on its face and fur. Then he set it back on its mother, where it set about finding a nipple. The mother cat simply stared at the human observers, an impenetrable, wary gaze.

"That one," Danny said.

"Ok," Janet said, smiling. "We'll save her for you."

Two weeks or so later Danny brought home his new kitten. He was all prepared. Beside his bed he had a cozy shoe box in which he had placed a warm water bottle wrapped in a fuzzy towel, a tiny saucer of cream (wedged in so as not to get tipped over), some soft, puffy cotton balls, and a small alarm clock whose regular ticking was meant to mimic a mother cat's heartbeat.

At bedtime, he brought the kitten (that he had decided to name Feather after her fine grey fur) into his bedroom and set her in the box. He stripped out of his clothes and slid into bed, reaching over to pet the little being once, and then he snapped out the lamp. He lay back and sighed.

Thirty seconds later he heard a soft scrabbling, then felt a miniscule tug on his bed clothes, and a moment later sensed the weight of the kitten on his chest, where it dug in its claws and burrowed into the warmth. Danny felt its tiny weight rising up and down with his own breathing and heard the reassuring grumble of its tiny but nonetheless outsized purr.

Well, so much for that stupid magazine Cat Lover, he thought. He reached his hand out tentatively to cup his palm over Feather's little back. The purr strengthened.

Danny yawned. Just before he fell to sleep he thought, *Who knew a cat could make you so happy?*

CHAPTER TWENTY-ONE

Satisfaction

I can't get no, Satisfaction; I can't get no, groovy action...
—the Rolling Stones

Charlie Watts' driving drumbeat made Danny shiver, and as he drove along I-25 toward Yellow Cab, he sang along. "Hey, hey, hey; that's what I say; I can't get no; no, no, no!"

The singing was primal and fun, and the song tapped into a wellspring of motivation that seemed to Danny to be everywhere in society. "Grab that cash with both hands and make a stash!" seemed the universal prescription.

He thought of the ball game he had attended only the previous week, a Triple A game with a local team against San Antonio. One of Denver's savings and loans had sponsored a contest for its customers. Any person opening a new account at one of their branches received a chance to be drawn for the Cash Grab! contest at the San Antonio game. Two winners had been chosen, and during the 7th inning stretch, a representative of the bank had marched out to second base carrying a sports bag stuffed with five thousand $1 bills. He dumped them haphazardly around the bag, allowing them to flutter and settle in a chaotic spread. The two drawn winners were stationed at first and third base. At the sounding of a whistle they were to run to second base, gather up as much cash as they could grab and carry, and get back to their starting point before two minutes passed. If either of them didn't get back to his base by the whistle, he would forfeit his cash.

The crowd, hyped up on beer, pretzels, and stolen bases, was wildly excited, placing bets on the first or third base contestant (neither of whom appeared particularly fit). After a raucous introduction to the contest over the stadium intercom (...proud to present Cash Grab! sponsored by Chief Idaho's Savings and Loan, your source for the best deals on car loans and mortgages...), the two players (one a slightly overweight, middle-aged man wearing dark-rimmed glasses, and the other an obese black woman wearing track pants and sneakers) were given their "Get Ready!" On the whistle, they were off.

The man got to second base before his opponent, and he began sweeping piles of bills toward himself with his arms and stuffing them into his pockets. Arriving only seconds later, the big woman bowled into him (on purpose? who could tell?) as she fell to her knees, thrusting her big hands into one of his piles, and thrusting the cash into her cleavage, where it began to bulge in the sweater she had purposely tucked into her sweats. The crowd went nuts, cheering and cursing.

"Fuckin' greedy bitch!" one spectator had yelled, only to be hit from behind by a popcorn box from further up the stands. He looked around, but everyone behind him was focused on the action, shouting support or invective.

With 20 seconds to go a warning whistle sounded. There was still lots of cash on the ground. The black woman looked longingly at it a moment, but then lumbered as quickly as she could toward third base, two or three bills escaping through the bottom of her sweater where it had come loose.

"Don't drop it! Don't drop it!" someone was screaming.

At the final whistle both contestants had managed to return to base. The man at first base was grinning idiotically, and mopping sweat from his forehead with a handkerchief. The black woman tugged her sweater free, allowing a small cascade of notes to tumble to the Astroturf around her. Two young children, perhaps nine or ten years old, came to her, the smaller of the two hopping up and down with excitement, as his older sister and their mom gathered up the cash in a more orderly fashion. The man was met by a heavily made-up woman, who kissed him enthusiastically before leading him off the field by the hand, both glancing behind to ensure they hadn't dropped any bills.

"Remember! Come to Chief Idaho's Savings and Loan, for all your financial needs!" the announcer yelled. The organist spun out a flourish of arpeggios followed by a perfect cadence onto a loud, long, major chord. A groundskeeper with a rake gathered up the remaining bills and put them back into the sports bag, as the crowd jabbered and groaned. Finally, the home team trotted out to resume the field.

Christ, that was bizarre, Danny thought to himself, as in his imagination Mick Jagger faded off with "...no Satisfaction, no Satisfaction, I can't get no..."

All the while that Danny was signing out his cab he was thinking to himself, *The things people will do for money!*

I wonder how far people are willing to abase themselves for a few bucks? I've never seen something so self-humiliating in my life. And yet, they actually seemed proud of themselves. What if they'd been asked to mud wrestle? Or kiss a pig?

Still, it's funny, he thought, *here I am, rumbling around Denver in a stinking, old cab, just to accumulate enough bucks to keep going.*

The long afternoon had ticked by, measured off in hours and miles. Now it was nearly 8:00 pm. He had just dropped off a young, black mom and her little boy in one of the projects, the subsidized housing locations inhabited mostly by minorities and down and outs. They had been cruising down a street in the early evening light, and the little boy, staring out the window at a low, full moon had said, "Look, Momma, how the moon's followin' us."

"No, baby, the moon's not followin' us. It just look that way." She grinned at Danny in the rear-view mirror, and he smiled.

"But it's followin' us!" the boy insisted.

The mom raised her eyebrows and giggled indulgently.

You tell her, Danny thought. *It's followin' us, for sure!* And he grinned, too.

He helped her get her groceries to her door, where a tall, lanky guy with an afro and sitting on a lawn chair was sipping a beer and thumbing through an *Easy Rider* magazine. On its cover, a bikini-clad blonde in red high heels was leaning suggestively over a motorcycle, a kind of "come hither" pout on her scarlet mouth. The man looked up from the magazine and closed it, a kind of wary suspicion in his expression, but without comment. His wife gave Danny $5, and he obligingly handed her the fifty cents in change he imagined she needed more than he did.

I can't get no, Danny thought.

It was his last fare. Three quarters of an hour later he had checked his cab back in, paid his rental, and squirreled away the remaining $48 he had earned for an eight-hour shift. He decided to stop at Jasmine's, a trendy if somewhat down-at-heel restaurant just off Colfax Avenue that specialized in exotic sandwiches made with home-made bread.

The place was busy when he arrived, but he managed to squeeze into a small table beside the parking lot windows, not far from the kitchen entry. He ordered an avocado and cheese sandwich from a harried waitress and began to read *Zen and the Art of Motorcycle Maintenance*. It was rather a fascinating read, an attempt (among others) to reconcile the sometimes foolish romanticism connected with commercial logos and branding to the practicalities of everyday life.

In this chapter, one of the author's co-travelers was expressing his resentment at being expected to use a beer can tab as a shim to tighten his handlebars, even though it was perfect in every regard for the task, just the right shape, malleability and thickness. It was clear that Robert Pirsig, the author, was critically amused at his friend's sensibilities. Danny was struck by this example of how easy it is for an author to portray things in such a way as to make himself look more sensible, realistic, down-to-earth.

The waitress was just pouring Danny a coffee refill when he noticed an older man standing at the entry, scanning the crowd. The man stood uncertainly, frowning slightly, perhaps in disappointment. He wore a pair of faded but clean, grey coveralls over a pale, blue work shirt.

Danny could tell that the restaurant was full, young locals grabbing a quick supper out, some of the retail crowd from a department store a block or so away, two policemen eating soup near the cash register. He closed his book, got to his feet, and made his way through the tightly arranged tables to the man at the entry.

"If you're alone, I've got room at my table; you can join me, if you like," he said to the man. The man looked at him, a measured, measuring glance.

"All right," he replied softly. "Thank you."

He followed Danny back to the table and the two of them sat down.

Danny moved his book further to one side. "I'm Danny," he said.

"Wilf," the man replied.

The waitress, seemed to glide up to the table and deposited Danny's sandwich before him, a thick double-decker with lettuce and mayo leaking out one side. The aroma of the mayonnaise on fresh bread made his mouth water.

"Hi, Wilf," she said to the other man. "Same as usual?"

Wilf stared a moment at Danny's sandwich as the waitress poured Wilf a mug of coffee. Then he turned to her and said, "Yes, please..."

"So, are you from around here, Wilf?" Danny asked.

"Well, yeah, sometimes," he replied.

"Sometimes?"

"I travel some."

"Sure," Danny said. He took another mouthful of sandwich and chewed thoughtfully. "So, is Denver home?"

Wilf looked at him, a little shyly, it seemed to Danny.

"Some of the time," Wilf said.

The waitress returned and set down a plate. "Here you go, Wilf," she said. "Still travelin'?" she asked.

Wilf nodded and picked up what appeared to be the end slice off a bread loaf. The waitress moved to the next table. "Everythin' all right here?" she asked.

Danny looked more closely at Wilf's plate. Bread ends. Just half a dozen bread ends. He was about to make a small crack, something like, "Man cannot live by bread alone," but a sudden wariness prevented him. He stared a moment, then said, "They make good bread here, don't they?"

Chewing steadily, Wilf simply nodded. He took a couple of sips of coffee.

"So where do you travel?" Danny asked.

"Wherever the trains are going," Wilf said. He looked at Danny, and then, seeming to have decided to explain more fully, said, "I'm what you might call a hobo. I just travel on the trains, to where there might be a bit of work, maybe."

Danny stared at him for a minute, trying to fathom some of the mystery of this stranger in front of him, chewing bread ends and drinking coffee. After a moment, he thought to ask, "Can I buy you a sandwich?"

"No, no, this is good," Wilf said. He smiled faintly at Danny. "I'll be satisfied with this." Then he asked, "What do *you* do here—in Denver, I mean?"

It was a question that popped up every once in a while, one that always made Danny wonder, *What ARE you doing here, anyway?*

"Right now, I'm driving cab. And two days a week I work in a health food store."

Wilf nodded thoughtfully and swallowed some bread. "Is that a good life?" he asked Danny.

"It's ok for now," Danny said.

Wilf nodded some more. "For now..." he said.

"Do you mind my asking," Danny said, "how come you're a hobo? I mean, why do you live this way?"

Wilf ceased chewing and looked up, thinking, it seemed.

"Well," he finally said, "it's the way I want to live. It's... it's free. I don't owe anybody anything." After another quiet pause he said, "I like it this way."

"Do you have friends when you're travelling?"

"Sometimes," Wilf answered, "but mostly no. Being alone is best."

"Really?" Danny asked. He was a bit incredulous.

Wilf set down his coffee cup, and steepling his fingers, he looked at Danny. "Sometimes," he said, "when I'm alone in the doorway of a boxcar, somewhere way out in the wilderness—maybe looking down into a mountain valley, or staring off into a sunset on the Great Plains—sometimes it's like God is right there, like His arm is around me, like He's holding me tight. There's no feeling on Earth like it. It's a kind of ecstasy. I never found that in a church. Did you?"

Danny thought of his family's church, the one they attended regularly during his childhood, the painting above the altar of Jesus knocking on a door. It had been part of his fear, he was sure of it, the mystery of this supposedly holy man, knocking on the door of his heart, as their pastor had explained it. *For sure,* he thought, *there's something to be feared in everything, not in the 'I'm terrified,' way that brought me here, but in the sense that we're never going to know everything we need to know. It's never gonna' happen...*

"No, I don't think I did," Danny said. He wiped a couple of crumbs from his chin with a paper napkin.

"Thank you for sharing your table," Wilf said as he got to his feet. "It was very kind."

Danny looked at him a moment. Then he got up himself and extended his hand, which Wilf took and shook briefly, smiling faintly. Then Wilf turned and left the restaurant.

The waitress came to clear up the table. "Anything else you'd like?"

"You know that guy Wilf?" Danny asked.

"Sure," she said. "He comes here when he's in town."

She took the plates, balancing them on one arm and grasping the cups in the other. "He's a decent guy," she said, and she turned away to the kitchen.

Danny looked down at the cover of his book, a man beside a motorcycle staring off toward some mountains where the sun was setting, like some god of the wilderness.

Satisfaction...no satisfaction...

CHAPTER TWENTY-TWO

Ambulance Service

Sometimes people get where they need to go to find the help they need; sometimes they don't. One might think that being a kind of "Johnny-on-the-spot" in the position to help save someone's life could be a terrifying responsibility. Others might see it as an opportunity to shine, to demonstrate one's sterling character. Danny could have told such imaginers that situations like that hold neither romantic appeal nor trepidation. Occasionally life simply presents people with emergent problems, and they either rise to the occasion or they don't. It's only later, reminiscing after the events, that responders really learn the value of their experience.

One Tuesday evening, already dark, Danny was parked in his cab far into the northwest corner of Denver, where he had just delivered an emergency legal document to a local lawyer's residence. It was a posh neighborhood composed of large properties, with houses set well back from the street beyond manicured lawns and lighted driveways. It seemed almost in the country. To Danny it was the country of the rich.

In his bathrobe and slippers, the lawyer was waiting at the wrought iron gate in front of his property, holding a flashlight. Danny was aiming a flashlight of his own, his cab moving at a crawl while he tried to illuminate address numbers on gateposts. From about twenty-five yards away he suddenly noted the swinging light beam signifying his destination, and he pulled up to the drive. He lowered his window, scenting cut grass and the light, dry breeze drifting from the mountains to the west. The lawyer stepped up to the car.

"You have the package?" the man asked in a low voice. When Danny nodded the man said, "How much?"

"Twenty-eight bucks," Danny replied, extending the thick, brown manila envelope to the man.

The man took the envelope, slipped it under his arm, and handed Danny some bills. "Keep the change," the man said. He flicked his flashlight beam into Danny's eyes momentarily and stared at him, as if to memorize his features.

While Danny counted the money, the man examined the envelope under the halo of his light. "We good?" he asked.

"Yessir," Danny answered. He rolled up his window, backed up a few feet, and did a U-turn in the dim street. Looking back just before he drove off, he watched the lawyer tugging his gate shut behind him and dropping a bar into place.

Now, cab stationary at the curb with the engine off, Danny was sitting eating a burger, hoping for some kind of bell to be called nearby. *I'll give it ten minutes*, he thought. *If there's nothing, I'll head back into the city.*

The burger had some sweet relish that, though tasty, dribbled out from the bun onto Danny's jeans. *Shit,* he thought, trying to wipe the mess away with a paper napkin. He took another bite, wondering just how bad the stain was going to be, when the radio squawked.

Golden, Colorado...5, 4

"254!" Danny snapped into his mike.

254, where are you right now?"

"I'm in northwest Lakewood near the park."

254, go under I-70 onto South Golden Road. Follow it until it becomes Ford Street and continue 'til you see the Coors Brewery. Do NOT, I repeat, do NOT go into the brewery. You'll see a picket line out front. Union's on strike. You need to pick up a fare there and take him to the hospital. He'll tell you which one. Someone named Terry, ok? Got that?

"Roger. Picket line on Ford Street near the Coors Brewery for Terry."

Right.

The radio squawked static, went silent for a moment, then resumed its usual mutter.

Danny shoved the remains of his burger into the paper bag beside him. *I'll have to ditch that someplace*, he thought. He fingered a piece of gristle out from beside a canine and flicked it out his window. Then he started the car.

Using his flashlight and the overhead light, he examined his city map. There it was, South Golden Road off Ellsworth Avenue, which wasn't far away. He snapped off the interior lights, turned on the car's headlights, and pulled onto the empty street.

Toward I-70 the streets were better lit. It took less than ten minutes to get to the picket line, where a dozen or so men, some carrying signs ("Unfair Employer!" "We Want a Contract!") stood around a barrel containing an open fire. Danny pulled up to the nearest of them, a tall, blond man wearing a leather vest. He stood gesticulating to a shorter man, who was listening with his eyes cast down toward the pavement. Danny rolled down his window.

"I'm looking for Terry," he said.

The man in the vest looked over at him and said, "About time. He's over here." He pointed to a brown van parked at an angle to the street. It sagged toward its left front tire, which was flat. Another man, presumably Terry, sat on the pavement, leaning against the van's side door, his head lowered, almost as if he were sleeping. He had an improvised bandage wrapped around his upper left arm. Blood had seeped out beneath it.

"Some fucker shot him," the man said. "Maybe one of the plant guards. We don't know for sure. Gotta get him to the hospital."

"Have the police been here?" Danny asked.

"Huh! Probably some off-duty cop who shot him."

Danny stared at him, wondering at the irony, and at what he might be getting himself into. After a moment's hesitation, he got out of the cab, and the three of them walked over to the seated man, who didn't move. The one in the vest squatted beside him, placing his hand gently on the man's right shoulder.

"Terry," he said. The man groaned and opening his eyes, looked up.

"We got your ride to the hospital here. Come on, let's get you up." He tugged on Terry's good arm, helped him to his feet. Terry looked around, a bit bewildered. They led him to the right front seat of the cab and gently settled him in.

"Thanks, Joe," Terry said. They closed his door and he slumped against it, his face pale, his eyes closed.

The man named Joe turned and stared balefully toward the brewery a moment. Then he said to Danny, "Take him to Lutheran Hospital in Lakewood, to the Emergency there. Billy, here," and he indicated the shorter man he'd been talking to, "phoned from the call box down the street. They're expecting you." He handed Danny a ten-dollar bill. "That should cover it."

Danny frowned, unsure what the fare would come to, but he clasped the bill and slipped it into his pocket. "Okay," he said.

He sped them through the nearly empty streets, engine loud in the suburban quiet, and he found the hospital in about fifteen minutes. Emergency was clearly marked, and he swung into the ambulance driveway. Sure enough, an orderly was standing by with a gurney. Danny hustled out of the car to open the passenger door.

"Is this Terry?" the orderly asked. At Danny's nod, he shouted back through the entrance, "A little help here!" A young, Korean-American wearing a white jacket like the orderly's stepped out.

Between the two of them they gently guided Terry out of the car and got him up onto the gurney, while Danny watched, a bit anxiously.

"They pay you?" the first orderly asked.

More thoughtful than I'd have imagined, thought Danny. "Sure. Yeah. I'm all right."

"Thanks, then."

The two orderlies wheeled the gurney through the open doorway.

Labor relations in the good ol' USA. Yowsers, Danny thought.

In another incident, a few weeks after Danny moved into the house with Carolyn and the others, he had been wakened suddenly by Carolyn, who was shaking him by the shoulder.

"Whaaa!..." he yelped, sitting up abruptly.

Carolyn was kneeling beside his low bed, staring intently at him. She put her fingers to her lips. "Shshshsh..." she whispered, looking back over her shoulder. "Daddy'll hear."

Danny rubbed his eyes a moment, then said, "What?"

"You gotta take me to the center," she whispered. "Daddy's in his car, watching the house. He's come to get me."

"What are you talking about?" Danny asked, softly this time.

"Just help me get away. You can't let Daddy get me."

"Lemme get some clothes on," Danny said. "Wait outside," he added, and he nodded toward his bedroom door, which stood open to the hallway.

Carolyn looked at his window, where a crack of sunlight was angling between the cheap curtains.

"Daddy could be lookin' through that crack," she whispered urgently. She got to her feet and stepped softly to the window, where she pulled the curtain completely shut. Then she turned and said, "Hurry up. He's here someplace. I know he is." She stepped out the door and closed it behind her.

Jesus, Danny thought. *What the hell?*

He climbed out of bed in his underwear and slipped on the jeans that had been lying in an irregular pile where he had shucked them off the night before. He rummaged in a cardboard box at the foot of the bed and pulled out some clean socks and a t-shirt with Haagen-Dazs Ice Cream emblazoned on it, a promotion he had picked up at the store for $4. He slipped them on, as well as some sneakers, and opening his bedroom door, crossed the hall to the bathroom to relieve himself. A few minutes later he entered the living room, where Carolyn was standing beside the closed drapes, peeking out a narrow crack she had made so she could watch the street.

"We have to hurry!" she said in an urgent whisper. "He's not out front by your car, so maybe he's around back. I can feel him. He's nearby, I'm sure of it."

"Your daddy?" Danny asked. "What's he doing here? I thought he was in Louisiana."

"He's here to get *me*," she said, looking at him as if it were a self-evident conclusion. "Come on. Take me to the center."

"Let me get my keys," Danny said. He returned to his bedroom, fetching his keys to the Volvo from beside the second-hand lamp on the box that served as a bedside table. Once back in the living room he said to Carolyn, "Where are the others?"

"Louise is I don't know where, and Mac took my boy to school."

"Ok, let's go," Danny said.

He couldn't figure out what was really going on. He couldn't imagine Carolyn's father being here, and he had no idea what the man looked like, anyway. Some redneck cracker was the impression he'd always had from Carolyn's stories about his meanness, his obsession with NASCAR racing, and the white-faced terror she had shown when she told Danny about the rapes by this evil prick, as well as by her older brother. Maybe her brother was here. He tried not to think about it.

They got into the car and Danny headed for the center. "Are you seeing Jane again today?" he asked. Jane was the therapist who had been working with Carolyn for several weeks.

Carolyn nodded wordlessly, a couple of tears slowly leaking down her cheeks. She wiped them away with the back of her hand and turned to look out the back window.

"Is that Daddy back there?" she said. "Shit, I think it's Daddy!"

"Where?"

"That car back there! I gotta hide!" she said, squeezing down into her bucket seat. She was panting with fear now.

"I don't think it's your daddy," Danny said. He turned right on a red light. Seconds later in his rearview mirror he could see the car she had indicated turn to follow. *I guess it could be*, he thought with some alarm.

He pulled a quick left and then another right down an alley and into a further street from where he could maneuver into the center's parking lot.

"Is he there? Is he there?" Carolyn asked, almost a little girl whine.

Danny stopped the car beside the door to the therapy building.

"I don't see him," Danny said.

The door to the building opened and Jane was there. She came over to the passenger door, which she opened, and she said softly, "Come on Carolyn. Let's get you inside." She nodded at Danny and said, "Thanks, Danny. I'll take it from here."

She took Carolyn by the hand and led her inside.

Danny looked around carefully, using all the mirrors as well as the windows. He was sweating, a bit fearfully, as if Carolyn's anxiety had leaped across the gear console and infected him. There was no one to be seen.

Much later, after he had returned home and spent the day on some perfunctory cleaning chores, Carolyn returned. She was back to her old self (whatever that was), humming to herself and making a cup of tea when she began to tell Danny what had happened.

"I really saw him," she said. "I mean, I don't think he was here, but I saw him." Her eyes went far away for a moment. "In my session, I remembered him standing by the bed, wiping himself off, looking both proud and ashamed at his little girl." She let a few tears escape and she sniffed hard. She pulled a paper towel off the roll hanging beneath the kitchen overhead cabinets and blew her nose.

"He was just so awful—just so awful."

Danny simply had nothing to say. He knew what hallucinated memories can do. He just looked at her, a kind of tenderness toward her invading his being. He nodded.

Only three days later, and Danny was running the 'ambulance' again, once more in the Volvo.

He was sitting at the kitchen table, devouring a sandwich for his evening meal and reading, as usual. Louise came into the kitchen, a hangdog look on her face, and she sat down opposite him.

"Hey, Louise, what's up?" he asked, not really interested, but polite enough to recognize her presence. When she didn't reply, he looked up from his book. She was sitting back in her chair, her eyes wide open but looking at nothing in particular, gripping the table edge with both hands. "You ok?" he asked.

She nodded silently but looked around the room vacantly as if she hadn't really heard what he asked. Then she said, "You studied medicine for a while, didn't you?"

"Yeah, but just for a year. Why?"

Her eyes were still roaming around the room, as if seeking something reassuringly solid to fasten on, something worth looking at.

"Oh..." she said, a kind of drawn-out syllable. "Oh, I'm kind of..."

She stopped looking around, and then focused on him, on his face. "What happens when your heart starts going really fast—kind of jumping around?"

He stared intently at her a moment. Then he asked, very gently, "Have you taken something?"

She sat silently. Tears started forming at the corners of her eyes. She nodded slowly, and then smiled uncertainly. "My heart's going really fast," she said slowly.

"What did you take?" he asked.

She reached into her pocket and tugged out a small bottle. The cap was missing. She set it on the table.

"My heart keeps jumping," she said once more, and then she yawned, really deeply.

"Shit, Louise, how many of these did you take? What are they?" Danny asked, nervous now. He looked at the label, some prescription called 'Temazepam.'

She was closing her eyes. "Some," she said vaguely.

He got quickly to his feet. "Come on," he said, taking her by the arm. She slumped a bit in her chair, and he had to muscle her to her feet. "Come on," he said again.

She stumbled a bit, leaning against him, and he led her out the front door, the screen banging behind them, to where his battered Volvo was parked at the curb. He settled her into the front seat, belted her in, and went around the front to climb in himself. Her head lolled forward, her eyes closed.

The Volvo started immediately, a reassuring purr. They pulled away. He sped north on Holly Street, left on Cherry Creek Drive, and then west to Colorado Boulevard. Moments later he pulled into the medical center. He had to slap her awake enough to get her into the Emergency room.

"She's taken some pills," he said to the nurse at the desk, who looked up in alarm. Louise was swaying beside him with her eyes closed. "I don't know exactly what. Sleeping pills, I think." He handed the nurse the empty bottle.

She got quickly to her feet and came around to help him. "Bring her this way," she said, holding Louise's other arm and tugging them toward a bed beside a cloth partition. "Doctor!" she called, and a young woman with a stethoscope looked up from a chart a few feet away. "Pills!" the nurse said.

She helped Danny get Louise onto the bed, then turned to him. "Wait in the waiting room," she said. "Through there." She pointed.

Christ, he thought. *I hope she's going to be ok.*

He wandered into the waiting room through smells of antiseptic and body odor. A fearful looking woman in curlers looked up from her magazine, and then away. A lanky black man was stretched out snoring, his big feet seemingly yards from his chair. Danny found a seat against the wall and sank into it, only just realizing that his own heart had been going pretty fast. He took a deep breath and settled in to wait. He wondered whether or not he had thought to lock the door at the house. Then he thought, *Shit, I better get my car out of the ambulance lane.*

He got to his feet and slipped out into the low darkness. He recognized the crumpled rear deck of the Volvo, and he went over to it. *No ticket yet*, he thought gratefully.

He started the car and maneuvered it into a Pay Parking lot around the side of the building. He tugged a couple of quarters out of his jeans and plugged the meter. Given the Volvo's battered appearance, the likelihood of its being stolen was virtually nil, but Danny actually loved the car—its comfortable bucket seats and the steady hum of its wonderful engine. He would take no chances. He locked the car and returned to the waiting room.

Every so often he would get up and pace around the room, glance at the rack of brochures offering medical advice on everything from chicken pox to unwanted pregnancy.

People came and went. At one point the sleeping man started awake, looking around with a fearful, almost angry expression. A nurse came in and called softly, "Mrs. Akins?"

The woman in curlers climbed heavily to her feet, nodding to the nurse, who led her away.

Finally, after about three quarters of an hour, Louise came into the waiting room. Danny got quickly to his feet and went over to her. The cheeks below her eyes were swollen as if she had been crying. She had difficulty meeting Danny's eyes, but finally looked up, where he stood a little uncertainly.

In a low voice, Danny said, "So, are you ok?"

Louise nodded, but didn't say anything.

"Should we go home, then?"

She nodded again.

She followed him out to the car, the evening cooler now, in the lot the Volvo looking abandoned and tired next to the newer vehicles, which shone mutely under the halogen lighting. He unlocked her door and held it for her as she belted herself in. Moments later they were back onto Colorado Boulevard, heading south through its neon circus, back toward home.

"What happened?" Danny asked.

Louise looked away from him, out her side window, as if Muffler Man were somehow compelling her attention.

"I just wanted it to stop," she finally said. "Just to stop."

"But not really, not that way," Danny said. "Or you wouldn't have come into the kitchen."

"No," she said. Then she added, "They shoved a rubber hose down my throat into me, pumped my stomach, got out most of the pills. Then I puked when they pulled the hose out, and they helped me clean up."

Her description was blunt and inelegant. He could still smell the puke, the insistent acid sweetness.

No euphemisms, Danny thought. *Maybe life shouldn't have euphemisms.*

CHAPTER TWENTY-THREE

Now and Zen

Danny had never thought too much of the various kinds of "age of Aquarius" bullshit that were all about. He loved the song, but the notion of a naked man leaping through French doors in the Broadway musical *Hair!* just kind of turned his stomach. *Let the sun shine in, indeed*, he thought. *Where the sun never shines?* Sometimes it seemed as if every new psychological fad was simply a variation on the rest, a new set of terms addressing a generally held, insatiable desire for some kind of liberation through pleasure.

Still, his interest in the nearly unfathomable complexities of consciousness had never really diminished, even in light of the growing confidence he felt with regard to managing his own anxieties. *The Origin of Consciousness in the Breakdown of the Bicameral Mind* had been a thrilling read. There seemed so much explanatory power in Jaynes' elegant theory, and yet no one seemed to be doing anything with it aside from commenting on its quaint peculiarity.

Now Danny was reading *Zen and the Art of Motorcycle Maintenance* for the second time. It was a riveting work, made more so by the author's self-confessed mental breakdown. The fact that the author of a spectacular book like that could also have been mentally unstable gave Danny a feeling of personal support, an unspoken reassurance that although anxiety and psychic pain can be truly debilitating, they may not prevent exceptional achievements, even though Robert Pirsig's intellectual brilliance had failed to prevent his utter personal collapse. In a way, it further reassured Danny in his choice for personal treatment, his own recognition that thinking alone is an insufficient path to stability. But his failure to characterize in some kind of definitive way the role of his body's tortured physical responses to his efforts to release his anxiety made him understand that feelings alone were insufficient avenues to understanding, as well.

He reveled in the various conversational lectures in Pirsig's book, elaborate excursions of mental exploration the author called chatauquas. *Chatauqua*, he thought to himself. *What a cool word!* These sections of the book were a kind of thinking through to the heart of things, a mental wondering and wandering that contrasted the various appeals of a romantic imagination to the prosaic but functional methods of industrial pragmatism. *Ah, romanticism*, he thought, but he rapidly abandoned Pirsig's preoccupations (with what seemed foolish idealism) for memories of his own sexual gratification (or lack thereof). Thus it was, when the phone rang one morning he was heartened and surprised to hear Penny's voice.

"Hey, handsome, whatcha been up to?"

"Penny?" he said. Then, capturing his poise, he said vaguely, "Oh, this and that. What about you?" Despite celibate horniness, he wasn't sure at all he wanted to get too connected to this woman, whatever her intentions might be. Her husband might own a gun.

"Oh, I just wondered if you'd like to meet for coffee someplace, catch up."

Danny thought a moment, running through a dozen possibilities from a chaste tea at the Bluebird to raunchy, drunken sex on a trampoline, all within the space of a few seconds.

"Coffee sounds ok," he said, noncommittally. "Any place in mind?"

"There's a health food place on Federal Boulevard and Alameda called *Nirvana Eats* that makes great smoothies and stuff. Wanna meet me there? Say, 2:00 o'clock?"

"Sure, ok. 2:00 o'clock. See you there."

Danny had to catch a bus to their rendez-vous, as his car was being tuned up. The only other passengers were a grey-haired elderly woman with two grocery bags beside her and, two seats further away, an obese man in his twenties whose extreme strabismus made it appear as if he was reading something on the ceiling while watching the bus driver with his other eye. He was also singing, out of tune, in a foreign language. Danny watched the driver roll his own eyes in the big, rear-view mirror. *No wonder no one takes the buses here*, he thought.

Despite the unfamiliar bus route, he got to the appointed place at about 1:45. He had made sure to leave plenty of time for the bus, not wanting to be late. *Could I be keener on her than I think?* he wondered to himself.

He picked up a loose magazine from a side display, moved over to one of the tables dedicated to customer food service, and sat down to wait. *CoEvolution Quarterly* the magazine title proclaimed, published by *The Whole Earth Catalog.* The cover featured a full color drawing by R. Crumb, variously ugly, buxom young women seeding and cultivating a field.

Weird cover, Danny thought, and he opened it and began to thumb through it. *But there's some cool stuff in here.*

When Penny plopped herself down on the chair opposite he was engrossed in a page devoted to reviewing gardening tools. He wasn't much interested in yard work, to tell the truth, but he was amazed by the variety of tools and gizmos that were available to those so inclined. He looked up at her, the same cheerful face under her tangle of curls. She grinned at him.

"So, you gonna buy me coffee? Or do I have to do *all* the work?"

"Hey, Penny." *Damn, but she is pretty*, he thought. "Sure. What would you like?"

"There's this kind of French coffee drink I'd never tried before yesterday called a 'latté,'" she said. "Really good! I had two of them. I'd like one of those."

Danny had never heard of a latté, much less had one, but he stepped quickly over to the counter, where a serious-looking young man (*a college type,* Danny thought) was manipulating a strange looking machine that hissed and clanked and emanated odors of dark roast coffee.

"Two lattés, please," Danny said. The young man nodded and replied, "You're number 4. We'll call you. That's five bucks."

Danny grimaced at the sticker shock, but he peeled a bill from the meager stash in his wallet and handed it over. He turned back to the table, where Penny was seated, back to him, looking around the room. Rather than wait some indeterminate time for their coffees, Danny returned to talk to her.

He gave her a measured glance and then said, "So, how's your husband?"

She scowled at him a little, then grinned. "Same as always. He's out of town, gone to New York for some business reason. As they say, absence makes the heart grow fonder, and when he left I got this fond feeling for you." She grinned some more.

Danny felt a mild genital twitch and smiled at her despite his misgivings.

"I was thinking of going over to Boulder," she remarked. "There's some cool stuff happening there over the next day or two."

"Like what?" he asked.

"Tomorrow night John Lilly, author of *Mind of the Dolphin*, is giving a talk at one of the community centers. And the day after, the Naropa Institute is sponsoring the first of its lectures in a series on linguistics, some guy from MIT who worked with Noam Chomsky. What do you think?"

"Number 4!" called the barrista, shoving a pair of paper cups forward on his counter.

"Let me get the coffee first," Danny said.

When he set the two cups down on the table she scrutinized him amiably and said, "We could stay at my cousin's in

Boulder. He's got an apartment near the university, and he's out of town, as well. We have an arrangement. I can use the place when he's not there." She eyed him mischievously.

"Well, I don't know..." he began, but she cut him off with a wave of her hand.

"Look, Danny, I'm not asking you to run away with me or something. I just wanna have some fun, and you're fun." Then she grinned again and said, "Don't you think I'm fun?"

"Better than fishing, that's for sure," he replied, and she giggled, a free-spirited breath of musical pleasure.

"Good. So that's settled, then. Will you come?"

Danny thought a moment, eyes directed at her ample shirt front, and then looked back to her smile. "Ok. Sure," he said. "Have you got a car? Can you pick me up? Mine's over with my Korean mechanic getting a tune-up and some new brake pads." The explanation made him seem somehow important, as if he had a mechanic that belonged personally to him. He smiled at his own foolishness. But Penny seemed not to notice.

"I've got my Beetle. Where do you live?"

"Pick me up at my work place, *Healthy Body Natural Foods* over on Grey Avenue, east of the university, just off Colorado Boulevard. I'll pick up some snacks and stuff. Say 9:30? Would that work?"

"Ok." She reached over and took his hand, squeezing it in her soft fingers. "I don't know what it is about you," she said, "but you make me horny as a hoot owl."

Danny blushed.

"Maybe it's your blush," she said, laughing. She swallowed the last of her latté. *Boy, that five bucks went fast*, Danny thought.

"Look, I've got some errands to run. I'll see you in the morning," she said. She squeezed his hand once more and got to her feet. She bent over, teasing him a bit with her cleavage, and she kissed him gently on the cheek, then let go of his hand and headed for the exit. Danny watched her go, momentarily lost in a sort of happy lust, wondering when he'd be detumescent enough to get up and walk without looking totally stupid. He watched her pleasing bottom disappear through the doorway, and thought to himself, *Here we go again*. But he certainly wasn't disappointed.

True to their agreement, Penny appeared at *Healthy Body* about twenty after nine the next morning. She wore tight cut-offs and cork-soled high shoes that accentuated her long legs. She pulled off her big dark glasses and looked around. Pauline stared at her a moment, then turned to Danny, who was stuffing some yogurt and fruit into a paper bag for a customer. Pauline whispered to him, "There's a woman who's hot to trot if I ever saw one."

"That's Penny," Danny said. More loudly, he called, "Hey Penny, come meet Pauline, my boss." He handed the customer his change.

Penny sauntered over, blinking in the comparatively dim light. "Hi Pauline," she offered.

"Hi."

There was a moment of uncomfortable silence. Then Danny said, "We're going to Boulder to hear John Lilly tonight."

"Wow, John Lilly, huh? You read his dolphin book?" Pauline said to him, but kept her eyes on Penny, a kind of measured assessment.

"Sure," Danny said. "And *The Center of the Cyclone*."

Penny grinned obscurely.

"Be sure to tell me all about his talk when you get back," Pauline said.

"Ok," Danny replied. "See you in a couple of days."

Penny gave Pauline a half wave as she turned and led the way out of the store. Once outside, she said, "There's a woman who's hot to trot if I ever saw one."

Danny laughed.

"What? What's funny?"

"She said the same thing about you. Anyhow, she's married."

"So am I."

Danny just looked at her and grinned.

The route to Boulder was becoming familiar. It was Danny's fourth or fifth trip to the university town. It had some of the best bookstores around, and occasional trips up the back roads into the mountains were always exhilarating. Heading up the turnpike toward the town, he often imagined what the experience would have been like for mountain men or native Sioux, riding their ponies toward the massive westward barrier, the vast, empty plains stretching away behind them. The thought of the lonely wilderness left him with a kind of pleasant ache in his heart, and if it were merely nostalgia for a fantasy, he didn't care. He had little enough in his own real experience to remember with such sadness and affection (or so he thought).

He and Penny whiled away the afternoon in one of the local bookstores. Penny didn't seem bored, despite the fact that she worked in a bookstore. The store included several deep-stuffed armchairs and a sofa, into a corner of which Danny curled up with Lawrence Durrell's *Justine*. The writing electrified his imagination with its descriptions of the sweat and dust of Alexandria, of the exotic customs and the unique characters. He was rapidly taken by the mystery of Justine's child, and of the tantalizing danger inherent in the narrator's infatuation with Justine, a powerful banker's wife, a situation not sufficiently alien to his own with Penny to be ignored.

At some point Penny climbed onto the sofa beside him and curled herself under his arm. She held a book of Sylvia Plath's poetry and hummed softly to herself while reading, an affectation that Danny found curiously pleasing, even though it interrupted his own concentration. At first, he couldn't tell exactly what she was humming, but within minutes he recognized the tune, *Long and Winding Road* by Paul McCartney, the song that marked the breakup of the Beatles. "*Still they lead me back/To the long winding road...*" For a moment or two he felt intensely sad, yet here he was, curled up with a pretty girl who was soft and warm, and for the moment, his.

After a leisurely supper of pizza and beer from a local pub, they wandered down the avenue to the hall where Lilly was supposed to speak. Plenty of other young people, and a few grey-haired hippies, were making their way in the same direction. *It's like going to church used to be*, Danny thought, *everyone joining in assembly to hear—what? A path to salvation?* He imagined them all as dolphins, racing through the water to hear their guru. He gripped Penny's hand and smiled at her.

The hall was in some kind of community center. The arriving crowd was milling about in the process of finding seats on stacking chairs that had been arranged facing a stage. The hardwood floor beneath was marked with lines for various sports, and a basket and backboard that normally would have hung in front of the stage had been cranked up and out of the way. On the stage itself, a lanky man in a large, stuffed armchair sat calmly facing the crowd, a bemused smile on his face as he watched them.

No one flicked the lights or tapped on a microphone to draw the crowd's attention, and Lilly simply waited calmly until what might have been the aura of his passive patience finally caught the crowd's curiosity. Suddenly, it calmed to silence. Lilly raised his right hand in an effortless greeting and got to his feet.

He spoke for over an hour, without notes, describing his California house that had a seawater pool in its living room, a pool that connected to the Pacific Ocean, so the dolphins could swim in and out. He talked of the dolphins' quickness, their curiosity, their playfulness, their predictable but almost unknowable intelligence, and their sexiness. Danny imagined himself and Penny as copulating dolphins, twisting their way to orgasm through the salty water. He smiled.

Then Lilly spoke about the mind as what he termed a 'biocomputer,' an almost magical information processor we carry around in our heads. He closed his talk by recounting his experimentation with 'consciousness without an object,' his mental excursions while under sensory deprivation, a state that allows the mind to range freely without having to attend to sensory stimuli.

The audience was almost spellbound. The standing ovation at the end of the talk was long and heartfelt. Penny held his hand throughout the talk, letting him go only to applaud, and then grasping it again as if to anchor herself. It was a wonderful evening.

About 10:00 pm, after parking her VW on a narrow residential street, Penny led him up the outside stairway of a walkup apartment building. Perhaps it had been refitted from an old motel, although it was off the main roads. On the third floor landing she turned to Danny, grasped him behind his neck, and kissed him with deep longing. He felt an instinctual rush of pleasure and desire, and he held her close to him, his heart racing.

"Come on," she said. Three doorways down she inserted a key into the door lock of her cousin's apartment, and pushing the door ajar, led Danny inside. A dim light shone over the stove in a cramped kitchen off to the left. There was a residual smell of what might have been hot dogs or popcorn, and beer. She pulled him by the hand toward a cozy living room, then pulled up short.

Across the living room a bedroom door was open, lit by a bedside lamp. On the bed was a naked female, back to the bedroom door, riding her partner, who lay supine. Each of them was emitting soft moans of pleasure.

"Shit!" Penny said. "You asshole!" she said more loudly.

The girl, a lanky black woman with a frizzy afro rolled off her partner and grabbed at some bedclothes to hide groin and breasts.

"Who're you?!" she demanded.

"Oh, shit is right," the male said, his head stretched up from the pillow. "What're you doing here, Penny?" Then he noticed Danny, who stood staring incredulously.

"New York, eh?" Penny demanded. "You dumb shit! You know you don't have to lie when you want to pick up some easy piece. Jesus, David!"

"So, is this your latest tool?" the man said, indicating Danny.

Danny felt a stab of fear, a sense of getting in way over his head.

"I think I'd better go," he said to Penny.

She turned to him, a look of pleading on her face. "No, don't, please."

But he was already moving toward the street door, the ghostly sensation of his fear roiling up and down his spinal cord, his breathing rapid.

Penny followed him.

"He's cute," the black girl said.

"You think everyone's cute," the male voice said. "Penny? Penny?" he called.

Penny had taken Danny's hand again to slow him down. "Listen," she said. "I know this isn't what you signed up for. I'm sorry. But I think I've gotta stay. Here," she said, thrusting the car keys into his hand. "Take my car."

Danny stared blankly at the keys a moment, a sense of bleak disappointment washing over him. He looked back at Penny, at the searching expression behind her glasses— sorrow, anxiety, her own disappointment.

"Leave the car at *Healthy Body*. Shove the key under the back of the right front tire. I'll get it tomorrow." She looked at him, trying to gauge the depth of his reaction. Then she kissed him once more. "I'm so sorry, in more ways than one."

There was the sound of someone moving in the living room. "Penny?" David's voice said, anxious, angry, unpredictable.

He looked at her face once more, then nodded and left the apartment. He could hear the raised voices of the three of them as he descended the stairs.

By the time he got to the car he was feeling a mournful burst of freedom, a sense that he had narrowly missed something significant yet dangerous, a trap. He felt a tear on his cheek but brushed it away. He got into the car. In the front seat he could feel the long muscles of his back slipping in and out of spasm, and for a moment he thought he was going to slip into his contortions there and then. But he gripped the wheel hard, bent forward, started the engine, and pulled away, pushing his fear down, and only allowing the occasional tear to roll down his cheek.

All the way back to Denver, through the rushing of the tires he could hear the black girl's voice. "Who're you?" and, "He's cute!" David's harsh shouts at Penny.

And in the background of it all was, *You left me standing here/a long, long time ago/ don't leave me waiting here/ lead me to your door...*

CHAPTER TWENTY-FOUR

Neither Here nor There

If in some ways the Boulder trip had been a bust, slamming a door in Danny's face, in others it was another new beginning. John Lilly's presentation had been fascinating, if a bit on the outer end of "far out." Something that had really intrigued Danny was Lilly's references to "consciousness without an object," a state of internal reflection brought on through meditation or isolation from physical, perceptual inputs. The most efficient key to this state, according to Lilly, was the isolation tank.

As it happened, Terry, an athletic red-haired guy Danny had met at the nuclear demonstration, dropped by the store two days later when Danny was working.

"You gotta try it, man," he said to Danny, between spoons full of ice cream.

"Try what?"

"Those isolation tanks. Three-dimensionally weird, but so cool."

Danny immediately perked up his attention.

"What tanks? Where?"

"Over on South Grant," Terry said. "Remember that bookstore that used to be there? The one that went tits up?"

Danny immediately flashed on images of the store, of Doug Battersea, sleeping in the loft above the *History* section.

"Sure," he said.

"Well, some guy from Boulder has set up a business there renting tank time. It's called *Floating Nirvana*. You should check it out."

Danny had never been fond of being advised with the word "should" (even though he used it extensively on himself and others), but he resolved he would follow this recommendation, nonetheless. It was something too avant-garde to be passed up. *Danny Dolphin*, he thought with amusement.

The whole theory of "consciousness without an object" held an insistent fascination. It seemed self-contradictory. How can you be conscious if you're not conscious of anything? It seemed that the whole idea was "no things, just awareness." Various practitioners of Zen and other meditational disciplines had spoken or written about this condition, this "nirvana." He wondered what it might be like, whether or not floating in an isolation tank might bring it on.

The tanks themselves relied on basic physics to allow or create the experience. They were to be set up in very isolated places where sound was completely insulated out, and mounted as they were on coils of rubber hose, even vibration from passing vehicles (like trucks or buses) would not be felt. The inside of the tank featured a supersaturated salt solution maintained at skin temperature (or very close—conceivably different humans had slightly different skin temperatures due to metabolic differences), and all light was filtered out with a series of baffles. The air temperature, too, was maintained roughly at body temperature. Thus, once you had stripped naked, climbed into the tank, lain down to float and pulled the lid shut, all physical sensations rapidly disappeared. It required no energy to hold up your body because you were floating. It was utterly dark and silent. You might taste or smell a little saltiness. The sensation of the water, because of its nearness to skin temperature, tended simply to vanish.

The next Thursday he drove down to *Floating Nirvana* to talk to the staff. He was familiar with the building. The sign advertising *South Grant Books* had been taken down from above the door, but it still leaned, a dusty plank, against the brickwork under the front window. It had been replaced above the entrance by a hand-painted sign with the name of the new business, and beside it the silhouette of a meditator "floated" in lotus position, with radiance emanating from around the body. *That's a bit pretentious*, he thought, as he pushed open the doorway.

A pretty blonde wearing a pale blue blouse, dark blue neck scarf, and what might have been nearly transparent pajama bottoms (opaque up around the "naughty bits," Danny noticed) got up from the armchair beside the desk where she had been reading a magazine on hatha yoga. Her bare feet had been tucked up under her, and she had hoop bangles on her left wrist. She gave Danny a half smile and said, "Hello." Then, as if she had just remembered her sales pitch, she asked politely. "Have you ever tried floating before?"

Her desk was curiously empty, just some kind of day timer journal, a pen in a holder, a note pad, and a telephone.

"I haven't," Danny replied. "But I'm curious to try."

She moved around behind the desk, and seating herself in the desk chair there, rolled it forward. She picked up the pen and made an elaborate show of checking some time slots, pointing to them one at a time, although from Danny's angle the day's schedule appeared empty except for two hours late in the afternoon.

"I'm Angela, by the way. And you are...?"

"Danny."

"We appear to have some time available right now, if that works for you." She looked up and smiled again, tapping the tip of the pen against the empty page.

"How much does it cost?"

She gave him a look of cool appraisal, as if estimating his net worth.

"Because we're a business start-up in an unusual new service, we're offering some bulk time at a considerable discount. Twenty-five hours in one or two-hour sessions for a hundred dollars."

Danny thought a moment. "How much is it per hour?"

"Normally it's ten dollars an hour."

"Suppose I try it for an hour. If I like it, can I apply that hour to the first of twenty-five? Or, if I don't like it, I'll pay you the ten."

"We can do that."

She looked at him some more, not really moving or adding anything for a few moments. Then she said, "It's a truly unique experience, and some people find it amazingly relaxing. A number of corporate business people who are in high-powered jobs with a lot of stress come in here once a week or so to wind down. That new lawyer next door, too, for example. She bought a hundred hours!"

She took a deep breath, then continued. "I'm instructed to warn you, though. Despite its many benefits, some people do not react well to the experience. Sometimes the isolation stimulates pretty wild hallucinations, the "creepy crawlies," as my boss calls them. People in the tank have to remember that all they have to do is to push up to open the hatch, let the light in, and wake themselves out of wherever they've gone. These hallucinatory episodes aren't all that common, but we feel obliged to inform our clients, just in the event that something weird evolves."

She twirled the pen between two fingers and waited for Danny's response.

"I'd like to give it a go," he said.

For a moment, he considered that given his proclivity to having anxiety attacks (although these had become considerably rarer as his therapy sessions had tapered off), perhaps this kind of experimental behavior might not be a good idea. But the possibility of its potential calming effect also appealed to him.

"We provide showers and towels for afterward," she said. "You want to get the salt off your skin. And if you have a scratch or cut you don't want to do this until you've healed—the salt can drive you absolutely wild, and we don't want to spread any possible infection."

"Ok," Danny said. "No scratches. Let's try it."

She got up, reached into a drawer and took out a key.

"Come with me," she said.

She led him down a short corridor toward the rear near what was once a room devoted to science fiction. *Pretty appropriate*, Danny thought.

She unlocked the new door and led him through. Two shower stalls had been plumbed against the far wall, and the room was complete with teak benches and rubberized floor mats.

To the left was another door, this one unlocked, and she opened it and clicked on the light. The room was only about 10' X 10'. A few feet away against the far wall was a large, plywood box. The air in the room was moist and warm, unlike the usual Denver dryness.

"That's the tank," she said, indicating the plywood box. It looked almost like a coffin, but larger, and without the taper.

She opened the hatch lid into the dark interior. "On the end where your feet will be pointed is the baffled air exchanger."

Danny looked in, as if he were looking into a cave to the underworld.

Angela looked at her watch. "It's nearly 1:00 pm," she said. She pointed to a chair against the wall. "You can leave your clothes there. You have to go in completely nude." She smiled. "Some couples have tried having sex in the tank. It didn't go so well."

Danny nodded, a smile of his own playing at the corner of his mouth. He thought of Penny.

"There's only six inches of water in there, so you'd have to try really hard to drown yourself. It's so buoyant that some- times you think it's lifting you toward the hatchway above, but when you're lying down you have about three feet of clearance above you. You'll have to keep the door to the room unlocked. I'll come in after an hour and knock on the lid. It's amazing how rapidly that simple sound can pull you back into the here and now. Then I'll go back out, you can dress, and we can discuss your experience afterward if you like."

Danny nodded again. "All right," he said.

Angela looked at him and nodded, then turned and left, closing the door behind her with a latch click.

For a moment Danny had several misgivings. *Suppose she steals my wallet while I'm floating? What if she's a secret ax murderer?* But he dismissed these ideas as paranoid foolishness. He was likely in much greater danger driving his cab.

He unlaced his sneakers and placed them under the chair. Then he stripped out of his clothes, leaving them neatly folded on the seat. He stepped gingerly over to the tank and climbed over the two-foot ledge that held the water inside. He was astounded at how quickly the water sensation against his skin disappeared! He squatted down, then sat on the bottom on grit he assumed was rock salt and extended his legs toward the far end of the tank. He lay back, pulling the hatch shut over him, allowed his arms to drop to his sides, and felt the water buoy him into an extended floating posture.

The darkness was complete. For a few seconds, he could sense the water settle against his limbs, and then, after he completely relaxed his arms, all went silent. The sense of wetness vanished. He could feel his heart beating, the tick of a pulse in his temple, and he could sense the wetness in the air only momentarily. He took a breath and closed his eyes. He opened them again. It made no difference. There was simply blackness. He felt the rest of his musculature go completely slack, as if someone had turned off a muscle switch. And then suddenly, he went 'away.' It was the only word to name it. He was there and not there simultaneously, thinking and not thinking, simply being. It was an astonishing condition, one of calm amazement and utter detachment. He could have been on Jupiter, for all he knew, and yet the words didn't even occur to him. There were no words.

He seemed to be dreaming of some backlit, glorious nowhere when, without there having been any sense of time having passed at all, he suddenly heard two distinct knocks on the plywood hatch. A voice above him said, "Hour's up." He paused a few seconds, and then straightened up into a semi-seated position and pushed the tank lid open. Dim light flooded in, and he blinked. Stretching his head up, he looked around the room, which was empty, the door closed. His clothes lay as he had left them.

He pulled himself to his feet, feeling the salty water drain off him. Angela had left a large, fluffy towel on the lower end of the tank. He climbed out and clasping the towel, patted most of the water off his body.

In the outer room, he had a leisurely shower, allowing the warm spray to rinse away the salt. He dried himself all over and quietly dressed, dropping the towel into a hamper on the way out to the front.

In the reception room Angela was reading once more. A pot of tea and two cups were on a coffee table beside the armchair, and there was another armchair beyond, which she indicated with a wave.

"How was that?" she said softly.

Danny simply shook his head, still almost dazed. He felt languorous, yet tremendously energized, relaxed and alert.

"Have some tea," she said. She poured him a generous mugful.

Danny sat down in the further armchair, picked up the mug and sipped. "It was incredible," he finally said. "I've never experienced anything like it."

Angela smiled. "A lot of people say that. No creepy crawlies?"

"No, nothing like that. It was like I was there and not there at the same time." He gave a half chuckle. "I mean, I know that sounds stupid or impossible. But that's the way it was."

Angela just smiled and nodded. She picked up her magazine again, but before beginning to read, said, "Take your time. Enjoy your tea."

After ten minutes or so, tea drunk, Danny said, "I'll take twenty-five hours."

"Thought you might," Angela replied.

CHAPTER TWENTY-FIVE

Ghosts (1)

It was a quiet mid-afternoon at the store, comparatively cool inside, out of the high summer sun, which had fueled a relentless heat in the region for more than a week. Custom was slow, but it would pick up between 4:00 and 6:00 pm when people stopped by to grab a few organic essentials for the evening's cooking. Meanwhile there were always various important chores to attend to.

Danny was scanning a *Prevention Magazine* to compare their advertised supplement prices to those offered by the store. Pauline was on her stool behind the till, seeing to some paperwork. Overhead the fluorescent lights hummed their peculiar harmonies, counterpoint to the intermittent whine of the coolers.

Pauline put down the sheaf of invoices she had been checking. Seemingly out of the blue, she asked Danny, "Do you believe in ghosts?"

The question nudged a tiny chill in Danny, who knew only too well his own metaphorical ghosts. He felt the familiar twinge in his back, a personal signal that he had to admit to himself functioned like the proverbial rattling of chains or unexplained moaning that characterized the clichéd effects of cheap Gothic fiction. But he knew it was merely angst whispering in his musculature.

"Ghosts?" he replied. "Not really. Why?"

"You know that girl from Kentucky that comes in here for burdock root supplements once a month? She says they help her keep her blood pressure down. What was her name? Marian? Marie?"

"Marian, I think." He thought of the quiet girl with granny glasses, pallid as if she'd never been in the sun, checking out the herbal supplements. "She's pretty ghost-like herself."

"Yeah, she's pale, isn't she? Well, she's really interested in ghost stuff. Last time she was in she told me she's thinking about doing a radio series on Denver ghosts, reported poltergeist phenomena, unexplained, strange events—automatic writing, you know. People are fascinated by that kind of far out stuff. Remember *The Exorcist*? Talk about spooky. Anyway, she said she's looking for a voice, someone who sounds authoritative to do the voiceover and narration. When she said *that* I thought of *you*. You've got the right kind of timbre, kind of deep, the sort of sound that lends credibility to what you say." She grinned at him. "Even when you're out to lunch!" She chuckled.

Danny smiled. But he knew there was some truth to what she was saying. He could think of numerous occasions when he'd be explaining the virtues of some supplement to customers, and despite the fact that he felt nervous inside, he could tell that they were just eating it up, almost as if there was some hypnotic quality to his words. He wasn't deliberately trying to fool people or con them. His voice just seemed to hold conviction or trustworthiness somehow. He wasn't sure why.

He thought about Marian's project a moment.

"Did you talk to her about me?" he asked. "And what does she know about radio, anyway?"

A hint of a smile lifted a corner of Pauline's mouth. "I might have mentioned your name," she said. "She told me her brother used to work for NPR, you know, the public radio station. She said he's agreed to help her with the technical side of things."

Danny just looked at her. Pauline glanced aside a moment under his scrutiny, but turning back to him she said, "I've got her number. Why don't you give her a call?" Then she added, "She's not paying anything, she said. Except if she manages to sell the series. Then you'd get half."

Danny turned back to his magazine and thought a minute, watching from the corner of his eye as Pauline checked off one or two invoice items with a blue pencil. Then he asked, "How about you? Do you believe in ghosts?"

She looked up again and smiled. "Sure. Why not?" she said, as if it were no more remarkable than saying, *"Sure, I'd like a coffee—with cream, please."*

"I don't know," Danny said. His was a comment of blanket uncertainty that could have applied equally to believing in ghosts or to uncertainty about phoning Marian. To clarify, he said, "I mean, I've never seen a ghost, or even anything really like one, or like the way story-tellers have described them. Have you?"

"Nah. But 'There's more in heaven and earth than is dreamed of in your philosophy, Horatio.' That's from *Hamlet*," she went on to say. "Probably the only line from Shakespeare I remember—or understand." She grinned and doodled a bit with her pencil on the edge of a page. "I think it would be cool to see one, though. Don't you?"

"For sure." From uncertainty to conviction in a single bound, his reply surprised even himself. He was suddenly sure he would call Marian.

Three days later he met Marian for coffee in *Nirvana Eats*. He thought momentarily of Penny and her lattés, but when he and Marian sat down, espressos in hand, it was all business.

Marian surprised Danny. He might easily have mistaken her for a shy girl. She was soft-spoken in a deliberate way, sometimes so slow to reply to a comment or question Danny wondered whether or not she was paying attention. Soon, however, he came to appreciate that she was so thoughtful and considerate that not only did she contemplate the subject at issue carefully, she also took the time to plan her comments with Danny's personality in mind, taking care to avoid turns of phrase or vocabulary that was in any way likely to offend him. He wondered what Pauline might have told her about him.

"You have an interesting project here, that's for sure," Danny said to her.

She looked at him with big brown eyes, a silent focus. After eight or nine seconds, she said, "Do I hear a 'but' there?"

"Maybe," he said. "Do you believe in ghosts? Yourself? Or is this just a gimmicky way to make some money? I mean, are you really interested in their possible existence?"

She looked away, as if her answer was floating in semi-visible letters off above the display of carob brownies beside the big coffee machine. She said, carefully, "I'm not sure the word 'believe' is the best way to approach the topic. When people say, 'Do you believe in this or that,' usually what they mean is that in their view, the subject at issue has no evidence supporting its reality or its validity as an explanation for something real, that it's all an act of faith, belief as opposed to understanding." She sighed. "I think there's plenty of evidence that many, many people have experienced things that, for want of a better explanation, they attribute to ghosts. I don't necessarily accept their interpretations, I believe in their experiences. I think I'd be a fool not to." She sipped her coffee and wiped her lower lip with a paper napkin, waiting for Danny to speak.

Despite his basic skepticism, Danny felt a keen rush of agreement, as if she'd crystallized an idea that he'd always held but never verbalized. *Ghosts are referred to everywhere in our cultural past*, he thought, *from the Bible to Hamlet. There must be something behind it all. It's the same with religion*, he thought. *There may be no evidence for the cosmic 'gardener,' but there's plenty of evidence that many people, maybe even most people, have so-called religious experiences.*

"So what kinds of scenes or experiences or people or whatever do you want to build this series around? Have you got some in mind?"

Marian cleared her throat, thinking. "I've met a number of different individuals in the region who have mentioned various unusual locations where ghosts have supposedly been seen or where they claim to have seen them, and in my early research into this project I've heard mention of some people, putative experts to do with the paranormal, that would make good subjects for an interview. I've approached three or four of them already."

"Like who?" *Whom?* Danny corrected himself silently.

"There's a husband and wife team of psychologists here in Denver who specialize in counseling people about inexplicable, terrifying experiences they've had—poltergeist phenomena—weird sensations of 'spiritual' presence in their homes, things like that. I'd like to interview them, and maybe even people they've counseled. And there's an old guy who lives in a Queen Anne era house over by city park who claims to have had more than one ghost living in his house with him."

"Do you have the gear we need? Tape recorders and so forth?"

"Already done and dusted." She gave him a conspiratorial grin. "Sounds like maybe you're a go. Are you?"

"Ok. Listen. I've got a pretty filled up life, busy with lots of things. But if you'll make all the appointments and they fit into my kind of haphazard schedule of obligations, I'm willing to do the interviews."

She smiled again, nodding as if she had just won some bet she had had with herself. "We'll need to plan out some of our questioning ahead of time, but of course, as these conversations progress, we may just have to wing it later into the meetings."

That made sense. Danny supposed you could never know for sure where some of these stories might take you. But he felt kind of excited. It would beat bumping around town in a taxi.

"So," he said, "halves on any sales? That's what Pauline said you told her."

Marian reached a thin hand across the table, a cool, tender gathering of slim fingers decorated by a mood ring. "Shake on it," she said.

It was a few weeks later that Marian phoned him at the store. So much time had passed he had begun to think she'd abandoned the project and not had the nerve to tell him.

"Hey, Danny," she said somewhat breathlessly. "If you can make it, we can interview Dr. and Mrs. Nicolescu, the counselors I told you about, tonight at 8:00 pm. They just called me back. What do you think? Are you free?"

Danny felt a slight tightening of his diaphragm.

"Nicolescu, huh? Sounds eastern European, Romanian maybe."

"His wife told me they came from Bucharest seventeen years ago, did some work in New York, and then made their way across the country. She's a historian, and he was a Ukrainian student of Carl Jung who later, after World War II, became a psychologist at the university in Bucharest. He did a lot of research about the old vampire myths in that country. You know how Jung was fascinated by myth. Interesting background to this guy, anyway. We'll have to find out how they came to be involved in this counseling gig."

"Where will we meet them?" Danny asked.

"They have an apartment in the Capitol Hill area. I've wangled an invitation. You're free, then?"

"Yeah, ok. Should I pick you up? You're not that far from Capitol Hill, and I've got the car."

"I was going to ask, so, yeah, thanks. About 7:30, ok? I'll have all the gear."

The old, brick apartment building on Grant Street just off Colfax must have been imposing in its day. Its six stories rose from behind a narrow strip of grass between its front wall and the sidewalk. On each side of the glass-doored entrance were tall, mullioned windows that despite their frosting, emitted a soft, warm glow into the gathering evening. The windows of the apartments above were clear, but most were obscured by drapery. Danny hoisted the tape recorder, and he and Marian approached the doorway.

"I've got notes and questions here," she said, waving a spiral scribbler at him.

He nodded and opened the door for her.

The dimly lit lobby had a polished, marble floor, surprisingly clean. All was quiet. In Danny's imagination it was the kind of setting in which some dangerous character, Oddjob maybe, is hidden someplace, just waiting to jump out and kill them in a grotesque and grimly violent fashion. He looked around. Nothing. He smiled at his own silliness.

They rode in silence in the elevator up to the fourth floor, and one after the other they went out into a spacious hallway whose worn but once high-quality carpet runners led off to the right and left.

"This way, I think," Marian said, and she gestured to their left with a flutter of notebook pages.

After a few steps she said, "Here it is, number 407." She pressed a button beside the door, and moments later it opened, spilling light into the hall.

A foreign-sounding woman's voice said, "You must be Marian. Come in, come in."

The woman, rather severe-looking with a bun but a warm smile, stepped back. "I am Antonetta. And you're Danny," she said, as if she had known him by his photo, or perhaps ESP. "Slip off your shoes, please. You'll be more comfortable."

They did as instructed, Danny depositing his sneakers beside Marian's flats in front of what appeared to be a coat closet. When he looked up, Mrs. Nicolescu gave them an evaluative glance and looked down at the tape-recording equipment.

"You may use the recorder as we discussed," (she directed this instruction to Marian), "but in the event we ask you to turn it off you must comply. We may inadvertently reveal some details that should remain private. If we ask you to erase a segment, you must do so. Agreed?"

"Yes, of course," Marian said.

Antonetta nodded and indicated they should follow her.

Down a short hallway they emerged to their left into a spacious living room. Toward its rear was a small grand piano, open as if someone had been playing it. There was an assortment of soft furniture, a glass-topped coffee table, and some sentry palms, all upon a thick, Persian carpet of elaborate design. A balding, thin man looked up from some papers he had been reading, an open expression of interest on his face.

He set the papers aside on an end table under his reading lamp, and got up from his armchair, extending his hand to shake. "I am Dr. Nicolescu," he said, smiling noncommittally.

Danny shook his hand, and at his host's gesture, seated himself on a flowered sofa across the coffee table from their host's seat. Marian sat down beside him. Antonetta settled herself in a wingback leather chair at right angles to her husband and the guests, as if she might be ready to referee some contest from a neutral standpoint.

"You wish to talk to us about poltergeists, is that right?" he said, addressing Marian.

Marian nodded, and said to Danny, "Start the recorder, will you?" Then, with an apologetic gesture, she said to Nicolescu, "Sorry. Yes, that's right. Dr. Jacobs from The University of Denver informed me that you have had some unique experiences to do with poltergeist phenomena here in Denver, and that you might be prepared to share a description of them, and of how they affected you."

Danny had the recorder set up with the microphone on a stand between them on the coffee table.

"Is this ok?" he asked, and Antonetta replied curtly, "Yes, yes. Go ahead. You may turn it on."

Danny snapped the switch and the tape began to move on its reel.

Dr. Nicolescu watched the reel revolve a moment, then said, "Yes. We can speak about some things." He took a breath. "What do you wish to know?"

Marian nodded at Danny, and he began his questions using the notes Marian had prepared. "If you will, please tell

Alan W. Lehmann

us about poltergeists. We understand that you have specialized in counseling victims of poltergeist hauntings."

Nicolescu cleared his throat and said, "You must understand that poltergeist phenomena and hauntings are somewhat different. 'Poltergeist' is a German word meaning 'noisy spirit,' so named because these spirits' activities often include strange sounds, sometimes loud voices, and usually material damage, with everyday objects being strewn about, smashed, and so on. Poltergeists are associated with unhappy, usually female adolescents, who sometimes find themselves the unwitting channels for the spirit's destructive activities. Haunting, by contrast, is rather more associated with place than with a particular person. A poltergeist will often follow its channel person from place to place. Poltergeists can be very difficult to deal with, quite terrifying because they leave associated victims with a sense of helplessness."

Marian was scribbling notes into her coil book. Danny glanced over her arm at their question list. He asked, "Have there been many cases of poltergeist activity you have dealt with here in Denver?"

"Oh, yes, we have encountered at least three cases, one of them quite violent in that it resulted in several injuries to the family involved. I can't talk about that case, though."

"Can you elaborate on either of the other two?"

"Well," Nicolescu said, "you understand that I can't provide personal details. But yes, I can give you a general description. My wife and I received a call from a physician who had recently moved his family into an older house in one of the wealthier neighborhoods of the city. They have a teenage daughter, thirteen or so, who had been diagnosed with a learning disability and who was getting into difficulties at her school, physically fighting with other girls, insulting teachers, and so on. The parents finally removed her from school, hoping to engage a tutor to assist their daughter.

"A few days after the girl left school, the family, including their daughter, were eating a light supper in the kitchen at the rear of their house. Suddenly they heard a loud howling from upstairs, followed by a roar as if a great wind were buffeting the house—but it was calm outside. There were crashing sounds, loud bumps, scrapes as if furniture were being moved around.

"The father rushed to the stairs, only to be hit by a sports bag that came flying downward. He wasn't injured, but it was a shock, especially since there was no one from the family upstairs.

"As rapidly as they had begun, the noises suddenly ceased, having lasted only a couple of minutes at most. He and his wife cautiously ascended the stairs. The daughter's bedroom was in an utter shambles. The bed had been turned over, and the drawers had all been pulled from the dresser and emptied haphazardly on the floor. Clothes from the closet were strewn around the room, some of them tied in knots. Posters on the walls had been torn across and were hanging in shreds from their fasteners. The closet had been emptied out, with clothes and hangers tangled on the floor. But no one was in the room, and the window was closed and locked.

"The doctor turned back to where his daughter had climbed the stair behind her parents. She was backed against the wall of the hallway, alternately laughing hysterically and crying out, 'Oh, no! Oh, no!' Then she sank to the floor, her back against the wall, sobbing. It took them hours to straighten out the mess and to calm their daughter, who wouldn't speak for three days afterward."

There were a few seconds of silence while Danny and Marian absorbed this account. Then Danny asked, "How did you become involved? What did you do?"

Antonetta spoke up. "It is often thought that medical doctors are complete rationalists, practitioners of scientific medicine based on materialist science. This, of course, is humbug, for although perhaps a majority of doctors fit this description, many, many others are more open-minded. This gentleman's wife persuaded him to seek our help, despite his unfortunate belief that so-called paranormal occurrences are simply elaborate frauds. She had been something of a follower of paranormal phenomena when she was younger, and she knew of our presence in the city. Further, she had heard of my husband's reputation as a hypnotist."

She gestured to her husband, who spoke up once more.

"We visited their house twice. The first time I interviewed their daughter at length. She had been terribly shaken by the events. With her parents' permission, I used hypnosis to explore her memories and feelings, about the family, about her school (and the few friends she had had there). She told me of having been bullied by a particularly unpleasant girl in her grade. During an instance of being humiliated by this bully in the school washroom, she felt suddenly as if she had inhaled a great, smelly power, as if she could literally blow evil anywhere she chose. Naturally she was frightened of this sensation, realization, if you will. Sometimes she felt as if her body was occupied by some other being.

"As part of the hypnosis, I suggested that she instruct this being to leave her. She could thank this being for his attempts to help her and explain to it or him that he should go to assist someone else now, someone who needed his help more than she did any longer. Presumably she did so, for she sat under trance for some minutes, mumbling incoherent phrases that might have been some unknown or foreign language. She sighed and shook her head from side to side exclaiming, 'No. No.' Finally, she appeared to go to sleep. Her father picked her up and laid her on the sofa, covering her with a soft blanket. By his report, she apparently slept for eleven hours and woke, cheerful and happier than he had seen her for weeks.

"The second time I interviewed her a few days later she appeared completely normal and had returned to school, where she seemed to be doing much better. She didn't remember the events of our first session. The house has been quietly normal since. It was very gratifying to me to see that the hypnosis had worked."

Later in the car, Danny and Marian tried to absorb what they had heard. "This all seems pretty far-fetched," Danny said to her.

Marian didn't answer immediately, then she said, "I guess we'll see," although just how they were to verify any of this was problematic. All they really had was a story, although the counseling couple didn't seem transparently phony, but instead spoke as if they believed everything they recounted and expected their listeners to accept it, too.

"I'll make another copy of the tape," Marian said, as she climbed out in front of her apartment building.

"Ok," Danny said. "Call me when you're ready to move forward."

"I will," she said, and closed the door.

CHAPTER TWENTY-SIX

Tools for Conviviality

Conviviality—what an odd word! Danny thought.

He was sitting in a café down in Cherry Creek, nursing one of those latté coffees that Penny had introduced him to, and reading, as usual. The book, which he had just picked up at a yard sale, was *Tools for Conviviality* by Ivan Illich. Illich was a Jesuit-educated priest who thought and wrote about debilitating institutions, organizations that (according to his analysis) created "paradoxical counter-productivity." These included most professions including the medical establishment (doctors, hospitals, etc.) and education (formally sanctioned public schools, colleges and universities), both of which, Illich argued, caused more harm than the putative benefits they were designed to provide.

Danny had a rudimentary understanding of the etymology of Latin roots and affixes. *Let's see,* he thought, '*con*' means '*with*' or '*together*, and '*viv*' means live. *Tools for living together...*

At one time Danny had considered teaching as a career. But then he read Illich's *Deschooling Society*, an analysis that shocked him. In Illich's view, everything from curriculum selection to the physical organization of classrooms contributed to an overwhelming application of social power that in the process of delivering useful information and theories to children also delivered a *hidden* curriculum, one that trained them to be subservient to the state and to become unhealthily reliant on external definitions of their 'needs.' To Illich, this surreptitious conditioning was destructively antithetical to the touted purposes of schooling. Instead of freeing people to live for themselves within community, it bound people into conformist roles and isolated them as competitive individuals.

So, what was this new book all about? (New to Danny, anyway...) How did Illich put things now? *Something more positive*, Danny hoped.

> *Tools foster conviviality to the extent to which they can be easily used, by anybody, as often or as seldom as desired, for the accomplishment of a purpose chosen by the user.*

Wow, Danny thought. *That's real freedom.* He thought of the grand piano in the basement of the public library on South Grant Street, of how easy it was to drop in and play. It certainly fit the definition.

He swallowed the last of his coffee and got up to leave, dropping a couple of quarters on the table by way of a tip.

Beside the entrance was a bulletin board covered with an irregular mass of posters and notices. One in particular caught his eye. *Denver Free University! Call by our office for a catalog!* Beneath it was a strip of tear-off phone and address slips.

Serendipity? Danny thought, as he tugged one away.

Checking the address more closely, he noticed that the office wasn't far from the café, and rather than drive he walked the block and a half through the spring sunshine, mulling over the possibilities of access to tools.

The office was located on the second floor of a square, brick, office building. Danny missed the entrance at first, but he doubled back to where the *Free University* sign hung unobtrusively beside a single, glass doorway that led into a musty-smelling stairway to the upper floor. He trotted up the stairs and found himself in a small reception area furnished with a couple of futon couches, a stand lamp, a battered coffee table, and a desk with a telephone. A lanky black youngster in tank top and hi-top sneakers came in from a back room and sat down at the desk. Twiddling a pencil, he looked up at Danny and grinned.

"Yo, I'm Gary, what can I do for ya'?"

"I found your ad," Danny said. "Down at the coffee shop." He waved vaguely in the direction where he thought the shop was.

"Sure. You want to learn or to teach?"

"Teach?"

Gary leaned back in his sprung office chair and gesturing expansively with his left hand said, "This is a free university, man. Anyone can learn anything they want, and if they have something to teach, they can buy an ad in our calendar advertising their course. If enough people sign up (usually ten is the minimum), we'll find a space for you to teach your course."

"What kinds of courses are there?"

"Everything from flower arranging to Buddhist history. A doctor is teaching young women to prepare for childbirth. Twin sisters are teaching math and physics together. An old man from Louisiana is teaching organic soil preparation and gardening." He paused to take a breath. Fixing his eyes on Danny he said, "If you can think of it, we've probably got it."

Then he became more serious. "Now you gotta understand that this university doesn't have exams or degrees or anything like that. People who come here and who use our organization do it solely for the pleasure of learning something, hopefully something useful. Now you might think that some courses like," and here he picked up a catalog, and opening to a random page read, "*Reading Your Aura for Sexual Fulfillment* or *Do It Yourself Minor Surgery* are kind of weird and maybe useless, but, well, I mean, why not? If somebody can teach you how to clean out your own ingrown toenails, so much the better. And if something called an aura can give you great orgasms, who wouldn't want that? Tools for conviviality, man."

Waiting for a response, he stared up at Danny, who glanced back at him in surprise. *He's read Illich?!*

"Who runs this place, anyway?" Danny asked.

"You know, I forget his name right now. I've only worked here two days. He's cool, though. He used to be a manager for a composer, some guy who does comedy on stage, and writes some movie music. Maybe he still is for all I know. Lately he's branched out into this free learning stuff."

"And what does he pay you for?"

"Right now, I'm kinda just a gofer—go for this, go for that—and I answer the phones and talk to guys like you, explaining what we do. When the next semester begins I'll be signing people up into courses, collecting tuition fees, and so on."

"How much is tuition?" *Now we're cutting to the chase,* Danny thought.

"Whoever's teaching a course can charge however much or little he wants. We charge a fixed fee for a catalog entry, that's $25, and we offer space for classes at the property owner's rental cost plus 10% for our work setting it up. If a teacher should charge too much or doesn't interest people enough to have them sign up for his course, it doesn't run, but he's out the $25."

"Can I take a catalog?"

"Sure. Help yourself. There's a pile there by the door."

Danny glanced over toward the doorway where, sure enough, there were two piles of catalogs, each about two feet high.

"When's the next semester start?"

"Three and a half weeks, beginning of May."

Later that day he was eating a simple lunch at home, nose in a book, when Louise came in and sat down.

"Would you go out with me tonight?" she asked.

Danny looked at her, a number of unspoken questions lurking behind his eyes. Louise obviously read some of them.

"I don't mean anything romantic," she said.

Danny frowned, unsure whether or not to feel insulted.

"I want to go to the new Afghan restaurant over on Colorado Boulevard to see the belly dancer. I took a course from her three months ago through DFU, and I'm thinking about doing a second one. Anyway, she's performing on Friday night, but at that place there are always a couple of dozen weirdos in the audience drinking their coffees and raki, drooling over her and any other female they think they can get their hands on. If you're with me they'll leave me alone."

"Ah. You want a bodyguard," Danny observed.

"Well, yeah, sort of. But I'll buy your dinner. And you'll like the dancing, for sure. I mean, she's fantastic. Before coming to America, she danced for the Shah of Iran. She's really high calibre, one of the best."

"Ok," Danny said. "Deal. What time?" Then he asked, "DFU? Is that Denver Free University?"

"The same. It's a neat place. Carolyn's doing a rug-hooking course from there. Well, the course is over now, but you know that huge rug she's working on during *Monday Night Football*? She learned how to do that through DFU."

Go figure, Danny thought.

At 7:20 pm or so Danny held the door open for Louise at a restaurant called *The Khyber Pass*. Scents of fried onion and lamb drifted toward them as a swarthy maitre d' greeted them. He removed a toothpick from his mouth, bowed obsequiously, and said grandiosely, "Ah, welcome to the Khyber Pass. You are here for dinner? You would like a table?"

"We'd like a table near the stage," Louise said insistently. "If that's possible, that is."

He frowned. "You wish to see our dancer. Well, you know our featured entertainer this evening is very popular. Many people would like to be near the stage." He looked meaningfully at Louise. "Perhaps your escort would like to ensure such a table...?"

Oh, great, Danny thought. *Baksheesh.* But he smiled and extracted a five-dollar bill from his wallet and extended it to the man, who accepted it with another, shorter bow, and secreted it in a pocket with the dexterity of a card sharp or a magician.

"I believe we have such a table," he said. "This way."

He led them past a salad bar and between the haphazard arrangement of would-be diners to a smaller table for two beside the stage, which was dully lit by two footlights.

"I am afraid it is to the side," he said in mock apology. "But you will find the view exceptional, nonetheless."

He held a chair back for Louise, who nodded her thanks as she sat down. Danny seated himself to one side, ensuring that both of them could look directly at the stage..

"I will bring menus," the maitre d' announced, and he withdrew toward the dimly lit kitchen area.

"Thanks, Danny, honestly," Louise said. "You won't regret it. Guaranteed."

Danny nodded his acquiescence.

In due time a junior waiter appeared, smiling as if he were already totting up his tip, and tapping his pencil on an order slip. The two of them ordered some kebabs and sweet tea, and sat back.

"Excellent choice," the waiter said softly, a soft 'h' hissing after the 'x' and the 'ch,' a characteristic feature of his Farsi accent, Danny imagined.

Once the food had arrived and they had begun to eat, Danny asked, "How come Carolyn and Mac didn't want to come? Did you ask them?"

Louise looked at him over the rim of her tea glass. "Carolyn prefers keeping Mac at home. Mac has a bit of a roving eye, you know. He's tried it on with me once or twice. I wasn't having any of it, of course. Carolyn's my friend. But she keeps him on a pretty tight leash."

She sighed, remembering Mac's little sexual gambits. "He thought he'd tell me a joke to get me in the mood. He said, 'How do you do a mouse a favor? Eat a pussy.' Apparently, that was supposed to be hilarious. Yuk, yuk. Or utterly seductive. All I could think was, 'Stay away.'"

She looked at Danny as if searching for confirmation of her good sense. "But at the same time, I never thought having to keep a man on a leash was a good way to go about having a relationship," she added philosophically.

Danny thought about their trip to New Mexico, about Randy. He had seemed less than reliable, Danny thought, another rover. *But then again*, he considered, *having a suicidal girlfriend might just drive you away*. He wondered how long Louise had been suffering her depression. She seemed somewhat more upbeat these days. *Belly dancing as therapy,* he thought.

Just then the lights on the stage brightened and a spotlight was switched on from above, well to the back somewhere. The maitre d', who had donned a scarlet jacket for his role as MC, announced, "Ladies and gentlemen, the treat you've all been waiting for: the wonderful Zelda!"

Danny guessed it was going to be her first set, for they had barely finished their kebabs. But he could be patient. And he was curious.

Wild, rhythmic Middle Eastern music started suddenly, the kind with that nearly atonal nasality that's prone to make western listeners cringe. The maitre d' jumped forward off the low stage, and turning back toward it, began applauding vigorously as he backpedaled away. At this cue the audience followed suit, clapping enthusiastically, some of them standing. Seconds later a dark-haired beauty with kohl around her eyes and small finger cymbals chattering in her hands swept onto the stage from behind a side curtain, gyrating to the rhythms of the music.

Danny sat back in his chair, eyes riveted on her undulating form, her naked belly rippling and revolving as she moved, barefoot, in time to the music.

She was astonishingly lithe, muscles flexing and limbs moving with a startling fluidity and grace. Her eyes were lit with concentration, her face almost ecstatic, with an easy smile that occasionally was hidden by a cascade of her long, dark hair. Then she would snap her head sideways, the hair flowing away from her face, as she spun and writhed.

"I told you so," Louise offered, as Danny gaped at the woman.

After several minutes, the dancer began to move from table to table around the edge of the stage. She would sidle rhythmically toward a specific onlooker, eyes smoking into his, mesmerizing him with her rippling movements. One moustached man wearing dark glasses raised his hand toward her and tucked a bill into her waistband; then, a smiling GI at the next table did likewise. Never slowing her movements, she would nod, a gesture of recognition or gratitude for their gifts, and whirl away toward the next table.

"Here's a dollar," Louise said. "If she comes here, tuck it into her elastic belt." She extended the bill to Danny, who accepted it reluctantly.

True to anticipation, Zelda stepped toward their table, her belly vibrating madly, her hands over her head tinkling the cymbals, her eye on Danny, her expression one of amused joy.

For a moment, he felt an immense reluctance to move, an inertia compounded by his natural shyness. Louise slapped his forearm lightly, and as if wakening from a trance, he reached out with the bill. Just as he did so, Zelda turned away, her luscious bottom vibrating toward his face, almost obscene, but she stared down at him over her shoulder, smiling radiantly with what seemed to Danny an ecstatic happiness. With infinite care, he tugged the elastic away from her bum just sufficiently to slip the bill into its grip, and he let it go. She laughed lightly as she sprang away, spinning toward another table.

Christ, she's beautiful, Danny thought, and just as the thought occurred to him Louise said, "Beautiful, isn't she?" Danny nodded. He'd never experienced anything like this, ever.

"Better than sex?" Louise asked, a smile playing about her lips.

All Danny could say was, "Wow." And after a brief pause, "Wow," once more. Then, grinning, he added, "I wonder what Allah would think of all this," and he remembered his Iranian client with the Koran tapping his nose and murmuring to him, "Inshallah."

On the way home in the car, he asked, "So what do those belly dancing lessons cost you?"

"Twenty-five dollars for four lessons," Louise answered. "Worth every nickel. I mean, I know I'll never dance like she does, but just the dancing itself, and the movements she shows you—it's like nothing else."

She turned and smiled at Danny, a happy smile, Danny thought. Turning his eye back to the traffic, he smiled, too. *Conviviality*, he thought.

CHAPTER TWENTY-SEVEN

Ghosts (2)

Two days after the Afghan dinner, the phone rang early. Danny had the day off and was just pouring himself a coffee, looking out the kitchen window, thinking of the morning ahead.

"Yup, Danny here," he said into the receiver. He pulled the long cord toward the toaster where his breakfast had just popped up.

"Danny, it's Marian."

He felt a frisson of excitement. "Oh, hi. I'd begun to think you'd forgotten about the project."

"No way," she said emphatically. "Two things. First, yesterday I had a long talk with a woman real estate developer who's been working on a project to do with an old orphanage out in the west end. She had a really interesting tale to tell, and I'll bring you up to speed on that later. But second, are you free today? 'Cause I think I've just set up another cool interview, if you can be ready by about 10:00 am."

"Sure. It's my day off. Where are we going?"

"It's down here again, not far from City Park. It's that guy who claims to have had, and still to have, some ghosts in his house. Pick me up?"

"Ok. I'll be there about 9:45, all right?"

"I'll wait out front this time. Ciao." She rang off abruptly.

Danny made sure Feather had some cat food in her bowl and some clean water. Then he sat down to read until it was time to go. It was *Hamlet* this time. After Pauline had mentioned "Heaven and Earth" and "philosophy" he had picked it up at a garage sale, and he had just opened it up last night. He had fallen asleep on the first page, so he thumbed it open at the beginning once more.

Who's there? the opening line read. Danny paused and thought, *Damn good question. It could be the guard talking to the other one, or it could be Shakespeare talking to me, the reader. God he was a clever sod.* He remembered reading the play in his English class in high school, the weirdness of the language, and yet the tremendous tension in the plot, and the amusement he had found in Hamlet's acid wit. He had almost cried at Hamlet's final remark—*the rest is silence.*

Due to his unexpected immersion in the play, he was five minutes late to pick up Marian, who stood on the curb in front of her apartment building, an irritated expression on her face. But once she had deposited the recorder in the back seat and taken her place in the other bucket seat beside him, she greeted him civilly with, "Good morning."

"Which way?" Danny said.

"Just stay put a minute, ok? I want to tell you about that woman at the orphanage."

"Sure, ok."

Marian took a deep breath. "The woman I talked to is someone from the upper echelons of a real estate development company here in Denver. They're quite the outfit. You know that avant-garde new office building just down from the Oxford Hotel? They acquired that property, designed the structure and built it. Won some kind of architecture award. Anyway, they've been looking to acquire an old building out in the west end that used to be an orphanage. It was built in the late 1920's, a solid, brick, three-story building. It probably held between two and three hundred orphans at a time in its busiest period. A charity sponsored by a group of protestant churches operated the place, but there was a series of scandals, and they closed it down in the early 1960's. Now this woman's company wants to turn it into condos. Apparently, the structure is sound, and it has a great view overlooking Sloan's Lake, making it a very desirable location.

Danny could see how appealing that might be. *I wonder how people ever come to have enough money to buy these things?* he thought.

"Management of the company suggested that this woman go over there and have a look through the building. She has some expertise in preservation planning and materials conservation. You know, what are some of the old building's features that they'd want to keep just because they add character or have some historical significance that should be preserved?

Danny nodded. "I get it," he said.

"She drove over to the building about two months ago and went in to have a look around. One of the striking features of this old place is a bell tower that rises from the central entry hall. The bell is just visible from the parking lot out front. She decided she'd like to have a look up there.

"It took her some time to find the correct stairwell, whose entry was nearly hidden behind a supporting column for the tower. The door to the stairwell wasn't locked, and she climbed the fifty or sixty steps to the belfry. She said the old bell was rusty and corroded, but still solid, and she wondered when it might actually have been rung last..."

Marian sighed, as if listening to its tolling in her imagination. "Pigeons had been nesting up there for over a decade since the orphanage shut down, she said, and there was dust and pigeon shit everywhere, but no sign anyone had been up there for years. But the climb was worth it, she said, as there was a fabulous view out over the lake and to the city beyond."

"But something happened to her there that scared the bejesus out of her. She was just at the top of the first narrow flight of stairs that would crisscross the tower back down to the lobby. She suddenly felt a cold breath on her neck and cheek. Just as she turned in alarm, she felt a push in the small of her back. She grabbed the old handrail, which came partly away from its anchors, and she fell about eight feet, spraining her wrist and getting a number of ugly bruises."

"She gathered her breath and looked back up the stairs, but there was no sign of anyone, not a sound. She was terrified! She got to her feet and hurried down to the lobby. Once she was out in the parking lot she looked again up at the bell tower to see if anyone or anything was visible. There was nothing to be seen, of course. She thought about calling the police but decided against it. She imagined they'd probably put her experience down to hysterical fantasy or give her some other sexist put-down."

"She *did* mention the event to one of her co-workers back at the office. He said to her that the old place had a reputation, that he'd seen stories in some of the research he'd done on the history of the place that could make your skin crawl! Allegations of child abuse, violence, untimely deaths, that sort of thing. But he'd written it off as probably old hokum embellished to sell newspapers, that sort of thing. Wild, huh?"

Marian took a deep breath. "Anyway, I'm hoping to arrange to interview her at length, maybe do a whole episode on the building and its history. What do you think?"

Danny thought a moment, listening to the buzz of nearby traffic, imagining the woman's fright. "I think it's just the ticket, exactly the sort of thing you had in mind when you first came up with this idea."

"I don't mind telling you," she said, "these stories are spooking *me* a little—more than a little. But, well, let's go forward. Let's find today's appointment." She looked ahead out the dusty windshield.

"Drive up the block just to the parkway that runs along the north side of City Park. We'll run east along there a few blocks and then turn north on Madison. I know the house number. I'll watch for it. Number 9386, on the west side of the street."

Marian's directions were spot on, and a few minutes later Danny pulled them into a parallel parking space only steps from the door. "Looks like this is it," he said. The two of them took a long look at the house from inside the car, as if reconnoitering some possible danger.

The neighborhood was decrepit. Several of the houses along the street had been boarded up, their yards weedy and unkempt behind twisted chain-link fences. The curbing was cracked and uneven.

The house, too, was a strange-looking old place, run-down if apparently still inhabitable. It had the traditional two stories, with its main entrance to the right and what was probably a parlor or living room behind a large, heavily draped window on the left. The concrete steps appeared sagged and worn, and the once proud siding was now an irregularly faded tan color. Above the second story under the gable was a tiny, round window, probably merely decorative, Danny decided.

"Well?" Danny asked. It was more of a suggestion, really, but it sought agreement.

"Sure. Let's go."

Danny retrieved the recorder from the back seat, and the two of them trudged across the street and up onto the porch. A spider's web stretched between the stair rail and the porch overhang, wavering back and forth in the light breeze. Danny noticed a captured fly, struggling in a corner of the sticky net. Despite the air movement, there was a slightly unpleasant odor emanating from somewhere. Marian wrinkled her nose, but she gamely reached up and knocked three times on the painted door.

For a few moments there was no sound. Danny looked at the spider's web once more. *I wonder what a fly thinks when it gets caught?* he wondered. Then, without any expected footstep's warning, the latch clicked and the door swung silently inward. A short, stout man in jeans and a plaid shirt stepped forward. He looked to Danny like a small-town prairie dweller from the 1950's.

"Yes?" the man said. It was a soft but rather deep voice, almost shy-sounding, as if it had been muted by experience.

"I'm Marian, the woman who called you last night?"

"Oh, yes, of course. I thought your knock might be a few of the neighborhood children. They sometimes think it's fun to bang on my door and run away." He paused, frowning, as if momentarily disappointed that he hadn't caught those nefarious little perps. Then he said, "Please, come in," and he stepped back to indicate that his two guests should go into the living room." To Danny's ear the man's speech was unexpectedly correct, well enunciated compared to the more casual accents he commonly heard in Denver.

Inside the door to the right was a narrow staircase leading to the upper floor, and between the staircase and the living room a dark passageway extended toward the rear, presumably to a kitchen or some similarly functional room. There was an odor of coffee and fried bacon.

The house seemed even older once they got into the living room and had a chance to sit down and look around. The whole place had a worn-out feel. A stained, threadbare rug was centered over what might once have been a fine, hardwood floor. The walls featured ugly floral wallpaper above an aged wainscot of some dark wood. The light switch was an old, bakelite, round one, with braided wiring running up the wall from a hole in the floor-level coving. Presumably some of the wiring, at least, ran underneath the house.

Their host settled into a stuffed armchair of indeterminate age that didn't quite match the sofa on which Danny and

Marian had seated themselves. Danny set the recorder down on the shabby coffee table before him while Marian took out her notebook.

"What would you like to know?" And then, looking at Danny, he said, "I'm Franklin."

Danny nodded and replied, "Danny." He switched on the recorder and positioned the mike more or less midway between the three of them. "Is it ok to record this?

Franklin nodded.

Marian passed a list of questions to Danny, who asked, "How long have you lived here in Denver, and in this house in particular?"

"About twelve years, give or take a few months. I came here from Witchita in the early sixties."

"How did you acquire this place, if you don't mind my asking?"

Franklin scratched briefly behind his ear and said, "This house belonged to some distant relatives of my mother. It was left to her in 1957 as a remnant from my great aunt's estate. When my mother took possession, various people lived here as renters, as our family was comfortably off in Kansas. But when the company my father worked for went bankrupt, he became depressed and shot himself." Franklin paused to reflect. There was no sign of loss or sorrow in his demeanor. It appeared to Danny that he had apparently come to terms with these events a long time ago.

"You can imagine that this event greatly troubled my mother and me (I was an only child, although I was more or less grown up), but soon after my father's passing she developed breast cancer and died only eight or nine months later. After my dad's death I had gone back to college in Pennsylvania. But when my mother's health deteriorated and then she suddenly died, I had to drop out of my program in order to come back west to get my parents' affairs in order. I decided to sell our home in Witchita and come here to Denver. I'm really not sure why. It's one of those decisions a person takes partly on a whim. I guess I wanted to forget about the sadness back in Kansas. I've been here ever since."

Marian took a breath and then asked, "When did you conclude that there were ghosts in the house? How did that happen?"

A hint of a smile crossed Franklin's face. "It wasn't long after I moved in here that I began to realize that there were some other beings present. I would hear people moving about upstairs, for example, although I knew there was no one in the house. The master bedroom upstairs was always cold, even after I brought in a separate electric heater. I sensed that someone was watching me, all the time. I wasn't afraid, exactly, but it was a little unnerving, nonetheless. Finally, I began to speak to these beings (I say beings, because I'm sure there was more than one).

"The master bedroom still had a few pieces of old furniture in it that had belonged to previous occupants, including a credenza near the window. In a small, compartment that the executor must have somehow overlooked, I found a series of love letters to a woman named Iris from a man who had obviously been in Europe fighting in World War II. At the bottom of the packet was a telegram from the U.S. Army informing Iris that her husband, Henry Unger, had been killed in action.

The usual phrases of gratitude for his service to the country, and all that, were included.

"For one reason or another I began to speak to this Iris, calling her by her name. When I did this, I would hear flutters and creaks from various parts of the house, as if she was moving about. I said to her, 'Iris, please don't stay attached to your loss here, you must move on, for Henry undoubtedly awaits you on the other side.' I said this to her more than once. Finally, I heard a sound like a great, distant wind, and seconds later I was sure that she was gone. Very strange. But I've never sensed her here again." He looked at the two younger people and gave them a sort of apologetic smile as if to say, *I know it sounds weird and unbelievable, but it's true.*

Danny said, "You referred to more than one ghost's being in the house."

Franklin nodded. "Oh, yes, there was one more who has since left, and there's still one here as we speak. In fact, he could be in the room with us right now." He smiled at Marian's obvious discomfiture and she looked away.

"Can you tell us about them?" Danny asked.

"One of them was the ghost of a young woman, perhaps an adolescent. I'm sure she died a terrible and painful death on these premises. More about that later. I did eventually convince her to move on in a similar manner to the way Iris left.

"The other ghost is the spirit of a retired farmer from Nebraska who lived and later died here in the 1930's. Apparently, he managed to sell out his farm before the great crash in 1929 and the subsequent Depression, and he lived here until sometime before the war. I've *seen* him."

"*Seen* him?" Danny exclaimed, and Marian drew her breath in sharply.

"Yes, a couple of times. He's often wearing coveralls and chewing a piece of grass. He chuckles from time to time, as if he's a man who likes a joke. In fact, he pulls a number of different stunts, little practical jokes on *me*. I don't mind having him around. He's good company, in a way."

"What kind of jokes?" Marian asked.

"Sometimes he'll flick the lights on and off, for example."

At just that moment the overhead light flicked on, flickered two or three times, and went out again.

Marian emitted a little half moan. Danny stared at Franklin to try to see where the switch was that he was manipulating the lights with, but Franklin's hands were on the arms of his chair.

"He is a bit of a rascal," Franklin said. "Aren't you?" he said to the room in a louder voice, and the lights flicked again.

Marian looked wide-eyed at Danny, big saucers of incomprehension.

Now Danny was really interested. "How did you do that?" he asked.

Franklin didn't reply. The three of them were silent for twenty seconds or so, Franklin smiling as if he'd just told a fine joke, and Danny staring at him with a fascinated skepticism. Marian reached over and briefly took Danny's arm, then let it go once more.

"What about the third ghost?" Danny asked. "You had something more to tell us about her."

"Sure," Franklin said. He raised his hand in something like an instructive gesture as he gathered his thought.

"I was sure that this adolescent girl died violently in the house. (I never got her name, or the farmer's, for that matter, even though we're kind of friends.) But I failed initially to sort out exactly how it happened, the girl's death, I mean. I spoke to this young woman a lot, but for a long time could never get any clear reply, imagined or otherwise that held any conviction for me."

He looked at the two of them, as if to gauge the depth of their credence. "You know how terrible care was for the mentally ill earlier this century?" He stared intently at the two of them.

"Yes," Danny said. In his own efforts to understand himself he had read many accounts of the atrocities committed in asylums for the mentally ill—rapes, beatings, and so on.

Franklin said, "For one reason or another, I began to think that this young lady had been mentally ill, and that her parents had kept her hidden away somewhere in the house, for her own protection as much as to obscure the scandal from the neighborhood. A few months after I moved in here, I decided to try to examine the attic, but I couldn't find an attic door anywhere. After a thorough search, I located it by stripping off the lathe and plaster on the ceiling of the master bedroom closet. There was a trap door hidden there through which I broke into the attic. What I found confirmed my theory."

"Really?" Danny said. "What did you find?"

"There was once a fire in the attic. All the studs, especially at the front nearer the street, are charred to a greater or lesser degree, although they're still sturdy. At the front of the house, where that small, round window looks out over the street, is a boxed-in room whose framed door opening is more like a third the size of a regular doorway. I think this girl was kept away in this little room, probably locked in. Who knows? She may have knocked over a kerosene lantern or something, starting the fire. I think she died there." He paused, then said, "Would you like to see?"

Marian touched Danny's arm again.

Danny said, "Sure. If it's no trouble."

Franklin got to his feet and said, "Follow me."

"Are you sure?" Marian whispered to Danny, and he nodded.

Franklin was at the living room entrance, and he said, "Come on," and led them to the front stair.

The two young people followed him up the stairs where he turned to his left and into a large bedroom. Against the far wall they could see an open closet with a ladder fastened to its back wall.

Franklin looked at Danny and said, "Go ahead. Have a look." He smiled. "There's nothing to be afraid of."

Marian stayed at the bedroom door, her hand on the jamb, watching.

Danny crossed the room and slowly climbed the ladder, poking his head up through the trap entry to the attic.

It was just as Franklin had described it. All the surface wall materials of the little room had presumably burned away, and the studs were all charred and blackened on their inside faces. A wan light shone through the little round window. Everything was quiet.

"Danny!" Marian called.

He stepped hurriedly down off the ladder. Franklin was reclined on his elbows on the edge of his big bed watching the two of them, a faint smile playing about his lips.

"Danny, I think we'd better go now," Marian said.

Danny looked at her. She seemed suddenly frail in the weak light through the translucent bedroom curtains.

"Yeah, ok," he said.

Danny didn't hear from Marian for several weeks. Late one afternoon he decided to call her, see what was going on.

"Hey Marian, how's it going?" he asked when she picked up the phone.

"Ok," she said.

"I was wondering," he asked, "what's next on the agenda for our ghost project?"

There was a moment's silence. Then Marian said, "I don't think I want to do this project any more. Nothing to do with you, you've been great. It's just not for me."

Danny felt momentarily deflated. But he said, "Well, if you're sure. I thought we were getting some good stuff there, but..." He paused, remembering the fear on Marian's face when the lights flicked, and the alarm in her voice being left at least partially alone with Franklin in the bedroom.

"Ok, I understand," he finally said.

CHAPTER TWENTY-EIGHT

Just My 'Magination

Danny used to love singing to himself—in the car, in the shower, walking along a sidewalk, nearly anywhere. *What is it about lyrics and music*, he wondered to himself, *the way they can speak as if from deep inside us, even when they were written by somebody else?*

The Temptations' hit *Just My 'Magination* was swirling through his own imagination as he whistled its melody, walking down Atlantic Avenue toward home. *Runnin' away with me...*

Just before he reached the house he noticed a nondescript grey sedan parked in front. That was unusual. He had left the Volvo out front, as well, and this car was parked right in front of it, only about fifteen yards from the corner. As he approached the two cars he further noticed that two men were sitting in the front seat of the new vehicle. That *was* strange. He felt a frisson of unease, and he picked up his pace, hastening up the front walk to the house's front door, and slipping inside, closing it firmly behind him.

Walking into the kitchen, where Carolyn was dishing out some stew for her little boy, Danny asked, "Know anything about those two guys in the parked car out front? What are they, JW's or Amway or something?"

Carolyn set the pot back down on the stove top, placed the steaming bowl and a spoon in front of her son, and asked, "What two guys?"

Oh shit, Danny thought, *I hope she doesn't think it's her daddy again...*

Carolyn slipped into the living room and from the side of the window where she could not be seen from out front, peered at the vehicle.

"I don't recognize them," she finally said, looking back at Danny. The two of them went back into the kitchen. Danny took a Michelob out of the fridge, popped it open, and had a drink. He sat back down. Carolyn just watched him, then said to her little boy, "Come on, eat up your stew, now. 'Sgood for you."

Jody scowled a little, took another mouthful and chewed resentfully.

"Hey, buddy," Danny said, trying to be helpful, "I wish I had a mom to make stew for me."

Jody just glared at him.

Danny resumed thinking about the strangers outside. He knew that his own tourist visa to the US, as well as that of Mac, Carolyn's man, had expired. Technically they weren't supposed to be in the country. He suddenly shivered. Could these guys be after him? But then why didn't they simply come to the door to inquire? He sat at the kitchen table, mulling over the possibilities. He didn't want to blow up what might be a simple coincidence into some danger that wasn't even real. He thought of Louise carrying money into Mexico to get Randy. *It's a crazy world*, he observed to himself.

He got up again and went to the same observation spot Carolyn had used and looked out. The two men just sat there, less than forty feet away, staring ahead through the windshield. One of them sipped coffee from a paper cup. Then he turned and glanced over toward the house, a kind of speculative assessment in his expression. Danny remained still, the barest sliver of his profile perhaps visible from the car (but unlikely), and the man turned away.

Back in the kitchen he said, "I'm going to call a lawyer."

Carolyn looked at him. "Ya think?" she said.

Danny tugged a thick phone book out of the drawer under the desk telephone that sat on the end of the counter.

"Where's the Yellow Pages?" he asked, a bit of urgency in his voice. *Where ARE the Yellow Pages?* a little voice queried in the back of his mind.

"I've got that big book downstairs," Carolyn replied. "I was looking at antique shops. I'll go get it."

She went quickly down the stairs.

Jody was stirring his big spoon around in the thickened gravy in his bowl, making circular patterns, lifting out globs of meat and dropping them back into the bowl. Plop! He hummed a nondescript melody to himself, off in some other world of childhood imagination.

Carolyn returned with the thick volume of phone numbers and advertisements. "Here," she said, thumping it down on the counter.

Danny flipped through the contents looking for 'lawyers.' He was referred to 'attorneys,' and he flipped back toward the front of the heavy paperback. He ran his finger down a column, tapped it once, and picked up the phone. He dialed a number.

"Merrick and Jones," a female voice answered.

"Hi. My name's Daniel Kerrigan," Danny said, inventing a last name. *Where the hell did Kerrigan come from*? he wondered. "I'd like to speak to an attorney, please."

"I can put you through to Mr. Merrick, if that's alright?" the voice said.

"That'll be fine."

There were a few seconds of silence, followed by the click of the receiver opening the line. Behind was music and some laughter. "This is Dave Merrick," a male voice said. "How can I help you?" Another gust of laughter in the background, then silence. Danny could imagine Merrick waving his hand to shut up whoever else was in the room.

"Hi, I'm Daniel Kerrigan," Danny said once more.

"Yes."

"I have a kind of delicate inquiry, if you don't mind."

"Go ahead. What can I do for you?"

"I'm a Canadian citizen here in the US on a tourist visa. I've accidentally allowed it to run out, but I'm not ready to leave the country yet. I'm in a rental house here in Denver. We've got two men in a parked car in front of our house. They've been there for, oh, a couple of hours now. I was wondering if they might be immigration officials or someone like that."

"Huh. Immigration, huh? Where do you live? I can make a call or two and ring you back."

Danny hesitated a moment. Then he said, "5538 Atlantic Avenue, just by Holly Street."

"Give me your number. I'll get back to you shortly."

Danny supplied the number and hung up. He went back to the table and sipped his beer, now warm and somewhat flat.

Carolyn had sent Jody downstairs and was wiping the table that she had already cleared.

"So?" she asked.

"He's going to call back."

Danny tapped his fingers on the table impatiently. Carolyn sat opposite, leaning on her elbows. They waited.

A couple of minutes later the phone rang. Danny got up.

"Hello?"

"Mr. Kerrigan?"

"Yes."

"I made a couple of calls for you. You've got nothing to worry about. Unless they get out their guns or something."

Danny's heart skipped.

"I mean, they're not after you or anything like that. They *are* police. There've been a string of holdups at convenience stores recently. They're staking out the 7-11 across Holly Street on the opposite corner." He chuckled. "If there's a holdup, they're Johnny-on-the-spot to take out the crooks."

"Wow," Danny said. "That kind of explains things."

"Sure. Besides," Merrick said, "Immigration aren't chasing down Canadians. They don't care about you and wouldn't even if they knew you were here. They're after wetbacks."

"Wetbacks?"

"You know, illegal Mexicans. That's who they'd be after."

Danny took a breath. "Well, Jeez, thanks," he said. Then, after a thought, "Do I owe you anything?"

Merrick chuckled. "Don't mention it. It's the most amusing work I've had all week. But maybe check into getting your visa renewed, don't you think?"

"Sure thing," Danny said. "Yeah, I'll do that. Thanks a lot. You've calmed down some grim imaginings."

"No problem." Merrick hung up the phone with a click.

Danny replaced the receiver in its cradle and turned to Carolyn. "No problem," he said. "For us, I mean."

"Well, good," Carolyn said. "So, who are those guys?"

"They're cops, staking out the 7-11."

"Jaysus," she said. "*The Rockford Files,* huh?"

"Yeah, just about."

The lines played themselves back in his head, James Garner at his most casual: "This is Jim Rockford. Leave a message. I'll get back to ya." BEEP

Danny thought of the lawyer and plugged Angel into a smart grey suit, talking to him on the phone. He grinned. Then he got up and headed for his room.

CHAPTER TWENTY-NINE

Stories of the Street

"So how did you decide to lead the club jack there?"

The question was addressed by an excited, university age young man to an older, elegantly dressed woman as they descended the entry stairs of the Brown Palace Hotel toward Danny's cab. The woman thought for a moment as she opened the taxi's rear door.

"I thought it prudent to uppercut the trump king on the table," she said, smiling. "Down one!"

Looking skeptically at a stain on the back seat cover, she nonetheless slipped inside and settled herself, brushing some imaginary lint from her sleeve. The young man hustled around to the other side to climb in beside her.

Danny looked above the hotel entrance, where beneath some red, white and blue bunting, a banner proclaimed, *COLORADO ACBL REGIONAL TOURNAMENT, March 8 - 17!*

Bridge! he thought to himself. He considered momentarily his weekly bridge game with Dick and Janet, and he remembered his high school English teacher, the draft dodger, explaining the game to him and a group of his friends one day after school. Danny had stared at the layout in dummy, utterly uncertain how to proceed.

"Don't lead that ace!" the teacher warned, as Danny had reached to pick it up. "It's your last entry to the board." *What a puzzle!* Danny had thought.

"Where do you want to eat, Ma?" the young man asked as he leaned back in the car seat. "Maybe down in Larimer Square?"

"Sure," she said. "You pick."

"Where to?" Danny asked, impatient to get moving. *Time is money*, he muttered in the back of his mind.

"How about Marco's? You know, the Italian place, on the corner of 15th there?"

"Sure thing," Danny said.

He pulled the cab away from the curb into the light evening traffic as, jabbering about suits and slams, more bridge players spilled out of the hotel entrance.

How do people afford to do this kind of thing? Danny wondered. Staying in a luxury hotel to play cards was a concept of expenditure that was way out of his league. Turning onto 15th, he thought of some of the other trendy hangouts where he picked up customers and dropped them off. Who could afford to eat out at these places? *I guess I've just become more or less accustomed to near poverty.* He glanced at the shabby jacket on the seat beside him, one he had picked up at the St. Vincent de Paul where he bought most of his clothes. There was little to nothing wrong with the clothes. They were just second hand. Who could argue with a shirt priced at a dollar fifty? He didn't feel he was suffering. If anything, he enjoyed the beauty of a bargain. Yet he also had the sense that there was some vast inequity at work there, acted out in the city's leisure locations and high-rise office buildings.

The young man in the rear was scanning through a large, duplicated handout. In the mirror, Danny could see bridge hands laid out on its surface in neat squares. He turned his attention back to the traffic.

The older woman said, "You played that heart game on board 13 really well. Your finesse of the heart queen and then the end play was really inspired..."

"Thanks, Ma. That was a fun hand."

Danny pulled the car into the curb in front of Marco's, where beside the restaurant entrance, a tall black man held the hand of a shorter blonde white woman, the two of them waiting to be seated. She beamed up at his face, said something, and he chuckled happily.

Taking one look at the two, the woman in the back said in a disgusted tone, "Not here." To Danny she directed, "Go on to the pizza restaurant down the street."

Her son, who had been about to climb out of the car, looked back at her, then pulled his leg back in and closed the door. Glancing at Danny's face in the mirror, he said nothing, his own face giving nothing away.

Danny looked back at them and nodded. They pulled out once more, stopped for a minute while the light down the street hung red, and on the green proceeded to the new location. At the curb, the young fellow handed Danny a ten-dollar bill across the back of the front seat. "Keep it," he said.

"Thanks."

Danny climbed out to hold the door for the woman, who acknowledged the courtesy with a bare nod. As the two headed to the entrance, Danny heard her son say, "Really, Ma, you've got to get over this thing you've got with niggers. Negroes," he corrected himself. Danny watched them enter the restaurant.

It wasn't the first time he had encountered this kind of racist animosity, from all sides of the racial spectrum. Cab driving provided an ongoing cabaret of racist slurs and denigrating comments. "Look at those god-damned wetbacks," a black basketball player had commented one day as Danny drove him past a Mexican restaurant where a family was waiting to get in. "Fuckin' country's goin' to hell." Grinning at his own bigotry, and expression of grim amusement, the basketball player had looked at Danny. "You a honkey," he said. "Don't tell me you want those spics on our streets," he accused, and turned back to the window. "I sure don't, anyway."

Later that evening, Danny was cruising down North Broadway toward downtown. "Sixth and Logan," the radio barked. "Five, four..."

"Two five four," Danny called.

"Two five four, go to Capital Arms at 575 Logan. Meet a Dr. Parks there and take him to Porter Hospital."

"Roger."

Four minutes later Danny pulled into the apartment house entry drive. A grey-haired man stood waiting under an awning, holding what appeared to be clothing folded on his left forearm.

"Dr. Parks?"

The man nodded through the open right window. Danny leaned across and opened the door. Dr. Parks slid onto the front seat and tugged the door shut beside him.

"Porter Hospital?" Danny asked.

The man nodded. He appeared to be thinking hard about something, so at first Danny didn't initially intrude. Instead, he concentrated on his route. "Harvard and Downing, right?" he asked after a moment. Dr. Parks nodded once more.

Stopped at a red light, Danny noticed that the doctor had slipped his hand out from under the clothing, which appeared to be a pair of flannel pajamas. He was gripping a toothbrush in a transparent plastic container. With his other hand he set a tube of toothpaste down on the pajamas and lifted an elegant finger to scratch his nose.

"Packing light?" Danny said lightly.

"The natives are restless tonight," Parks said thoughtfully. "There was a gun battle between rival gangs over in the Chicano area west of Federal Boulevard late this afternoon. Seventeen young men with gunshot wounds! Four killed! Can you believe it?" He stared Danny in the eye a moment. "I'm going to be doing surgery for three days."

Wow, Danny thought. *You always think you're safe out here on the streets, but it's an illusion.* He thought of the dispatcher's earlier warning to stay away from S. Federal Boulevard. He hadn't considered it deeply at the time, just obeyed.

When he stopped at the hospital entry, the doctor said, "Go around to Emergency. There's an orderly there who'll pay you." Parks clambered out of the car and stalked into the building.

Danny had been to Porter before. He remembered being paid the same way when he had delivered a human heart in an icebox that had been flown in by private jet to Stapleton. A college student killed in a car accident had donated his organs, and the heart was for some cardiac patient on a wait list. The blue styrofoam box wrapped securely with duct tape had sat meaningfully on the floor, chilled heart waiting while Danny navigated from the airport to the hospital. Before that job he would never have believed something so important would be delivered this way. But he was well familiar with the payment routine.

Later that night, early the next morning, really, he parked the cab in front of the pancake house on Water Street. It was a dimly lit place in a rundown area near the railroad tracks, right near the river. But it was cheap, and it had never-ending coffee. At least twice a month Danny would meet other drivers there for an end-of-shift breakfast.

A row of three other cabs was already parked out front, lights out, off duty. Today he had agreed to meet Heath there for their late-night meal. Heath had reconsidered his abject resignation from the business, despite the shocks he had endured earlier that year. That pleased Danny, because Heath was a decent sort, honest and trustworthy, as far as Danny could make out.

Sure enough, when Danny entered he spied Heath and two other drivers drinking beers and eating waffles in a booth toward the back. He wandered down to join them, inhaling the welcoming aromas of syrup and coffee.

"How's it going, guys?" he asked as he slid into the booth beside Jeremy, another cabby.

Grinning opposite, Heath said, "Tell him your story, Jeremy."

Jeremy snickered. "I was driving down Colfax Avenue this afternoon down by where those two porn theaters are. I stopped at the red light there. Ha-ha. Red light. Get it?"

Danny just looked at him.

"Well, anyhow, I had my windows open, and this guy came out of the Missile Theater there, you know, the gay theater, and he spots me and calls over, 'Hey, want some head?' Jesus, this is a strange town."

Another driver, a Jewish kid named Simeon sniggered.

"So," said Danny in a measured tone. "Did you get some?"

Jeremy punched him lightly on the shoulder. "Asshole," he said.

Simeon piped up, "Remember the stock show week last year? I got called down to that gay bar near Five Points, I forget its name. I was supposed to find some guy, take him to the airport."

He took a swallow of Bud.

"Well, when I get there and open the door the music is just rockin', louder 'n hell. It's pretty dark, too, and I knew I could shout this guy's name 'til kingdom come and he wouldn't hear me in that racket. But the weirdest thing was, there was nothin' but guys in there dancing with each other, some of 'em making out. And they were all wearing cowboy outfits! Roy Rogers necking with Wyatt Earp. What a bunch!"

Nothing like what happened to Heath, though, Danny thought. He looked over at his friend, who was watching the others with a faintly amused smile.

Danny wondered how Simeon had become part of their group. Usually he stayed aloof. He had developed a reputation as a true hustler, a driver who would take any fare, anywhere, as long as he could make a quicker buck. He was usually lucky, too. Last winter he had scored two trips to Vail and one to Aspen, all from the airport, each a nice long trip worth more than a hundred bucks.

Simeon also had another gig on the side. When he wasn't driving he was home in his little apartment practicing counting cards for blackjack. Once every two months he would drive to Vegas, and using the edge his counting provided him, he'd do pretty well. (He'd have about a 1% advantage over the house—or so he tried to explain to Danny one day.)

"It takes a lot of concentration," he said at the time. "It's hard to count cards when some waitress is rubbing her thigh up against you offering you a free drink, or the hot chick dealer is exposing her cleavage to advantage. They're always trying to distract you, get you making stupid bets. Of course, if the management even get a whiff that you're counting cards they're gonna escort you from the premises with a stern warning never to come back, sometimes accompanied by a punch to the gut." He sighed. "But they haven't caught me yet. Last time I was there I netted about $6500. Not bad for a weekend's work. But that was from five different casinos. And I didn't get much sleep."

Another entrepreneurial angle, Danny thought. *Jerzy and his loopy church. Cheating at cards—well, not exactly cheating, but kind of fixing the game. Everybody seems to be chasing an edge, and if you're not, you're something of a sucker, one of the only guys paying full freight.*

It reminded him of a joke an insurance salesman had told him once: Why did God make Anglo-Saxon protestants? Somebody has to pay retail. Yuk yuk.

The conversation tilted from work to sports to politics and back again, but Danny remained fairly quiet. He was yawning heavily before he finished his waffle, and he climbed to his feet.

"Gotta sleep. Gotta go," he said, leaving five bucks on the table for Heath to pay with.

Heath nodded and scooped up the fiver.

"See you next time."

CHAPTER THIRTY

Crash

They say that 70% of car accidents occur within 20 miles of home—something like that. *Well,* Danny thought, *I suppose it's true.*

He lay in his bed after eleven hours of sleep, nursing a bruise on his left shoulder where he had slammed into the door frame of the cab the previous night.

What a night! he thought, still groggy, and sore.

It was the weekend, and the usual deal for cab rental was available: one day's cab rental for the weekend from Friday at 6:00 pm until Monday at 6:00 am. Drive, drive, drive, and take home the extra loot.

The cab office smelled of onions, for some reason, or perhaps unwashed bodies, Danny wasn't sure. He sat impatiently as other drivers were called out for their weekend cabs. He watched Simeon leap up at the call of his name, snatch the key from the hand of whoever it was who kept them, and head for the yard, probably off to grab a trip to Chief Idaho's

Hot Springs or Estes Park. Who knew? He was always getting the good fares.

Danny drummed his fingers on the vinyl upholstery of the cheap office chair upon which he uncomfortably waited. He seemed to be sweating through his pants. It was still 87 degrees outside, according the plastic thermometer outside the window behind him, cooler than the 94 it had been earlier in the day, but everyone still seemed to be suffering. And there was a full moon predicted. The shadows were already turning the cab yard behind him into a gloomy place, although the city lights beyond were at least somewhat cheering.

It was 6:48 pm, and the day driver had still not returned his car. *Must be a ball game or something,* Danny thought.

"Danny!" the call finally came. It was 7:10, probably $15 into the evening's take. He jumped up eagerly and went to the window where a hand was extending a key.

"Take car 342. The driver just got back from Boulder."

Danny took the key and headed to the yard. The cab was an older Checker model, surprising, because Checker and Yellow Cab had once been serious competitors. The fact that Yellow Cab in Denver was using mostly Checker vehicles had always been an unsolved puzzle for Danny, one he had been simply too busy or too lazy to investigate.

These Checker cars were big, heavy cars with lots of legroom, front and back. There were no seat belts (are you kidding?), and although they weren't racing machines, they had plenty of power. With the automatic transmissions, they were a natural fit for cabbies, who would often have their right hands on the radio microphone since they didn't have to waste time shifting.

A small, cylindrical safe was bolted to the transmission housing, with a slot in the locked top for paper money and a round key hole. Drivers didn't carry the key to the safe, and they stuffed their spare cash into it. Prominent signs on the exterior of the car stated that, "DRIVER CARRIES ONLY $5 CHANGE!!" Cabbies were tremendously vulnerable to robbery. Drivers' having no access to the money gave them a protection they both wanted and needed.

Most drivers also carried a long, 6 D-cell flash light just under their front seat. Its power enabled them to scope out address markers that were otherwise difficult to see at night, and its size, about that of a police night stick, gave them something of a weapon were they ever obliged to use one.

Danny climbed into the car, cranked the motor (which started reassuringly), and headed out onto the streets.

His first call was way out on a commercial section of West 50th Avenue near Federal Boulevard, just north of I-70 and not far from Regis College. He was cruising down the avenue, which was brightly lit and full of pedestrians out for Friday evening festivities. *TGIF*, thought Danny, as he stared ahead, looking for the 7-11 where he was to pick up his fare.

Seeing he was still three blocks from his destination, he picked up speed marginally. Just then, however, he saw a lanky black man a hundred or so feet away rear back and throw a half empty beer bottle toward him from the sidewalk. He instinctively ducked, but he kept his hands on the wheel.

Smash!! The bottle rebounded from the windshield of his car, leaving behind a star-shaped corona of cracks and crumbled glass. *What the...!* thought Danny, pulling the car to a halt.

The man who had thrown the bottle straightened, gave a whoop of laughter, and then bolted down an alley. Danny watched him disappear. *You shithead,* he thought.

He called in to the dispatcher.

"Base, some jerk has just destroyed the windshield of 342 with a beer bottle. I'm out on West 50th. Over."

There was a moment's silence. Then, "342, you better bring that car back in here and pick up another cab. Can't drive it that way. Over."

Shit! Now it was past 8:00 o'clock, and he hadn't made a nickel yet.

Back at the yard he had to wait for another twenty minutes to get another car. It was 9:15 pm when he once again hit the streets in 449.

Danny had managed to get three fares under his belt and was carrying his fourth down E. Colfax toward Lincoln and Broadway when he got another call. His passenger was volubly explaining to him the perfidy of his overweight girlfriend, and Danny was trying to catch the dispatcher's countdown.

"City center, 1-0-9..."

"Four four nine!" Danny snapped, knowing he was dropping his fare off on Arapahoe, not far away. The drivers' unwritten rule was, if you could manage it, 'a fare in your car, and one in your pocket,' meaning someone to pick up near where you were dropping off. He stepped on the gas. Then his heart skipped as he sped into the red light before him.

The car that hit his cab at about 35 mph plowed into the left front quarter panel and wheel, driving his car sideways down Lincoln about forty feet. For a moment, Danny was dazed. Another half second and the T-bone collision would probably have killed him. The passenger in the front seat beside him simply climbed out of the car and walked away— he wanted no part of this.

"You idiot!" someone was shouting through his open side window.

The police were there in minutes.

"So, you're admitting fault then, eh?" the officer said as he scanned Danny's Colorado driving license.

Danny nodded, a bit stupefied.

"I've already called Yellow Cab," the policeman said. "This man who hit you has all the details. The wrecker will be here soon. The cab company will tell you how to proceed." Then, as an afterthought, he asked, "You're not hurt, are you?"

Danny rubbed his shoulder a moment but said, "No. Nothing serious."

"Ok, then."

Back at the cab office he said to the supervisor, "What now?"

The man blew some smoke from his cigarette, turned behind him, and took another key off a hook. "I guess you get another car," he said, giving Danny a stare of minor appraisal. "Not a good night, huh?"

"No."

"The day supervisor will be in touch." He paused, then said, "Look, kid, these things happen. It'll probably cost you a few bucks, but the company's insured for this. Just hang in there."

Danny nodded.

Danny took a third car, an older one this time, and he managed to make another $43 before he was simply too tired to go on. *Tomorrow*, he thought.

He started driving south on Broadway to where he could link up with I-25 and head back to Atlantic Avenue. Broadway was nearly empty, only a few vehicles now, the anonymous wanderers of the late-night city. It was 2:34 am.

He stopped reflexively at a red light at Virginia Avenue. There were no cars at all. He stared at the glowing symbol. Then, out of all control, he began to tremble, all over, his arms and shoulders, and even the muscles of his calves. For a full minute, he couldn't stop it. Then the light turned green and the trembling ceased. Thinking a moment of his near death, he sobbed once. *Trust your body,* he remembered Mike saying. He took a deep breath, looked both ways, took his foot off the brake and resumed southward.

CHAPTER THIRTY-ONE

The Canadiens Come to Town

"Guy Lafleur! Are you kidding?" Danny was nearly shouting. "I kid you not," said Tony, another Canadian from the Center who had been in Denver for three years now. "Lafleur, Robinson, they're all here to play the Rockies."

"Those clowns! They hardly know which end of the stick to hold. How much?" Danny asked.

"About $16 for the upper tier. But the Colorado team is so weak, and the fans here so few and far between, that between periods you can go down into some of the empty seats nearer the ice."

Danny thought a moment. *When else will I ever get a chance to see these guys play?* "Are you going?"

"Sure. Should I get you a ticket?"

"You bet. Thursday night at McNicholl, right? Should I pick you up?"

"Yeah, great, around 6:30 pm. Bring the money."

"Ok, Tony. Thanks."

Tony started in on some details about the Colorado Rockies, but for a moment or two Danny tuned out, thinking about Tony's background.

Tony wasn't his real name, or at least, it hadn't been. Tony was an assumed identity.

"It wasn't that hard," Tony had explained over afternoon beers one day. "My visa was three months overdue. I didn't want to get married. But then I found the coolest article on changing one's identity in *Soldier of Fortune Magazine*! And it had a reference in the want ads for instructions on how to become, literally, someone else.

"So, Tony isn't your real name?"

"Nah. I'd tell you my real name, but then I'd have to kill 'ya." He smirked.

"How'd you do it?"

"Well, the public library has microfiche records of death certificates. In fact, the one here in Denver has records for six states! I went down there and trolled through hundreds of pages and then I found what I was looking for: a baby that died the year I was born, 1948. His name was, wait for it, Anthony Burns."

He looked sideways a moment, gathering his thoughts.

"I got all the details I could from the death information, as well as from an obituary I was able to locate in a newspaper from the town where he had been alive. He was born in a small town in Utah down in the southern part of the state, and he died of measles six months later. So, I wrote away to the government department in Utah that issues birth certificates using a post office box pickup out east of town in Aurora as the return address. I claimed that I had lost my birth certificate and asked if they'd be kind enough to issue another one. I gave them the mother's and father's names that I got off the death notice as bona fides. Ever helpful and cooperative, the civil service of Utah hopped to it and sent me a new one. Step one done."

"Wow," Danny said. "They didn't know he was dead..."

"No. Remarkable thing. They don't cross-reference births and deaths anywhere." He sipped his beer and smiled. "Then I took my birth certificate into the drivers' license office, did a road test, and got a driver's license in the same name. With those two documents, I sent away for a social security number, claiming that for some obscure reason I had never been issued one. They were all apologetic, wondering how they'd missed me, etc., and they sent me one. Then I got a library card, moved into a new apartment to get accounts for gas and electricity, opened a new bank account with cash. I am now Anthony Burns."

Danny thought for a few moments. He was happy for his friend, who now had the legal status he had been seeking. Yet there was something stickily dishonest about the whole process, as well, that didn't sit well with Danny. True, it wasn't going to hurt the original Anthony Burns any, or even his family, who would likely never know anything about this new interloper or what he had done using their names. And it's not as if, as a cab driver, he was damaging the economy by taking a job away from some legitimate American. The economy was humming along just fine, as far as he knew (although he didn't pay too much attention to macroeconomics other than to the inflation that seemed to continue to eat away his earnings).

He remembered the policeman who had stopped him when he did an illegal U-turn at 2:30 am on an empty Colfax Avenue. The grumpy patrolman had scrutinized his license, noting the previous Saskatchewan registration.

"You Canadian?" he asked suspiciously.

"Yes."

"Got your green card?"

"Well, sure, but I don't carry it with me. You get so much crap thickening your wallet, you know. Too bad more of it wasn't money. It's safe at home, the green card, I mean."

"Huh. Well, watch your drivin'. I know there isn't any traffic to speak of this time of night, but the law's the law. Consider this a warning."

"Okay, I will, thanks, Officer."

The cop had sauntered back to his vehicle, hand on the closed holster of his big revolver.

Tony cleared his throat. "You thinking I've done something morally reprehensible here?"

"Aw, I don't know," Danny said. "It's a pretty grey area. You're not exactly stealing someone's identity because there is no such someone. Not any more, at least. But it's kind of fishy, you know."

His voice got a bit more wistful. "Amazing, isn't it, the lengths people will go to stay in this country. I mean, in many ways it's a wonderful place—full of opportunity, lots of cultural stuff—but coming from Canada it's not so great. I mean, shit, look at the war. When I was younger my English teacher was a draft dodger from Texas. A more unlikely soldier you never saw, but he'd have been shipped over to the jungle to die, just like so many of them. Remember that guy I lived with on South Grant? Totally fucked up by his tour of duty. There are some really weird things about this place. Assassinations. Guns everywhere." He thought of the little Beretta handgun one of the other drivers had shown him one night—"Nobody's gonna fuck with me," he'd said meaningfully.

"I don't give much of a shit about culture, frankly," said Tony. "There's just something about being in the center of the cyclone down here, you know? After 'Toronto the Good,' the US of A is so much more alive, don't you think?"

Danny *did* think (although he had only been to Toronto once, a summer trip to visit a friend of his whose wife had gone there to study dance). But to Danny the so-called culture was key to America's appeal. He thought of the intellectuals, the plays, the concerts he had seen here in Denver—on a cabby's pay, no less.

He took a long, malty swallow. He remembered listening to Buckminster Fuller, droning on about dymaxion cars and geodesic domes in City Park one afternoon. He thought of seeing Katherine Hepburn, still a knockout at about 70 years old, in some less than memorable play downtown. He had listened to speeches by Republican intellectual William F. Buckley Jr. and *L'il Abner* cartoonist Al Capp at Denver University, and thrilled to a Copland symphony conducted by the composer. And he considered the elation he had felt watching a ballet performance of *Carmina Burana*. And the time he had watched Max Frisch's *The Firebugs* at that pocket theater just off Colfax and Downing. He'd seen Mark Messier, a hockey whiz just waiting for his shot at the NHL, skating through and around his college opponents (*he's gonna be a good one*, Danny thought). Jerzy's dude ranch music weekend…it just went on and on.

"Lots of stuff happening here, that's for sure."

On the phone, he interrupted Tony's diatribe about the failings of Don Cherry, saying, "So, about the hockey game, I'll come get you in Maybelline (Danny's name for his battered Volvo) about 6:30. Game starts at 7:30, right? There's lots of parking at McNichol."

After a second of surprised silence, Tony replied, "Yeah. Ok. Sure."

Thursday evening, he and Tony left the car in the big, half-empty lot and headed for one of the gates of McNichol's Arena. It didn't look as if ice hockey was going to make it here in Denver, at least at the NHL level. They had hired Don Cherry as head coach for the unheard-of sum of $400,000 a season, and the best he could do to excuse his team's abysmal performance was say, "How can you fly with the eagles when you're saddled with a bunch of turkeys?" Danny had watched Mark Messier flying up and down the ice at a Denver University hockey game, no turkey, but the Edmonton Oilers had already drafted him.

When he and Tony located their seats, the teams were already skating around in their warm-up. The Canadiens had a fabulous lineup: Yvan Cournoyer, Ken Dryden in goal, Guy Lafleur, Bob Gainey (whom the coach of the Russian team in

1972 had called the best hockey player in the world), Jacques Lemaire, Peter Mahovlich, Larry Robinson, Serge Savard, Steve Shutt. A woman in a fur coat next to a man wearing a tuxedo just below them said to him, "These guys are meant to be just the cream of the hockey world." Her tone was almost reverential. The man merely nodded, as if his mind were elsewhere, perhaps on basketball.

The organ accompanist (*Why do they always have an organist at these games?* Danny wondered) completed a flourish with a grand cadence, and the MC declaimed, "And now, ladies and gentlemen, please stand for the two national anthems." Aside from a few individuals still looking for their seats in the half-empty arena, everyone stood still and to attention.

A young woman in an evening gown stepped onto a small carpet at the edge of the ice, clasped a microphone, and began to sing.

O, Canada, our home and native land...

Only these few sung lyrics, and Danny felt the most penetrating sadness and longing for home that he had ever felt. He felt tears sting the corners of his eyes, and he brushed them quickly away. *Is it conditioning from school, or cub scouts, or what?* he wondered.

The game was a rout. When the thrashing was finished, the visitors skated away with a 7-1 victory, hardly trying, as the frustrated Denver team scrambled around, trying to formulate some kind of opposition, their only goal the result of an accidental deflection of a shot from the point, ruining Dryden's shutout. Oh, well.

"Jeez, what a well of talent," Tony stated. "Amazing..."

On the way out of the arena, the two found themselves walking beside the referee and linesmen from the game.

Curious, Danny asked, "What's it like being an NHL referee?"

Continuing his steady pace, the man said, "Oh, it's well paid, and I like the game. But it's crazy, you know, always travelling, waking up in one hotel room or another wondering what city you're in. Not exactly a career for a family man. But it's good for now, while the legs stand up."

It's good for now, Danny thought.

CHAPTER THIRTY-TWO

Bullets and Last Breaths

The cab office was raucous and noisy, with drivers swapping bullshit, listening peripherally to bells and responding calls that were broadcast through the drivers' lounge from a couple of speakers mounted near the ceiling. It was November. The Stock Show was over, and now, a week later, it was cold, only about 17 degrees Fahrenheit by the thermometer outside the window over Danny's shoulder. He was waiting patiently for his regular car, enjoying the office warmth, the familiar jocularity.

Skiing had begun up in the Rockies, and all the drivers were hungry for a trip to Vail or Aspen, ferrying some lawyer or businessman from back East with cash to burn on a vacation to the western wilderness (which aside from the ski slopes—groomed daily—largely consisted of a fancy condo or hotel with a big fireplace and hot, spiced wine). *Wow. What passes for roughing it these days,* Danny thought.

There had been a wild blizzard a few days back. Used to cold winter weather in Saskatchewan, Danny had walked to work at the health food store, keeping his face out of the wind, especially when it was cutting down along I-25's corridor. There hadn't been much point in opening the store. Only two customers came in all day (although the quiet gave him an opportunity to do an extensive inventory of the shelves full of supplements). Out on the Great Plains to the east a road grader that had run out of diesel had been temporarily lost under a 20-foot snowdrift, with only its blue beacon light mounted on the cab roof visible the next morning. The driver had been found to be all right, sleeping, wrapped in a thick seat blanket over his parka, with his head in a toque and his feet in big, fur boots. In town, the snow had been light, although Stapleton had been closed for sixteen hours. Now about eight inches of snow remained on the yards and beside the city streets. Everything was coming back to life, fueled by gasoline and grid electricity.

Some of his regular driving comrades were in the room. Heath, who had finally gotten over his angst, was back driving nearly full-time. He sat in a corner, brow furrowed in concentration, reading the instructions for some assemble-it-yourself furniture he had recently purchased. Jeremy was there, too, bored, spinning a yo-yo up and down beside his chair. Simeon had left about fifteen minutes ago, eager beaver that he was, chasing the elusive fare. In casual conversation one day he confided that he had been inspired by an uncle who had driven cab and who had once had a fare from Denver to New Orleans carrying a stage magician up front and three cages of birds in the back seat! "So, you just never know," Simeon had said. "There are always surprises in this job."

Suddenly the relative quiet of the room was interrupted by a shout from the dispatcher. "What!? What did you say?" All the drivers paused whatever they were doing and shut up, turned to listen.

There was some staticky interference for a moment. The dispatcher turned the volume way up on his receiver. Then they all heard it: "Help, help, they're shooting me!"

"511, where are you?"

"278! Hooh, haw! I've got a trip to Vail!" yelled a female voice.

"278, get off the air, NOW!" the dispatcher shouted. "511, where are you? Over."

Silence.

"511, over!"

"Don't do that, you little shit! Don't..." Then there were two distinct gunshots.

"511! 511!"

"278 to dispatch, did you get my message?"

"Shut the fuck up, 278!"

Everyone in the room was on edge now.

The dispatcher shouted to the room at large, "Anyone in here know where Simeon was headed?"

"He said he was headed for the airport," Heath said.

Two of the telephone girls who usually handed the dispatcher the bells stood uncertainly beside him. The dispatcher grabbed a phone and dialed 911.

"Police! Police! Right now." There was a moment's pause, then, "One of my drivers is in a violent confrontation, somewhere between Yellow Cab and the airport. Cab number 511." Pause. "Yes, Stapleton Field. He's probably somewhere along 32nd Ave or in the vicinity." Pause. "Yup." Pause. "He called in, said someone was shooting him." Pause. "We heard gunshots over the radio." Pause. "Ok." He hung up the phone.

He turned to us and spoke through the dispatch window. "They've put out an APB, all-points bulletin, and four squad cars are looking for his cab." He looked down a moment, then up again and said, "We'll just have to wait for news."

In 511 all was quiet. It sat immobile, headlights still beaming against the chain link fence at the back of the empty lot in which it was stopped. One of the rear doors hung forlornly open. The motor was still idling, although with the open back door, despite the car's heater (on low), the interior was rapidly cooling. The ceiling light lit up the driver, Simeon. His head, mouth open as if to say something, but eyes closed, was flopped back over the flat seat back. A bit of blood still leaked out of the two holes in his chest. His left hand clutched the wheel; then suddenly it dropped into his lap. A trail of scarlet blood drops, lit by a streetlamp not thirty feet away, brilliant in the snow, led away from the front right door of the cab. A bright smear of blood was on its external handle, as well.

In the cab office, the drivers sat silently. For a few minutes, the dispatcher remained off the air. Then, when he saw the pile of bells accumulating beside him, he took up the mike again.

"Twelfth and Colfax," he began, "9, 8, 7...two sevens, get Barry at the 7-11. Grant and Alameda, 3, 2, 1, 0...four ten, get Mrs. Anderson at 4318 Alameda and take her to Lutheran Hospital."

Shit, Danny thought, unaware that the same thought was drifting repetitively through the minds of all the other drivers, as well. *Simeon...it could have been any of us.*

Heath got up and came over to sit beside Danny. His Australian accent had diminished considerably, but it was still detectable, even in his husky whisper.

"He used to take a lot of chances, you know," Heath said.

Danny nodded. Simeon's eagerness for a trip, any trip, was legendary around the cab office.

"He probably picked up some flag," Heath went on.

"Yeah," Danny responded. But he didn't really want to talk much.

A couple of minutes later the phone jangled, and the dispatcher grabbed it.

"Yeah?"

He covered the mouthpiece for a second and said to the room, "They found him." A pause, then, "He's dead."

Lifting his hand once more he listened intently. Finally, he hung up the phone and said, "The car's in an empty lot on the way to the airport, just north of the main road there. He was shot twice in the chest. There's a good chance they're going to catch somebody. They'll let us know."

"Fuckin' A, man," someone in the corner said. There were nods and murmurs of assent.

Cab drivers stick together. Danny remembered the time somebody tried to stiff him on a fare. A stressed-out looking guy in a sports jacket had asked Danny to drop him off at a dry-cleaners beside an alley, instructing Danny to wait and to keep the meter running. Something didn't feel right to Danny, so he backed up just enough to watch down the alley. Sure enough, the client slipped out a side door and started walking down the alley, away from the front street.

Danny radioed in, "A guy's trying to stiff me behind the dry cleaner on Cherry Creek Drive and Ellsworth. Pass it on?" He pulled into the alley and idled along until he caught up with the man. He lowered his window and said, "Somewhere else you wanted to go?"

The man blushed, hustled around the front of the car and climbed in. "Yeah," he said. "Cherry Creek Inn."

"I think you'd better pay me up front this time, don't you?" Danny said. He pointed toward another Yellow cab that had entered the alley, facing them. The driver lifted his hand in a half wave.

The man sheepishly tugged a wallet from the back pocket of his chinos, removed a bill (a twenty), and handed it to Danny. Five minutes later Danny let him out in front of the hotel. The other cab was pulled in right behind them.

"The meter only says $16.20," the passenger said.

"Don't you think you're pushing it?" Danny replied. "Off you go." He felt uncharacteristically powerful at the moment, and he was ready to reach down for his flashlight.

The man looked at him a moment, a hangdog expression on his face. Then he opened the door, climbed out, slammed it behind him, and ascended the three low steps into the hotel. Danny got out and walked back to the other driver, who rolled down his window.

"Thanks," Danny said.

"All for one and one for all," the other driver replied. "Got your money?"

"Yup. Coffee's on me next time."

Another time one of their night compadres called over the open mike, "Some bastard has jumped out on me without paying a $35 fare! East side of Washington Park!"

Within ten minutes there were eleven taxis cruising the nearby locale, including the curvy interior roadway where people regularly washed their cars on sunny Sundays in the summer (a kind of urban ritual). Four minutes later two of them had the fare jumper pinned in their headlights, shielding his eyes against the glare, up beside the concrete block wall of the tennis rental shack. The driver got his money.

"Any of you guys gonna go to work tonight?" the dispatcher asked caustically.

No one got up. One driver in a flannel shirt got up and said, "Not me, man. Not tonight. I'm goin' home to snuggle up to my wife."

Heath and Danny sat together for a while. "Let's wait for some more news if there's any," Heath said.

Finally, around 10:30 pm, the phone rang again. After a murmured conversation, the dispatcher hung up and said, "They've made an arrest. Three black kids. Oldest one's thirteen. Go figure."

Ten days later a Grand Jury was convened in the courthouse downtown. At least a dozen cab drivers, including Danny, were in attendance.

The room was brightly lit by overhead fluorescents and by pale winter light filtering in through long, vertical windows in the south wall. Before proceedings began, the crowd milled around, engaged in hushed conversations. Some were obviously family of the accused boys. Hunched on a front bench were Simeon's parents, holding hands and staring at the floor. His younger sister kept glancing over at the accused with undisguised hostility. Three scrawny adolescent black males sat shoulder to shoulder between two sharply dressed men who were probably their lawyers, Danny thought. One of the accused was heavily bandaged on his left shoulder, and his arm hung in a sling. He was nodding intermittently to the older man to his left.

The cab drivers were sitting on two benches behind Simeon's family. They were a comparatively scruffy bunch, wearing anoraks and heavy flannel shirts.

There were fourteen people in the jury box. Five of them were black. Seven were women. One was an elderly man, perhaps in his seventies. He fiddled with his hearing aid.

A complete surprise to Danny was the opportunity the District Attorney gave to members of the audience to see some of the photographic evidence, which was laid out on a table between the judge and the defendants and supervised by a couple of beefy bailiffs. Most of the drivers filed by. One of the photos, a polaroid taken the night of the arrest, showed Simeon's body, sitting upright in the driver's seat, head back and mouth open, eyes closed, skin a yellowish grey in the illumination from the flash. He must have been dead for some time when the photo was snapped. Danny found it difficult to reconcile this waxy figure, looking for all the world like some Hallowe'en caricature, with the abrasive, hyperactive, devil-may-care young man the drivers had all known, at least to some degree. There were also photos of a blood trail through the snow outside the car. It was this trail that detectives had followed across an alley and over a wooden fence into the yard of the house where they confronted the boys and located a recently fired pistol under the mattress of the eldest. The police had forced the door over the objections of a woman, his mother, who had been trying to stanch a bullet wound in the boy's shoulder.

It seemed pretty open and shut, and the jury found sufficient evidence had been collected to justify criminal charges.

But the most unnerving part of the proceedings was the distribution of the audience. Most of the left side of the courtroom behind the defendants was occupied by negroes. The right side of the courtroom was completely white. When Danny saw the obvious racial antagonism in the room, he became very uneasy. *It's time to leave this place*, he thought. *Not just court. The damn country.*

CHAPTER THIRTY-THREE

Hitting the Road

The decision to leave came surprisingly easily to Danny. Despite the urgency and planning that had brought him to Denver in the first place, all under the naïve assumption that the duration of his stay would be short—a few months at most—he had been in the city just shy of three years. With sudden clarity, Danny realized that it was time to go home to Canada.

In some ways, Denver had become home. If families are communities of intimacy knit together through genetic ties and mutual understanding, at least the second of those had been achieved there, amid the gathering of damaged misfits at the primal center. True, if the theoretical underpinnings of the therapy often approached a fervor of near theological intensity among many, the kinds of mutual support given and received among the clients had been welcoming and reassuring, especially as much of the time, many of the participants were trapped in emotional states that were vulnerable and nearly incomprehensible without that theory. The center was a physical manifestation of safety for the clients, in much the same way (if less imposing) that a cathedral is the physical anchor of catholic belief and spiritual relief.

The staff, too, were a dedicated group, often grappling with their own problems, which seemed, to Danny at least, honest and therefore acceptable. He had no time for psychological theorists of whatever stripe who protected their own royal roads to the unconscious and claimed unambiguously that theirs was the only map to salvation. He rarely saw Mike any more, and now they were more like acquaintances who had met on the same train than like doctor and patient.

Was he ready to leave the safety valve of therapy? Even after nearly three years he still felt the ghosts of his terror, occasionally filtering into an anxiety-driven consciousness like an old, ugly and dreaded intruder, knocking threateningly at the door or peeking, unwanted, through the window. Yet when these episodes occurred, he was always able to retreat to a safe environment—a private bedroom, usually—in which to sink into the cramping twists of bodily contortion that after twenty minutes or so would predictably bring relief, even if it was unfulfilled with cerebral insight.

The logic of his experience laid over the framework of the psychological theory of the therapy suggested strongly that his body was "remembering" physically some terrifying experience to do with the processes of his birth, a preverbal stage that would have defied explanation then. Memory is plastic and unreliable at the best of times. So now, quite naturally, there was no evidence-based, verbalized memory that could confirm his interpretation. It didn't really matter. Over time the reactions of his body had provided sufficient relief to enable him to function. If that functioning wasn't perfect, it was nonetheless a vast improvement over the condition that had driven him to Denver in the first place. And the episodes of anxiety were becoming fewer and fewer, and farther between. He felt considerably stronger, and he was coping much better.

The communal houses on South Grant Street and on Atlantic Avenue had been more than convenient shelters. The inhabitants (including Danny) had been brothers and sisters in both practical and emotional struggles of varied intensity, leaning on one another as needed, hopeful even in periods of despair. Sometimes he looked back in astonishment at the connections he had made to the people there—Louise in her suicidal horrors, struggling on despite them, and Carolyn's efforts to make a living for herself and her little boy, all while wrestling with the hallucinatory memories of her father and brother.

And then there was Penny, from outside the "family circle" of the center, cute as a bunny (as John Sebastien put it in *Did You Ever Have to Make Up Your Mind?*), warm, sexy Penny, who had slipped into his life like honey into tea, only to disappear into the stirred complexities of her own psychosocial melodrama. He had never seen her again after the Boulder fiasco, nor had he spoken to her. She had been an object lesson on the Zen of loss, the temporality of pleasure.

The city itself had been an incubator that cushioned Danny (and at least some of the others) through a needed period of maturation. *Healthy Body Natural Foods and Vitamins* had provided a wonderful (if ill-paying) job, with amenable company and endless opportunities for meeting unusual people and learning scores of facts and theories about the relationship of nutrition and lifestyle to health and well-being. Pauline had been a steady friend and a fair employer, and Danny realized that he would miss her.

The job at Yellow Cab had opened his eyes to the staggering variety of people in the world, seen from the underbelly of the city. He and his fellow drivers had been an unofficial brotherhood, a minor gear in the great urban machine that constituted the city, like mice in a vast field, scurrying from place to place, scratching out a living, often overlooked until snatched by some hawk of violence (like Simeon).

Danny spent a number of hours reviewing the wisdom of his imminent departure, even though when he was honest with himself he knew he had already made up his mind.

"I'm thinking of going home, back to Canada," he said one morning to Carolyn, testing her reaction. He knew he had already decided, but he didn't want to burn any bridges just yet.

Carolyn had been drinking coffee at the kitchen table and reading her horoscope, a foolishness focused on nonsense she really didn't understand and that she consequently overrated. But it was one of the free rituals that made up much of her habit-driven life. She looked up at Danny, who was watching her. She frowned and stubbed out her cigarette.

"You think you're ready?"

Danny looked at her, silent a moment. Then he said, "Is there a defined end point for any of this?"

She stared at him, a kind of uncertain defiance, or at least readiness for disagreement. It was a question that she could interpret only through her own experience. She lowered her eyes in thought. One thing about Carolyn: she was a good listener, and she considered serious questions with her own attentive gravity.

Suddenly Danny became aware that Carolyn would probably never leave Denver. Where would she go? Back to her redneck community in Louisiana? Denver provided more safety than she had probably ever experienced.

When Carolyn looked up she had wetness in the corners of her eyes. She said, "This place won't be the same without you." She wiped her hand across each eye and did her best to smile. "You know, we've kind of been a family, in a strange way. Jody'll miss you. I know he doesn't talk much, but I know he loves you. Weird, huh? Kids..." Her voice trailed off. Then she said, "You told Louise yet?"

"No. Not yet. Soon."

Carolyn sniffed.

"When you thinkin' of goin'?"

"I want to go back to school, make some kind of career, or a decent living, anyway." Danny frowned. He hadn't meant to suggest that his life in Denver wasn't "a decent living." *Decent is as decent does*, he thought. He felt momentarily guilty of seeming to dismiss Carolyn and the rest of the household as impoverished losers, although he hadn't really done that, he thought. He said, "University will start again in September. I want to get back to Canada in July some time to make some decisions about my future there."

"Doctorin'?"

Danny sighed. "Probably not. It would take too much time. And I don't have much money. University can be expensive." He thought a moment. "I could probably get some loans, but doing six or so more years of school, and then paying back all the money owed...it's just too long. It'll have to be something else. Anyway, it's May. I still have time to think and plan."

Half an hour later Danny climbed into his old Volvo and fired up the motor. He had people to see before he left, that was for sure. *Me and Bobby McGee* was wailing out over the radio as he navigated the back streets toward Heath's place. *Feelin' good was easy, Lord, when he sang the blues...* Danny tapped time on the edge of the steering wheel, thinking of the road ahead—not the tree-lined avenue here and now in Denver, but the seemingly limitless highways stretching north and west toward the lower mainland of British Columbia where he'd decided to go.

Two nights past he had spoken with his brother on the phone, sounding out the possibility of going to Victoria.

"Mi casa es su casa," his brother had said, and Danny had felt a flood of relief. He had always been able to rely on his brother. He wondered how his brother's wife would feel about his coming. She had always been generous and kind...

"How you holdin' up?" Heath asked him.

They were sitting on a pair of tatty lawn chairs out behind his wife's rented house, drinking instant coffee and watching a squirrel chasing birds away from a few peanuts Heath had tossed onto the patchy grass.

Determined little bugger, isn't he? Danny thought, watching, as two crows hopped and flapped away from the squirrel's ferocious approach. To Heath, he said, "I think I'm okay." He considered Heath's question some more, though, and added, "You know, guys like us, guys who nearly broke down completely, can we ever know for sure we're going to be all right? You've been in therapy more or less as long as I have, right? How're *you* holding up? I mean, how do we know we're any better or worse off than any other person scrambling to make a living in the great mess out there?" He gestured away from them, as if indicating some great indeterminate mass of unknown people, somewhere beyond the back fence.

"This stuff is shit, isn't it?" Heath said, tipping his mug to pour out the remainder of his coffee.

"I didn't want to say anything, but yeah," Danny replied. But he drank the rest of his down and set the mug on a flagstone beside him, one of a series of stepping stones leading to a forlorn looking shed at the side of the lot.

"I'm thinking of going back," Heath said. "To Australia."

"You, too?" Danny said, startled. "What about Sherry?"

"I mooted the idea with her. Even suggested that she come along." He paused, scratching the side of his nose. "Melbourne's a really beautiful city, you know. When you're not feeling totally fucked, it's a nice place to be. But I don't think she's interested. True love, huh?"

"Did you get what you came here for?" Danny asked, genuinely interested.

"Well, you know," Heath said thoughtfully. "There weren't any miracles, as we hoped and expected. But I feel stronger. I don't know if that's better, but it has its advantages."

"Uh-huh," Danny replied. Then he said, "Remember when you were going to quit driving that time, what, nearly two years ago? It really made me anxious for you, not that you didn't have good reason."

"It was sticking it out that made me stronger. Partly that, anyway."

"Sure," Danny said. Changing the subject, he added, "Let's get some Mexican food together before we go, you to the deep, deep South, and me home north to Canada."

"Yeah, for sure," Heath said. He looked back toward the house, and Danny tracked his gaze. Sherry stood there in the window, looking out at them, a serious, far-away expression on her face.

"Gotta go," Danny said. "Call me." He straightened, remembering something. "Say," he said, "I've got eight more hours of isolation tank time that I can't use. I'd be willing to sign them over to you if you want. Remember, I was telling you about that *Floating Nirvana* place?"

Heath shook his head, but then said, "I think Sherry would like to try it. The idea kind of spooks me."

"Check with her, and let me know, ok?"

He got to his feet, clapped Heath lightly on the shoulder, and headed out of the yard through the side gate.

"Sure," Heath said, watching him go. "Thanks."

It took only a few days before every acquaintance of any consequence in Danny's Denver life had been informed of his planned departure. Pauline simply nodded when he gave her his notice.

"It had to come sooner or later," she remarked to him philosophically. "When'll be your last day?"

"I thought week after next. That'll give you time to vet a replacement." He grinned. "I'm not sure I *can* be replaced, you know."

"No kidding," she said. She was serious. "Goin' with that hot-to-trot girl?"

Danny simply shook his head. Pauline looked relieved.

Back in the living room at Atlantic Avenue, Louise was standing by the living room window, looking out at Danny's car. She said to him, "I wish you weren't going."

It was her typical, straightforward message. When she wasn't silent, she had little or no inclination to beat around the bush. She scowled a little. "But I guess you have to," she added forlornly, and turned to look at Danny, who had just come in from the kitchen.

Danny thought of saying something like, "Stay off the pills, ok?" But he simply looked at her seriously and nodded. "Yeah," he said. "Oh," he added, "I have something for *you* though. A kind stranger gave it to me when I first came here, with instructions to pass it on one day. You have to promise to do the same."

Louise looked at him curiously.

Danny fished in his pocket and pulled out the native bracelet. "I'm not sure what it means," he said. "To me it kind of meant 'connection,' like we all have to remain connected. Anyhow, I think you're the right person to give it to." He extended the bracelet.

Louise took it from him and looked at it carefully, the shiny silver eagle profiles on the black background. She nodded, as if musing to herself. She didn't say anything, but she looked up, leaned forward and kissed Danny on the cheek. Then she turned and went into her room.

Jerzy held a minor music gathering for him. Half a dozen people showed up at his place to eat hot dogs, drink beer, and chat to one another, Chopin nocturnes punctuating the mood. PID gave him a hug and a copy of Lawrence Durrell's *The Alexandria Quartet*.

"Did you read this?" Danny asked.

"Of course not," she replied. "But Penny asked me to give it to you." She looked at Danny expectantly, smiling at his blush. Sure enough, on the inside Penny had scrawled her name beside an elaborately drawn smiley face and a smudged X— *Bad Penny 1978.*

Danny felt a moment's emptiness. Then he said, "Thank her for me, will you?"

Near the end of the month, the Friday night before leaving, he took stock. Aside from his clothes, toiletries and books, he had $171 in his wallet and another $400 cash secreted within a cheap copy of *Treasure Island* carefully stuffed into a box of books on the back seat. He had mailed a certified cheque for

$1200 to his brother for deposit into a new account once he reached Victoria. And he had the car, of course, for however long it might last. (He had checked the tires and changed the oil. The engine still just hummed its reliable song.) Otherwise he had nothing.

On Saturday morning, he shoved his suitcase and a couple of boxes of books into the trunk of his Volvo and wired it shut. (The disfigured rear deck would not allow the latch to work properly.) He exchanged hugs with Carolyn and Louise, who both wished him well. He tossed Feather into the back seat.

Louise turned away and climbed the dandelion patch back to the front door of the house. She turned there on the cement porch and stood watching.

Carolyn lifted her hand in a half wave as Danny settled into the driver's seat. He buckled on the shoulder belt, returned her wave, started the engine, and pulled away.

Driving down Holly Street toward the freeway, he had to push Feather away. She had given a few agonized meows, clung to his arm ferociously, and then leaped once more into the back where she burrowed in beneath the rear seat and out of sight.

For half a moment, he felt a strange vertigo, a sense of loss. Then, he turned on the radio to the strains of Willy Nelson's *On the Road Again*.

It must be a sign, Danny thought, and he sped up the ramp onto I-70, heading west into the mountains.

Printed in Canada